SHADOW TERRORS...

Victoria Angelucci's charcoal pencil swiftly drew the lean limbs of a model clothed in a mid-length shorts and a gauzy, sleeveless tunic top that covered the hips and was caught below the waist with a slouchy belt. Strappy legionnaire sandals wrapped up her ankles. With the slight gathers at the shoulders and the plain front, the piece screamed for one of Reggie's necklaces. Maybe even one of the pieces she'd made for Milan. On a whim, Victoria sketched in a hammered silver disc set with a single pearl and the outfit came alive.

Smiling, she flipped to the next page and was sketching a model in narrow-legged cropped trousers with a short, boat-necked top of heavier knit fabric when her door rattled. She paused at her sketching and looked toward the door. Tall silhouette. Male.

Danny?

For all she'd rejected him and sent him on his way, that kiss of his had left her wanting more.

She set the sketch pad down and slid off her stool.

The door rattled again, more insistently this time. Not a knock, but an impolite rattle as if whoever it was just expected the door to be waiting open for them.

She headed across to the door thinking up a quip she could tease him with, but two steps from the door she stopped.

Something wasn't right. The silhouette seemed to shift as if the edges weren't quite complete. A whiff of smoke caught her nose and a chill ran through her so that all the little hairs on her body stood on end. She took a step back.

Whoever was out there, she did not want to see. More *importante,* whoever was out there should not see her!

BOOKS BY THE AUTHOR

Romance
Ashes and Light
Shades of Moonlight
Judas Kiss
Second Spring
A Different Nightmusic
Shadow Play
Unlocking Her Heart
Unlocking Her History
Unlocking Her Grace
Unlocking Her Dreams
Unlocking Her Chances
Unlocking Her Doubts (Coming February 2016)

Fantasy
***The Cartographer Universe* series:**
The Warden of Power
Impossible
The Cartographer's Daughter
Afterburn
Aftershock
Aftermath
Afterimage

Terra Incognita
Terra Infirma
Terra Nueva

Also by the Author
Mutable Things
Emberstone
Ice Dragon
Crystal Courtesan

UNLOCKING HER CHANCES

Karen L. Abrahamson

For all those who love the lake.

UNLOCKING HER CHANCES

Prologue

The thing that was Johan Fehr hung up the telephone in his Berlin office. He felt weak, the physical strength of the Johan Fehr body not enough to overcome his disquiet.

His desktop was empty save for a computer screen and a single file folder—opened. It contained everything he knew about the blasted women in Peachland. Four. There had been four! But no longer, apparently. Somehow they had managed to draw others into their infernal cabal.

The office air held the chill, odorless, mechanical tang of air conditioning, but not enough to mask the burning scent that came with his anger. The walnut-paneled office walls held the carefully collected remains of two lifetimes—photos of Johan Fehr with various dignitaries at construction site inaugurations and political events in Germany and beyond. There were photos of Johan's father, as well. Guided by the thing that had inhabited him, Heinrich Fehr had risen quickly in the military and then with his business in the heady days of the rebuilding of Europe. Medals and commendations as well as letters of recognition from the Allied occupiers and the *Bundestag*, all framed and mounted, commemorated the Fehr contribution to the rebuilding of Germany. Law books and the classics lined shelves built into the walls—not that he had any need to read them, with teams of lawyers to do his bidding and no interest at all in human literature.

And all of it was worth nothing if he did not develop a plan to deal with the situation!

Afternoon sunlight filled the tree-lined streets far below his window. The sun glared off the glass of the other downtown towers like sunlight on shifting water, and for a moment he was amazed at what the humans had done. It was a far cry from the towers of Babylon or Giza's ancient pyramids. This was the true wonder of the world—that humans had created such a thing.

And since when had he admired anything about these lesser beings?

Johan Fehr's body shivered. The disquiet he felt had to be because of the abrupt ending of his last effort to reclaim the bracelet. The body had been killed while he had still controlled it. In his already weakened form, he had been left to coalesce as best he could. That had not occurred for eons—not since most humans had forgotten that they shared this earth with other beings. In the past he would simply have taken another nearby human, but the opening of the fourth door of the infernal bracelet had stripped him of too much of his power. It had left him restless and weak, the need for revenge coiling in him like a fire about to leap between buildings.

It had taken all his strength and five days to find his way back to this body again. The fourth door of the bracelet opened by the fourth couple forming and vanquishing the power that had long ago been stolen from him and locked in the bracelet. Only three doors remained—fewer than half of the seven—over half of his power, lost forever.

The body's hand closed into a fist. Those infernal women— they'd bested each of his emissaries. Perhaps that was the problem. Newly snatched bodies were not fully cooperative. Humans hired for their skills at killing had to be trusted to know what they were doing. The trouble in each case was that the body or the emissary was unable to get close enough to do the job—or too incompetent to finish it. There always seemed to be something that stood in the way of the woman trusting him—usually that something was the man she was meant to be with.

The man.

Now there was an interesting consideration...

Chapter 1

"Victoria! What have you done?"

Victoria Angelucci, late of Milan, Italy, looked up from the lovely silver bracelet around her wrist. Cleopatra-haired Reggie Lewis wore a worried expression on her flushed face—the flushing the product no doubt of the expert kiss of Victoria's one and only scoundrel brother, Cesare, who sat on the chair arm beside Reggie.

"Done? I am sorry. I simply try your bracelet on? It fell from your wrist, you know?" In the shadows of the broad front porch of the stately old red-and-white house, she angled her wrist this way and that, admiring the seven small, silver doors. Angled sunlight filled the early evening and patterned the waves on the huge lake across the street with the same patina of silver. Okanagan Lake, Reggie had said, was over eighty kilometers long, running north and south between ridges of low rugged mountains.

"Is this one of your making, too, Reggie? I have admired it since I saw it in Milan."

Reggie Lewis had come to Milan at the invitation of fashion designer Erminio Biondi, who had planned to use Reggie's jewelry for his fall and spring clothing lines. Unfortunately, the deal had fallen through due to a variety of circumstances. It had led to them seated here, on brightly cushioned furniture on the quaint front porch that extended the breadth of the old house in the sleepy Okanagan town of Peachland. The deep indigo of

Okanagan Lake and the red-gold gilding of the evening light on the sun-baked dry mountains across the lake sent a momentary pang of homesickness through Victoria. The scent of sun-warmed water was so like Lake Como in Italy and yet the dry hills were so not like the hills of her home.

Though there were copper planters on the broad front porch overflowing with red and white geranium and purple heliotrope, it was not the lovely bougainvillea flocked with pink, purple, and white blossoms that in some places around Lake Como covered entire estate walls. There was none of the thick, dark green pine on the mountains across the lake—these were barren, the product of a forest fire a few years back she'd been told, though hints of green said new life was coming back. There were none of the graceful old towns that had slumbered by Lake Como for hundreds of years. No, here there was a straggle of small shops, a bar, and a string of small beach bungalows gradually being replaced by condo developments and million-dollar monster houses that destroyed what might have been the feel of the town.

Reggie pulled away from Cesare. "Let me see," she said and grabbed Victoria's wrist most unceremoniously.

She flipped Victoria's hand over to expose the closure—a most clever, ornate keyhole that a small key slid through. Reggie tried to slide the key back through the lock. It did not work. She tried again. And again, and released Victoria's hand to slump back, eyes closed, in the loveseat next to Cesare.

"Oh, God. It's happened again."

Victoria shielded her wrist with her other hand, feeling momentarily hurt by Reggie's response. What was the problem? "I am so sorry, Reggie. If I had known that trying on the bracelet would upset you so, I would not have done it. Here. I give it back to you." She slid the bracelet around so the closure was on the back of her arm. Tried to slide the key through the keyhole.

It was as if, at the last moment, the key grew too large for the opening and confused her fingers. The closure refused to open. She frowned. "*Cos'è questo*? What is this? It was so easy to close."

Reggie's jaw was a rigid line, her knuckles white as she clasped Cesare's hands.

"Reggie. Please. Forgive me this. I did not understand this piece was so important to you."

But Reggie was shaking her head.

"It is not the bracelet, *cara*," Cesare said, his dark hair falling charmingly over his eyes. "Or perhaps it is. The bracelet is the source of trouble here in Peachland. Reggie wore it all the time because it would not come off. It was like you find it now—locked on her wrist."

"But why? How? The key fit through the lock. It must fit in reverse." She tried the stubborn bracelet closure again, but it still resisted.

"*Chepalle!*" In disgust she shook her wrist and the silver doors tinkled together most prettily. It really was a lovely piece, even if the fact it would not come off was a pain. "But Reggie, it just came off your wrist. And surely you can cut it off and repair it with no sign, yes?"

Reggie Lewis was a well-known jewelry designer on the verge of becoming internationally well-known if not for Erminio's actions in Milan. A little snip and a solder. Surely that would do the trick.

But Reggie shook her head. "I didn't wear the darn thing because I wanted to. I wore it because someone had to and it wouldn't come off. There's a story attached to that bracelet, Victoria, and it's not a good one. I guess with you back and forth to Milan, no one told you about the trouble that darn thing has caused around here. It's what led to the attack on Thalia and me." Thalia was Reggie's ten-year-old daughter. "'Course, it also helped get Cesare and me together."

She looked up at tall Cesare, who draped his arm around her to pull her to his side. It was still a surprise seeing him like that— yes, Cesare had had many women in his life, but Reggie Lewis was different. Not a flighty jet-setter, and not some random girl he had picked up off a beach. Reggie was an artisan, a businesswoman, and a partner in the jewelry store called *This and That,* which occupied the front of the main floor of the white-and-red house. She was also the mother of the very active Thalia, who was currently splashing in the lake across the street under Reggie's watchful gaze. Aside from the fact that Reggie was unusually beautiful with her black Egyptian haircut and her thickly lashed almost black eyes, she wore her difference from Cesare's other conquests in the two Celtic knot tattoos that encircled both her biceps. Both were visible in the sleeveless navy silk tunic blouse she wore with wide-legged trousers. It was simple clothing—something Victoria herself could have designed if she hadn't wasted her entire career letting Erminio rob her of her ideas.

Victoria sighed and shook her head. "I am sorry. I do not understand. It is impossible that a bracelet will not come off and must be worn."

"Not this one," Cesare and Reggie said in unison.

"You need to understand," Reggie followed up. "The bracelet isn't any design of mine. It came to *This and That* in a box of jewelry from an estate sale. Kylee found it and was the first one to put it on."

Kylee Jensen, the little blonde who was a marketing genius for the store.

"Someone tried to abduct her to get the bracelet. It only came off when she and Brett finally accepted that they were to be together. Chloe was the next. She put it on sort of like you did—not knowing. It wouldn't come off her wrist, either. She was attacked, too, and things were really touch-and-go until she and Jas Stone finally realized they were right for each other. Ally was next—that's Allison McVay, the international photographer. She was visiting and was nearly killed in a diving accident. It came off for her when she and her old flame Séamus worked things out. That was when I put it on. I knew what I was getting into, but there was no one else. You know what happened to me."

It had been a very near thing indeed, with Reggie's daughter abducted and both of them and Cesare nearly killed. Cesare still favored his side, injured from knife wounds.

The air was suddenly chill even though it was a warm evening with barely a breeze off the lake. Victoria's arms turned to gooseflesh. The sweet scent of heliotrope seemed suddenly smoky and the golden light on the mountains seemed to dim. She did not like the idea of an attack on her life. Not at all—and to have the bracelet only release when she had found her love interest—that was ridiculous, surely.

"But you can cut it off, yes? I do not fancy being a target." Sighing, she jingled the bracelet on her wrist again. It might be lovely, but she shivered with a fear that matched what she'd felt when she abandoned Erminio in Milan and brought back a box full of Reggie's designs that he had stolen. She'd been brave then, but she was not stupid.

"I'm not sure it can be done," Reggie said with a shake of her head. "More importantly, I don't think it *should* be. You see, there's something else. I don't know what it is, but there's something that wants the bracelet. If you talk to Danny Forester, he'll tell you that whatever it is, it's like an alien in your head. I think it was controlling Dietrich when he tried to kill Cesare and me. When he died it was—" She looked at Cesare. "It was like something came out of him. A huge grey cloud, like ash, that the wind swept away. Did you see it?" she asked him.

Cesare shook his head. "It seems that I was too busy convincing myself that I was not going to die."

"I'm a little happy that you didn't." Reggie leaned in to give him a peck on the lips that swiftly became something more. "Make that a lot happy."

And the thing of it was, by the look on Cesare's face, he was happy, too. The happiest Victoria had ever seen her older brother, and he was making plans to get on with his life—to work. To do something instead of wandering the world and wasting money—all that he had done for the past five years, ever since he began his feud with their successful industrialist father. Seeing his happiness, for a moment she felt envy.

But the bracelet...She looked at Reggie and felt a little baffled resentment. After Victoria had risked everything to get Reggie's files back, was removing the bracelet so much to ask? It was so typical of so many people. They used you and you could not trust them.

"But I cannot wear this thing if it brings danger. I cannot. I refuse." She stood up. "I will go speak to Lila and she will help me if you will not." Or she would cut it off herself. After all, in this world there really was no one else to depend upon.

She abandoned them on the front porch of the house and went down the porch stairs to circle around the side of the two-story house to the flagstone patio in the rear.

It was a festive place: Lila Weber, the tall, willowy, auburn-haired owner of the house had decorated the patio with tea lights set in the broad kitchen windows across the rear of the house, and small white lights hung in the maple tree in the garden corner and on the eaves of the low-slung building that was Reggie's work shop. A stainless steel barbecue smoked with the scent of skewers of tender lamb, and an aluminum foil packet that must hold the salmon Lila had said she was going to cook.

Petite, blonde-haired Kylee looked up from her seat on a turquoise-cushioned chaise with tall, beach-boy blond Brett at her feet. Kylee frowned as if she read something on Victoria's face. Her concern must have registered, for the two other women on the patio, Lila and Chloe Main, Lila's other partner in the shop, both turned in Victoria's direction. All three gazes fixed on her wrist and the happy conversations sputtered out.

"Victoria? Oh, my God!" Kylee sputtered. "How did the bracelet get from Reggie to you?"

How? How? "It was a mistake. An accident. Cesare came to the front to tell about possibly partnering with Brett in his winery. He and Reggie kissed and the bracelet fell." She told how she saw the bracelet fall and picked it up. "It was so pretty that I draped it across my wrist. Then I could not resist closing the clasp."

"And now it won't come off," Kylee said, scrambling up to catch Victoria's hands and lead her to a chair. "Sit. You look like you could fall down."

Feeling numb, Victoria sat and met the gazes of the people on the patio one by one. There was concern there and pity, expressions she was not used to. Lila found a lovely, soft, ivory pashmina that matched the flowing pantsuit Victoria wore. She draped it around Victoria's shoulders but it couldn't seem to dispel the freezing cold she felt. She didn't need this. She had enough problems—her career ruined and her name as well—at least in the Milan fashion industry; Erminio was seeing to that. Her father—always concerned for the Angelucci reputation—was furious. She already had two stormy voice messages from him but had held off returning his calls. Her "theft" to reclaim Reggie's files from Erminio's office likely meant she couldn't even go home to Milan without facing arrest, even if the files had been originally stolen from right here in Peachland.

And now this. A bracelet with some wild story attached. But there was no denying that the silver-door bracelet would not come off. She scanned the faces of those around her, but could not bring herself to ask for help. Too many people had always thought she was no more than her father's coddled daughter. Kylee looked anxious. Lila reserved, but concerned. Chloe was clearly afraid for her. Brett held Kylee's shoulders protectively as if he would stop her from getting involved. Jas Stone, the detective in the Royal Canadian Mounted Police and Chloe's lover, stood in reserve— help when needed. He had been there for Reggie, too.

And beside him stood the last of their number, Jas Stone's partner, Danny Forester, though the diminutive name did not suit him. He was a big man like Jas, just as broad of shoulder, but instead of Jas's dark, almost Italian good looks, Danny was every inch a Nordic redhead, with the high cheekbones, square jaw, and rugged good looks of Vikings. He wore a faded green polo shirt that brought out the color of his eyes. All evening he had stayed beside the barbecue tending the skewers. Danny Forester, who Reggie said knew about whatever wanted the bracelet. In the light from the barbecue flames, red glittered in his watchful eyes.

Chapter 2

In the backyard amidst the bevy of beautiful women immersed in the flickering tea lights, Danny kept his attention on the sizzle and pop of the lamb skewers he was tending—or tried to. It should be easy. He was a flexible guy. Easy going—that was his motto. In the often tense world of policing, that was the only way to get by. And this was a social event with people he liked. Throw in a little humor and easy-peasy.

The air was cool, the soft strains of classical music—something like Appalachian Spring—came from the speakers on the corner of the flagstone patio. As the sun fell over the mountains behind them, the dusky sky darkened toward night and from the street came the sound of voices calling—the beach was closing down and people were saying their goodnights. The breeze carried the scent of the lake, the heated sage of the hills, and the sweet of the petunias planted in pots around the garden.

He used barbecue tongs to turn the skewers. He'd volunteered for the job first of all because he was all about the grill and the meat. In fact, he'd made a bit of a study of it this summer on his long evenings at home alone and wanted to show that he could cook lamb without creating leather. At home there might not be someone to cook for, but he could experiment and it was a safe enough hobby. A hobby he could focus on while he tried to come to grips with exactly what had happened to him in June. Because he might be easygoing, but having something take over your flipping body was not something you could be easygoing about. Besides, he was a police officer—a detective, in the television cop jargon—and he prided himself on cool logic, attention to detail, and dogged determination in order to solve his cases. He and Jas as a team had an incredibly high clearance and conviction rate for their cases. All good, but that time in June when something had entered his brain and had him doing things that he would *never* do—well, that tended to put all his beliefs about himself in question.

The second thing that kept him focused on the juice-laden lamb skewers that he'd marinated all afternoon in lemon, olive oil, and spices was the latest addition to their little enclave of friends here at *This and That*. Beautiful women had never scared him off, and the first time he'd seen *This and That* when he was his own man and not some automaton driven by an external force in his brain, he'd looked forward to opportunities to come back. He liked women, and beautiful women most of all, and *This and That* had no shortage of them. Oddly, although he liked to think of himself as a bit of a ladies' man, he hadn't hit on any of the women here. It was the conversations that he'd had with the women and the friendships that he had with their men that had drawn him the most.

Until tonight.

Somehow, while everything was happening between Cesare Angelucci and Reggie, he'd missed meeting the gorgeous blonde that was Cesare's baby sister, a cross between Brigitte Bardot and Angelina Jolie, with thick blonde hair and a figure that made his mouth go dry. He'd had a tough time finding the words to do more than greet her with hello when they'd been introduced. And he'd stumbled over that and managed to cover it with a cough—he hoped.

Good going, ya idiot. Impress her all to hell and stand like a nimrod next to the barbecue all evening. That'll get to know her.

'Course, now that she had the bracelet on and was surrounded by Lila and the others, maybe he should just pack himself up home and to bed, because he clearly wasn't good for much around here.

There'd be some knight in shining armor sweeping in to save the glorious Victoria from whatever threats came her way, and that would be the end of his chances.

"You're being awfully quiet, friend. No quips? No mention of the fact that there's a good chance she'll meet her soul mate?" said Jas, out of nowhere.

Danny stiffened at the way the words reflected exactly his thoughts, but that could happen with police partners. Jas had sidled up beside him, from where, Danny couldn't say; and if that wasn't a sign of being outta sorts, well, what was?

"Got to tend to this meat. It'll burn if I don't. But then, perhaps you prefer shoe leather?"

He couldn't help himself—he glanced over at Victoria as Lila and Chloe and Kylee fussed over her. When he looked up at Jas, he found his partner studying him, his expression almost gloating.

"What? What's the problem?"

"Hey! Nothing, man." Jas held up his hands. "Just thought I saw something. Clearly, I didn't. Damn bracelet, though. I swear it knows just when there's a new wrist to climb onto."

Danny snorted and raised his brows. "You're believing an inanimate object has intention, now, are you?"

Jas shook his head. "After the past few months, I'm open to just about anything if it will explain what's been happening. I mean, shit, Danny. It's been a month and we aren't any closer to solving this whole thing. We've got bupkis except crimes—attempted abduction, break-ins, stolen files. The break-in at *This and That* and the attack on Chloe, we've got a 'file closed' stamp on, but we both know that's not really the case because the perp was effin' possessed at the time. We'll never know if the others all were. At least the guys who tried for Ally and Reggie had links to Germany. That at least puts their origins as the same country as our mystery man, Johan Fehr, but it still doesn't get us either Johan Fehr in custody or a better understanding of why *This and That* seems to be the eye of a storm."

Danny grabbed a plate and began shifting the skewers onto it. The foil-wrapped package of salmon he slid onto a platter. "That was a mighty big speech there, partner. You're sounding a little frustrated."

"Aren't you? I don't like that this is happening. It's wrecking our clearance rate, and I really don't like not understanding what's going on. Why the hell this bracelet? Why the hell now?"

Danny sighed and met his partner's gaze. Jas was as solid as a cop could get and yet he'd put aside his own "show-me" approach to life to believe in a crazy-ass story about possession because Danny had said that was what was happening. Of course, the fact that there had been suicide notes and two perps in the psych ward all talking about aliens in their heads had helped, too, but Jas had believed Danny when Danny could barely believe it himself.

That kind of partner was something you couldn't put a value on.

"And now we've got another woman vulnerable."

Jas thought a moment. "We could put a watch on her? Maybe we'd be able to pick up the bad guy before he had a chance to take action." He nodded. "That could work. What'd'ya think? You up for a little surveillance?"

Jas turned and Danny followed his gaze to the blonde goddess on the chaise. It looked for all the world like the others were her handmaidens. It would be an excuse, wouldn't it? A valid excuse to be around Victoria Angelucci. There were a hell of a lot worse ways a red-blooded man could spend his time.

"I could do that."

Jas chuckled and elbowed his arm. "I'll just bet you could, old man."

"What the hell's that supposed to mean?"

"Not a darn thing—except you've avoided her like the plague since you met her this evening and that ain't like you. Not when the woman's that good looking."

Damn. The last thing he needed was Jas Stone laughing at him. Laughing at a partner's romantic pursuits was more his own department.

"She looks like a lot of woman." Someone far too far above him—hell, she was almost Italian royalty.

"Yup."

"The high maintenance kind." Perfect manicure, perfect hair, perfect clothing, while he was more the throw-on-what-he-found-on-the-floor-that-morning kinda guy. If the tie didn't match the shirt, well, what of it?

"Yup again."

"She sorta dazzles the eye with that high fashion thing of hers."Just the graceful way she brushed a hair from her perfectly made-up face could take his breath away.

"She does that, too."

"What the hell am I going to do, Jas? I don't know if I can even talk to her." Danny stopped. Had he said that out loud?

A clap on the back said he probably had.

"Welcome to my world, ya poor bastard. Welcome to the lightning bolt."

§

Victoria sipped the glass of cool white wine that Kylee had given her, but her fingers felt wooden and her hand actually shook. As a matter of fact, her whole body felt wooden. It did not help that everyone—Chloe, Kylee, and Lila—were acting as if she had just been struck down by a serious illness. Was it truly that bad?

"But this is craziness, surely? It cannot be true." She held up her arm to examine the offending bracelet. A series of seven small doors made up the links, each one unique. A small, arched door had what looked like small vines coiled around the arch. One looked like a mysterious, North African door of heavy wood, bound in iron. Another was a simple door with a gargoyle knocker, and still another reminded her of the entrance of her family's musty old winery entrance. Another had leaf-shaped hinges over wood, like a door from a fairytale complete with a padlocked chain, while another had ornate iron hinges that reminded her of elves. The last, and the one that charmed her, looked like a classic Dutch door of plain lines. It was even made of two pieces, top and bottom cleverly fastened together by what looked like a small iron bolt. Charming. Utterly charming, and yet—not.

Given everything she had been told, the fact the piece of jewelry sat on her wrist terrified her. She might be bold in her meetings with Erminio and clients, but the prospect of physical danger—well, that took her from her fairytale world of fashion and design to somewhere real that she did not wish to go. Especially not with the tales of aliens and demons they had told her. It was against—against all her good Catholic upbringing.

Now there was a laugh. She might have been raised Catholic, but when was the last time she had gone to mass and meant it? The confessional?

Could the priests protect her? Perhaps they could get the bracelet off?

"Victoria? Is she okay?" Reggie rushed up to her, her daughter and Cesare in tow. Ten-year-old Thalia was wrapped in a bright blue-and-green beach towel, her blonde hair matted to her head and smelling of lake water. Cesare stood behind them like a protector—something Victoria had never seen before. Perhaps it was true—he had finally grown up and found what was important to him: this dark-haired woman with the concerned eyes. Was that the bracelet's influence?

Victoria caught Reggie's hand. "I am well. Fine, as you say. Just surprised and a little overwhelmed? Is that the word?"

Reggie nodded. "Overwhelmed is the perfect word. It's exactly how I felt when I put the bracelet on."

"That goes double for me," Chloe said.

"And me," Kylee chimed in. "I really thought I'd done something wrong because Lila had asked me to sort through the stuff in this shipment, not try stuff on. And then the darn bracelet wouldn't come off. I was mortified."

"Mortified." Victoria tried the word out. Yes, it fit. She had been so stupid putting Reggie's bracelet on. "I just don't know what came over me. It is yours. It should never have occurred to me to try it on, given it is not my possession. It was like a small voice in my head told me to do so." She shook her head. "Silly, I know."

Reggie shook her sleek black head. "The bracelet doesn't belong to me—to any of us, really. I think it came to us for a reason. Chloe talks about fate. Well, I think this was fated. Me. The bracelet. Meeting Cesare. The others and their partners. It's all worked out and now it's your turn."

"If it's any consolation, I remember that little voice in my head, too," Kylee said with a self-effacing shrug.

"My turn to meet a man and fall in love?" Victoria frowned and shook her head. "I am too busy—have too many other things to worry me. Men come and go. You cannot expect anyone to be there for you. Besides, why should I wish to settle down now?"

Reggie gave her the once-over and shook her head. "Sorry, Victoria. Ally was way more committed to having and discarding men, and now, after wearing the bracelet, she's back with her first love. I expect we'll be invited to a wedding sometime in the next year." She looked meaningfully at Chloe and Kylee and their men. "Maybe more than one. Who knows? The point is that you can't just kiss off the power of the bracelet. It won't let you."

"Won't let me? But it is a bracelet—not a thinking being."

Reggie shook her head. "I guess you're just going to have to live it. The big thing is that you need to be very careful."

"That's what concerns me," Jas Stone interjected. A *molto bello*—very handsome—man, he commanded attention even standing back by the barbecue with his equally good-looking, but silent, partner. "Whatever is after the bracelet, the attacks on the wearer of the bracelet have become increasingly deadly. The attempts are escalating as if the perpetrator is becoming more desperate. I don't understand why that's the case, but it means that whoever is wearing the bracelet has to be extremely careful. Victoria, I hate to say it, but you probably shouldn't go anywhere alone. Up to now the attacks have been subversive and opportunistic—catching you when you're alone and taking advantage of opportunity—until the last one."

"What he's saying is that he—it—whatever or whoever is spearheading these attacks—took a different approach with Reggie. He abducted Thalia to force Reggie to come to him, and he had a weapon." Jas's partner assumed the story, his intent gaze a heated weight on her skin.

"None of the others did that," Danny finished. He shrugged in his slightly rumpled looking shirt.

The way he kept looking at her, she couldn't meet his gaze. What was it about him that made her a little weak and a lot uncomfortable? She had never had difficulty dealing with handsome men before.

"No. Thank you for your concern, but I am a private person. I will not be accompanied by someone everywhere I go. I will not be a burden. It is enough that I impose on Lila's hospitality." Her fingers strayed to the bracelet; the silver now warm as if it felt her discomfort.

"You're absolutely no imposition," Lila said. "You fit right in; and besides, you said something the other day that piqued my interest—about you going out on your own with your clothing designs, given what has happened with Erminio. Rather than fight an uphill battle back in Milan, why not do it here? There's a great space that's come vacant in the little line of shops by the bakery café. I'll bet you could do a very good business given Peachland is becoming a bit of a destination place for restaurants and jewelry. If you're interested, we could work together on it while we sort through this whole mess with Reggie's lawsuit."

Someone had stolen the files Reggie kept to document her jewelry designs and then had claimed *she* was stealing the designs for her jewelry. The files had turned up in Victoria's employer's possession and he had planned on selling jewelry made from the designs as his own. Victoria had stolen the most important files back for Reggie, effectively ruining her career in Milan.

She shook her head. "It is a lovely idea, Lila, but is it even possible? There are visa issues and so on, surely. My brain is too full with all these stories and this silly bracelet that will not come off..." She scrubbed at her forehead. "It is too much to think about. Where does such a thing as this even come from?"

Lila shook her auburn head. Tonight, as in every moment Victoria had known her, Lila exuded an effortless beauty that Victoria could only aspire to. All the careless beauty Victoria showed to the world took hours of careful attention: the makeup, the hair, just the right clothing.

"That's what we've been trying to figure out," Lila said. "We know the previous owner, a British colonel, found it in the North African desert when he was a lieutenant during the Second World War. He called it his luck, and from the moment he found it, his career advanced quickly. He did well in business once he retired. Apparently he asked about the bracelet's provenance in Egypt, but experts there said it wasn't Egyptian and looked more like Mesopotamian, or something from the eastern Mediterranean."

"I got the test results back from the university," Reggie said, standing up from Victoria's side and accepting a wine glass from Cesare. Their fingers lingered as they touched. There was clearly something powerful between them—something that Victoria had never experienced because she had always been too busy.

"Sorry. With everything that's happened, I forgot to tell you," said Reggie. "The metal analysis suggests Italy—northern Italy to be exact."

The patio's gathering of people went silent except for the sound of the grill.

After a moment, Danny turned to platters he had filled and shifted them to the table. "Food's ready, everyone. Dig in."

Dig in, indeed. Food was not something to just be dug into. It required the right wines and a table set for friends. But aside from Danny, everyone on the patio was looking at her and at Cesare.

"I told Reggie that there was an old tale of a bracelet that our nanny told us when we were children," Cesare said, filling the pause in conversation. "*Tiricordi,* Victoria? Do you remember?"

Victoria frowned. She remembered the nursery where she and Cesare had spent too many days as children because they had been too much trouble for their busy father to deal with. Their mother had long been dead and so *Bambinaia* Maria had been the mother to them, fixing their cuts and scrapes, kissing better the wounds of their father's inattention. She had been a gentle woman of the Milanese countryside, with dark brown hair always drawn back tightly to a bun at the back of her head. It had been a severe hair style, one their father demanded, but her eyes had always been laughing. Though she was long ago retired to a small pension near Lake Como, Victoria visited her regularly. She needed to tell Maria what had happened. The elderly woman would be distraught if she heard only the stories from Erminio that the Milanese media would convey.

But Maria had told stories when they were children—the best ones in the world about kings and ravens and men turned to stone, and singing waters and talking doves. There *had* been one about a bracelet, too.

She looked up at Cesare. "I remember. It was something about lovers and an evil king who wanted the woman."

"That is the one. I remember it, too, but I don't recall the details," Cesare said.

"Are you telling us that there might actually be a story that will tell us what we're dealing with?" Kylee asked.

"A fairy story?" Danny was handing out plates while Lila opened the foil wrapped salmon, releasing a luscious, lemon-scented steam.

"Fairy and folk tales often hold a core of truth, whether as a teaching tale or a remembrance of history—at least, that's what I've read," Chloe said, returning from the kitchen with Reggie, both bearing salad bowls.

Lila opened another foil packet to reveal dill- and garlic-scented roasted vegetables. A bowl held fresh sour cream and another fresh salsa of local peaches, blueberries, red onion, and cilantro, and everyone began to fill their plates. Thalia ran inside and changed to khaki shorts and a blue t-shirt and then disappeared again to eat while watching the television in Lila's reading room. The low drone of the television came from the window at the far end of the house.

"Victoria, I think we need to know more about that story. Can you remember it?"

She thought a moment and shook her head. "Not details. It has been a long time. Perhaps Maria still remembers. I can give her a call."

"That'd be easier than all the reading it took to go through the colonel's journals. Aside from telling us where he got the bracelet, he didn't have much for us." Kylee said. "I really don't fancy having to read all of Italy's fairytales."

"Could you give her a call, then?" Lila asked.

"I would be happy to." Victoria sliced through a piece of the skewered meat. Not what she was expecting. Given the grill mark and char, she'd expected to have to saw into saddle leather. Instead, the meat was tender and the flavor was a lovely Grecian mix of lemon and licorice.

She looked up and found Danny watching her, his green gaze expectant.

"*Bene*! Good. Very good, in fact." She nodded in his direction and the compliments started flowing to the cook, but Danny had already sat back as if the only comment that mattered was hers. He started eating, chewing methodically, as if he ate the way he might conduct an investigation. Was he like that in all facets of his life? That could be—interesting. Or perhaps not. His rumpled shirt suggested that he did not pay attention to details, and in affairs of the heart, details were everything.

No, Signor Danny might know how to cook, but that did not mean he was good for anything more, and what was she doing thinking of him at all? He was not her type. Handsome, yes, but a Viking *poliziotto*—police officer? A rumpled one, at that. He showed none of the *passion* that was so a part of Italian life. This man hung back silently. Talking to him would be like talking to an echo. Where would be the vibrant arguments? The passionate embraces afterward and the claims of undying love? No. A quiet man like this Danny was not for her, and where the thought had even come from she was not sure.

The food was very good. The salmon cooked perfectly on a bed of lemon and herbs, with more lemon and herb stuffed inside so the tender flesh was succulent with it. The salsa was a perfect, crisp counterpoint to the salmon's richness and the vegetables were tender, but not overcooked; tiny sweet onions, vibrant green beans, whole baby carrots, and small yellow pattypan squash, all roasted and steamed with olive oil, garlic butter, and fresh chives over top. But it was the lamb that was the star, outdoing even Lila's salmon. The heaped skewers quickly melted away as the crowd devoured them. Even Victoria split a second skewer with Lila.

They drank Brett's chilled white wine and Cesare's red, brought all the way from Milan. That got her brother and Kylee's Brett into deep conversation about their plans for Elkhart Winery. Jas Stone and Danny spoke quietly together, but the way they kept glancing in her direction, she was certain she knew what they conversed about—and she was not having any of it.

She stood up and went to the two handsome *poliziotto*, catching them both by the elbow to lean over their shoulders as they stood over the now empty grill.

"What do you plot about, you fine men?" And they both were fine. Strong muscles in both their arms that pleased her. A clean scent of soap, water, and sunshine from Danny. A simple man of simple tastes.

"Plot? We don't plot!" Danny protested, but by the look in his eyes she had caught them.

"We're concerned about you, Victoria. It comes with the job and with what we've seen. The bracelet is bad news in so many ways, and Lila and Chloe say that it clouds the wearer's judgment. All we want to do is keep an eye on you."

"An eye? Yours?" She gave Jas a once-over. "Or perhaps yours?" She turned to Danny and a dark flush ran up over his fair redhead's skin.

Oh, ho! So that was the way of it then.

"No. I will have my privacy and you two brave men will fight the evils in the world. If I have need of you, I will call. Yes?" She patted both their cheeks and turned, smiling as she left them speechless.

These North American men had met their match in Victoria Angelucci.

Chapter 3

The sunrise the next morning was a couple of hours gone when Danny Forester sat slouched in his classic ice-blue Corvette across and down the street from the white house with the red trim on Beach Avenue. The morning was still young, barely eight o'clock, but the usual gaggle of joggers, seniors' walking clubs, and people with canines had caused a population explosion. The way the joggers slowed as they passed his car made him rethink his brainwave of getting the old car out of mothballs. He'd restored the classic '65 car seven years ago, but since then he had left it mostly in his garage. Sitting here, now, he wondered why he'd hauled it out of mothballs today when he was trying to go unnoticed.

Maybe he'd left it so long because seven years ago was when Emily had walked away and she had loved the car. But that didn't explain why today of all days he'd gotten over the old pain. He tapped his fingers on the steering wheel and inhaled the early morning lake water scent. A light breeze had shredded the thin mist that presaged the end of summer and placed a ripple on the water so it ran like silver. The air carried the white haze of the forest fires up in the hills. The long hot summer had seen a record number of fires, some perilously close to Okanagan towns. In the time he'd been sitting here, a fine dusting of ash had settled on the car's silver-blue hood and hazed his view of the mountain across the lake.

Just down the street, the Taste Bakery Café had finished setting up its cast-iron outdoor tables and the early-riser coffee addicts were settling in for their morning brew and the view—whether of the lake or the long-legged joggers, he couldn't say. He sipped his own mug of plain black coffee—Canada's favorite Tim's brand—bought with a donut breakfast as he drove into town. The donut was long gone but the honey glaze remained in a slight sprinkle down his bright blue polo shirtfront.

What the hell he was doing here? Yes, he and Jas had agreed that someone needed to watch Victoria Angelucci's back, but they'd agreed that when she was at home she had Lila, Chloe, and the others to help her out if anything happened. The trouble was, after what had happened with Reggie, he wasn't sure even the four women could counteract the thing that was coming for them.

Because it was coming. It was like a worm eating the back of his brain and he could hear the chomping, only in this case it was a sense of impending doom as if he sensed that other presence out there plotting.

Well, plot away all you want. We're waiting and we're ready for you. At least he was. The damn thing had ridden him like a Shetland pony at the start of this whole thing and he'd had no say about it because it had caught him unaware. Well, payback's a bitch. Anything came at him this time, he was ready.

He pulled out the black stone he'd started carrying in his pocket all the time. Chloe had given him the smooth jet pebble, saying it was protection against evil so the thing couldn't get him again. Too bad he hadn't had it when the whole thing started. She'd offered to give him a pendant and chain, but pendants and chains weren't exactly his thing—too reminiscent of middle-aged men with their heavy gold chains and their bad pick-up lines.

The stone was cool even though it had been next to his body. That had to be a good sign, right? But something was coming. He could feel it and he was pretty sure it involved Victoria.

He wasn't going to let anything happen to her.

Crap. His fingers beat a tattoo on the steering wheel.

The way he thought about her was almost proprietary, and that wasn't good. He was a good-time guy, not ready to settle down. Glad when Jas and Brett had done just that because it left more of the ladies for him.

Ladies like Victoria.

He found himself shaking his head. Nope. Victoria Angelucci was more than one of the ladies. She was—she was so much beyond anything he had ever aspired to she was almost a goddess. Yup. A goddess with golden hair and a body that aroused him just thinking of its curves. And then there was her smile. She had a good one, with good teeth and enough crinkles around the eyes to show she wasn't just some kid out of university, which was what he'd been dating of late.

A familiar green Miata came cruising down the street toward him, to stop in front of the red-and-white house. A petite figure climbed out wearing a bright summer dress of blue and yellow. She leaned back in the car—most likely for a kiss—and then, with a cheery wave of her hand, headed for the front door of *This and That*. Kylee Jensen was always an early riser.

So, apparently, was Brett, driving her down to the store. The little Miata left the curb to cruise toward Danny and he slouched a little lower. It didn't help.

The Miata slowed as it neared Danny's Corvette, then stopped beside him. The Miata's window rolled down and Brett's green gaze peered out at him.

Busted.

"So. Buddy. You're up bright and early," Brett said.

Danny shrugged. "Couldn't sleep. I thought I'd take a drive."

"And that brought you to Peachland. Funny thing, that."

He caught Brett's Cheshire cat grin and chose to ignore it.

"It's business. Someone's got to make sure the damn bracelet doesn't get taken."

"It's that important that the RCMP put their best man on the job, did they?"

At that, Danny met Brett's gaze. Brett might not be a cop, but he was smart and he'd lived through the fear of Kylee's abduction.

"We both know that's not the case. Hell, I'm still on probation after going missing this spring. To tell you the truth, I don't know why I'm here. I just have this sinking feeling trouble is brewing, and if it is—well, we both know it's going to involve that damn bracelet."

"And it just happens to be sitting on Victoria Angelucci's arm. You were awfully quiet last night, Danny. Not like you at all."

"I was thinking. A man can think, can't he? Or has someone changed the rules?"

Brett grinned. "My, we *are* testy this morning."

Danny shook his head. "Not testy. On stakeout and you're blowing my cover."

Brett started to laugh, but he revved his engine.

"In that case I'd best be headed back to the winery, but just so you know, an eye-catcher like that tin can you're in—it ain't exactly the way to blend into the background."

Another rev of the Miata's engine and Brett took off, but not before Danny saw him laughing.

Danny snarled and took another swig of the too-hot coffee. Burned his mouth. Just what did the people at his coffee place do this morning? Make their coffee radioactive? Or was it him? The coffee wasn't extra-hot or anything.

He set the cup down in disgust. When he looked up, there was movement at the front of the red-and-white house. Kylee was out sweeping the front porch, but then the front door opened again and out stepped Lila Weber, wearing an apricot-colored dress. She held the door open for someone and out stepped Victoria. She wore her mane of blonde hair stacked on her head, and a cream-colored shift that settled against her body in all the right places.

Danny sat up, his cup of lovely, overly-hot coffee forgotten.

The two women chatted briefly with Kylee and then left her to her sweeping and headed down the front porch stairs and through the white gate in the cedars to the sidewalk. Crap. His heart beat a quick tattoo. They were going to see him. Everything Brett had said was true, and just why had he chosen to bring his old baby out for a spin on this particular morning? What was he going to say when they came up to him?

Something inane like he'd just been out for a drive and stopped here?

No way they'd buy it.

He was considering starting the car and making a run for it when they turned away from him and headed down the sidewalk. The café. They were headed to the café, which might make sense given Victoria was Italian and likely would want something stronger than the North American coffee that Lila kept in her cupboard.

He relaxed back into his seat and watched the two women walk away. Both were a lesson in femininity the way their bodies swayed, but where Lila was a tall drink of water like a model, Victoria was as lush as a tropical island. Yup. That was it. She made him think of blue lagoons and a woman in a bikini and a sarong wading out of bathwater-warm turquoise water toward him.

Crap. The languid image of all that creamy flesh was just a little too arousing for an early morning. The car felt hot and claustrophobic.

Lila and Victoria had stopped in front of the little strip of shops in the complex where Taste Café, the tiny coffee shop associated with the bakery, was the cornerstone. It drew customers like flies and was busy all the time.

Last night there'd been some mention of Victoria and Lila opening a dress shop together. Could that be what this was about? A business deal?

The two women kept going and went into the café. Getting coffee to go?

They didn't come out again and he sat there uneasily. Sure, it was a coffee shop, but you just didn't know when something alien could take you over. Could it do that with more than one person? Could it do it to Lila?

He bolted upright. Here, he'd been thinking that Victoria was safe because she was with Lila. What if Lila was the alien's next target, because even though both Reggie and Jas spoke of something like smoke coming out of Dietrich before dissipating on the wind, it didn't mean that the thing couldn't come back again. It had every other time.

There was no way he was going to let something happen to Victoria. Not on his watch.

Without thinking, he shoved his car door open and climbed out into the light breeze that somewhat cooled the heat he'd built up in the car. Was he being stupid?

Well, he'd been stupid before, hadn't he? The car he was driving was proof of that.

He locked his door and headed out for the bakery café.

In for a penny, in for a pound.

§

To Victoria, each morning in Peachland was something of a dream. To get up without the clamor of the city around you. To look out the window and see the lake waters gleaming. It was like the best summer days she had had as a child at Lake Como, but instead of being in the stiffly formal villa of her father, she was here with these charming women in an environment that was totally about beautiful things and how to make women more beautiful.

It was actually funny when she thought of it—she'd had so many reservations about allowing Reggie's friends to become involved in the jewelry design process. They'd been far more astute than she had expected and each had her forte as well. Lila for the business, Kylee for marketing, Chloe for the stones and the *feel* of the item, and Reggie of Regulus Designs with the skill to make a vision come to life. At least in jewelry.

This morning the light breeze off the lake belied the heat that would come later in the day. It would be a good day to either lounge by the water or to stay indoors, preferably close to an air conditioner. The haze over the sky held a hint of smoke and the view across the lake was faded like a ghost as she came outside with Lila.

"It is really not necessary for me to see this shop space, Lila. I will take your word that it is good. I am just not so certain whether it is the right move, me opening a shop here when I have no credentials. I do not even have the right visa for such a thing." And she was not her father's little daughter who always needed someone to help her. In fact, she was exactly the opposite. Hadn't she proved that when she took Reggie's files from Erminio? Apparently not.

"All of that technical stuff we can take care of—if the shop is what you want." Lila brushed a stray curl away from her mouth with an elegant, beringed finger. "I lay awake last night thinking of what we can do. Let me buy you a coffee and we can discuss it more fully. Okay? Just a discussion, and if you don't like my idea, I'll leave you to do things your way."

It was like all things with Lila, a pleasantry and logical. To avoid a scene, Victoria allowed herself to be led off the porch and down the street toward the bakery café that everyone had told her about.

The morning was bright, but the sun was sullen over the mountain. The scent of burning curled her nostrils, but there were other scents as well—bread and something sweet baking, the roast of dark coffee. Espresso. Her mouth watered. That was one of the things she missed the most about Milan—the culture of espresso and something sweet devoured at a tiny café in the morning before work.

The grey stone and brick building filled up what could have been half a block in the city. It stood three stories high with what looked like two-story luxury condominiums on the second and third floors. At street level there was a small, specialty gift shop that had the scent of patchouli leaking out the door and fans already swirling to move the leaden air. A lawyer's office was next and then the bakery café on the corner. But at the near end of the building was a large space with broad front windows that were currently covered with "For Lease" signs.

Lila stopped in front of the empty space. "This is what I've been eyeing. It's a prime spot for Peachland—mind you, that's not

Kelowna and it certainly isn't Milan. But if you were interested in opening something—sort of a destination spot for shopping, perhaps with Canadian or Italian designers but showcasing your own designs—I think it could have a real draw. The shop's eighteen hundred square feet—certainly large enough to grow into and still have some design and production capacity on site. At least alterations.

"So what do you think? Is it worth even discussing?" Lila faced her with her hands on her hips.

Victoria wasn't sure what to say. The location was *bene*—far better and larger than any she would find in Milan. Who in Milan wouldn't want a shop across the street from such a lakeshore? But it was a summer place—not a place where people dressed in the latest designs. In Peachland she saw women mostly in t-shirts and jeans—except for Lila. Even in the shop, Kylee wore dresses that were not what fashion would endorse, though they looked wonderful on her. And Chloe had her own style that no fashionista was going to change.

She frowned and Lila draped an arm around her shoulders. "Let's go get a coffee and a pastry while you think about it."

The inside of the bakery café was not what she'd expected. Yes, it had tables, but they were hard, blocky, wooden things with thickly padded leather chairs for seating so that there was barely room to move inside. They joined the line for coffee—more orderly than she had ever seen in Milan, where the businessmen and women were likely to have shouting matches for their order to be heard first.

Lila chose a latte with a cinnamon bun and Victoria ordered a double shot espresso and something called a kitchen sink muffin. Where did these North Americans come up with such things?

They waited for their coffees and then Lila led them to a table by one of the large, sliding glass walls. Open now, it allowed in the lake breeze while they still enjoyed the shade.

Victoria settled herself into a low-slung leather chair across the coffee table from Lila.

"This is different than what I am used to. Both more civilized and—not."

"Hopefully the coffee's up to your standards. That's what I want. I figure if we can give the woman the coffee she likes, she'll be more inclined to want to stay." Lila grinned. "After all, coffee's important."

"More like a religion, I think. At least to the Milanese." Victoria picked up her espresso cup and inhaled. Very dark and with just the right hint of spice. Someone knew how to roast coffee properly.

She sipped the coffee's *creama* and the dark roast spread like butter on her tongue, the oils of the coffee perfectly balanced with just a slight tang of pepper and cardamom. She closed her eyes and relaxed back in her chair, the cup still in her hand. Heaven.

"I take it by your beatific expression that the coffee passes muster?"

Victoria opened her eyes and met Lila's gaze above her coffee cup.

"It is very good. I am surprised to find such in a small town like Peachland."

Lila nodded. "I think a lot of the locals were, too. Now people come to Peachland for the coffee and for one of the restaurants in town. Surprisingly, the town's becoming a bit of a destination point for more than the lake. *This and That* fits right in, too. People discover us by accident, but those who do come back again and again. We're starting to have summer people order online, too, now that Kylee has the store website up. We could do the same with a dress shop."

"You truly believe such a shop stands a chance?"

Lila smiled as if she had hooked a fish. "It's funny, but I had actually been thinking about a shop like that for some time. It would be a place where we could showcase the *This and That* jewelry as accessories and we could showcase the fashion at *This and That*. So the two stores would support each other. All it would take is the right designs and I think we'd have a gold mine. People want the authentic, the original. They're hungry for it. That's what *This and That* gives them. I've checked in Kelowna and there really isn't anything high-end and yet we have a number of millionaires in the population."

"Interesting." It was. In Milan, if she opened her own shop she would be one amongst many—a new designer on her own trying to be discovered. "Of course, in Milan the people are always looking for the new designer."

"And here they don't know what they've found. True, but if we highlight the fact that you are a designer from Milan, that would go a long way. You could, if you wanted, mention that you trained with Erminio. Anyone who's anyone knows that name."

"No. Erminio is the past. He robbed me of my ideas for too long." And she would not associate herself with him again. That was over and done, save for the court case pending about Reggie's designs.

She was just sampling the kitchen sink muffin—full of raisins and dates and sunflower seeds so it crunched like an unfamiliar buffet in her mouth—when a shadow fell across their table.

"Danny! Hi!" Lila said, looking up at the tall *poliziotto* standing beside their table, though he did not look like any *polizia* would in Milan.

Yes, he had the chiseled features of an Italian male, though he had none of the dark, five o'clock shadow that was almost a sign of Italian manhood. No, this *poliziotto* had rumpled red hair, sun-faded to blond at the temples. At this hour of the day, she'd expect him to be clean shaven, but a rust-colored tinge clung to his jaw. His blue polo shirt and tan trousers were as rumpled as his hair. Even the most disreputable of Milanese detectives would surely have a wife to press his clothes.

"Hey," he said and gave Victoria the briefest of pale green glances. "I saw you come in and thought I'd join you for coffee—if that's okay?"

"Of course. Grab a chair. I'm sure Victoria will appreciate a reprieve from my suggestion that we partner on a clothing store."

Odd, five minutes ago she would have agreed, but with the pale gaze of Danny Forester on her as he hooked a chair over with his foot, the thought of discussing a store seemed preferable. Just having him sit at the table with them placed a sizzle across her skin like new shantung silk. Even the silly bracelet felt hot for a moment and she found her fingers straying to it.

"So everyone's recovered from the wine and good food of last night?" He said brightly. "Lila, it was great. Thanks for the invitation."

"And thank you for bringing the lamb. I'd love that marinade recipe. I think it would go well on chicken, too, don't you think?"

He nodded. "Probably. If you try it, let me know. I've been playing around with it for a while trying to get the spices just right."

"By the way people cleaned up the skewers last night, I'd say you have." Lila sipped her latte. "Aren't you going to get a coffee?"

Danny nodded at the lineup. "Just waiting for it to die down."

Victoria eyed it and the people outside the café who looked like they might enter. There really was a good cross section of people, and the café seemed like a magnet, drawing them in as well as any top window display.

"I would say that the lineup will not shorten anytime soon. If you want coffee, I would go now." And preferably leave right after.

The *infernale* man did not take her suggestion. Instead he shrugged.

"I can wait. A good conversation is better than a coffee at wiping out the cobwebs." He leaned back in his chair and stretched out his long, lean legs.

She wondered if they were really as muscled as they looked. His shoulders were broad and he looked like he did not have an ounce of fat on him. No good Italian wife or mother to cook for him, then. Interesting. Her gaze slid down to his left hand. No ring.

And just why would she be interested in that piece of information? This man was very far from everything she liked. All of her men had been of a certain type. Suave, some would say. Certainly upwardly mobile in Milan's business world. A few had come from old money—the sons of her father's business associates.

And all had been interested in her as the daughter of Ernesto Angelucci, not as her own person. It had left her to her own pursuits unquestioned, but she was *sooo* tired of being nothing but her father's little girl. Looking at Danny Forester and feeling his not infrequent glances like warm caresses of her skin made her suspect that he was not the same kind of man. No, as a *poliziotto*—a policeman—he would be inclined to the stirring up of dirt and details she would prefer left undisturbed.

"So what brings you to Peachland so early on a weekday morning? I would have thought you and Jas would be out on some great investigation," Lila asked.

"Yes. Where is the most handsome Officer Jas?" Victoria asked.

Danny seemed to stiffen and his green gaze flashed in her direction, sending a shock of heat and something she didn't quite catch right through her. Then he settled back in his chair.

"Jas's working on the bracelet case. A little research into Italian folktales."

He turned the full force of his gaze on her and she realized his eyes reminded her of the haze that formed over the Italian countryside in the summer. Not just green, but the green-gold of early morning.

"You and Cesare spoke of one last night. A story about a bracelet. You don't happen to remember anything more about it, do you? Even the name of the story would be helpful. These days a lot of them are up on-line."

"I am sorry! I was to phone about this and forgot." She thought back to her memories of Maria, but shook her head. "*Scusa*, but it is gone from me. It was very long ago. When we get back to the house, I will contact Maria and ask if she remembers the story she told."

Danny shrugged. "Thanks. Let us know if she remembers. It can save us a lot of time and trouble. How are you doing with that bracelet of yours? May I?"

When she nodded, he reached over and caught her wrist, then leaned in to inspect the silver bracelet. His hand was surprisingly gentle for one so rough around the edges. His rumpled hair looked like it had been slept in and never combed, so a terrible cowlick twisted the crown of his hair all askew and a part of her wanted to do like Maria would have and straighten it with her fingers.

Would it be wiry, as red hair was said to be? Oddly, his fox-colored hair did not look it.

"All the trouble this damn thing has caused and would you believe that I haven't even looked at it up close?" He smiled up at her and at Lila and he really did have nice eyes when he smiled. All the official reserve of the *poliziotto* fell away leaving behind a very charming man.

He examined the small doors briefly and then turned her wrist to the soft vulnerability of her inner arm. For a moment she felt exposed and wanted to pull away from him, but the pads of his long fingers gently stroked the bracelet closure and her skin, sending small shock waves through her. The café seemed to shrink in around them until even Lila was just a photo on a wall.

"May I try the closure?"

Was that hope in his eyes? Did this foolish man actually think that he might be the one who could release her from the imprisoning silver links like some fairy-tale prince?

"Why not? You will likely not be the last. The thing is stubborn."

He deftly inserted the small key into the lock, but it did not work. He frowned and tried again and the frown deepened. He looked up at her, still holding her hand in his.

"Very strange indeed. I hope you're being careful. It can be dangerous, you know."

His expression was so earnest, as if he truly was concerned. But wasn't that just something they taught police officers to show when talking to victims?

"So everyone has told me." She pulled her hand loose and it was as if a curtain opened and suddenly there was noise in the café again and Lila was sitting right beside her with a bemused expression on her face.

Victoria looked from Danny—such a silly name, like a boy, not a man—and back to Lila's smile. Frowned.

"So you have not told us what brings you to Peachland, Officer Forester?" Keep it *formale,* for that would keep him at a distance.

His gaze dropped to his lap. "Would you believe the coffee? It's the best in the valley, or so I'm told."

Lila snorted softly.

"What is it, Lila?"

The auburn-haired shop owner shook her head. "I've heard it said that Danny prefers his coffee from a percolator—that he's sort of old school about his coffee."

Victoria turned back to Danny. "And what does this mean?"

A vivid blush flooded above his collar and into his cheeks. "It means that I don't really like the coffee here. Too strong and bitter." He glanced down at her espresso cup and the color in his cheeks seemed to deepen.

"So you are not here for the coffee?"

He shook his head. Then he sighed and looked her in the eye. "Not the coffee. You. We didn't get a chance to talk last night. I thought there might be a chance now."

Charming. Utterly charming. Doubly so coming from such a man—to admit vulnerability was not something an Italian man would do. No, they would bluster their way through. She wasn't sure whether Danny's admission was a sign of weakness or of strength. She would give him the benefit of the doubt. She sat back in her chair, still feeling his touch on her wrist.

"So. We have spoken now. Was it worth risking too-strong coffee?"

He smiled again, white teeth showing this time. A very charming man indeed—so it was not just Italians.

"Entirely." He checked his watch. "Yikes. I better be going, but maybe—maybe we could do it again sometime. We could meet for coffee. You could teach me how to swear in Italian." Another grin that made her skin tingle.

He climbed to his feet and nodded to Lila. "Great seeing you both." He looked down at Victoria. "You be careful. I want the chance for that cup of coffee."

For a moment it looked like he was going to touch her shoulder, but then he was gone, pushing through the tables on those long legs of his and then stalking like a Viking down the street until the wall of the café blocked her view. With a walk like that, he would have killed on the runway. She looked back at Lila, who still had her little bemused smile.

"So the store," Victoria said and glanced back at the sidewalk.

"You know he likes you, don't you?"

Victoria brushed her blonde hair out of her eyes. "He is cute enough in a rough kind of way. Not the manners I am used to."

"You flirted right back at him, you know."

"Me?" Shocked, she turned back to Lila. "That cannot be. I was only me."

"You mean your sexy Italian self? Believe me when I tell you that to a guy like Danny, that was flirting."

Victoria looked out to the sidewalk again. Beyond the road, the lake waters were ruffled by a light wind that was blowing away the misty fire smog. So she had flirted with Danny Forester. She looked back at Lila. Shrugged.

"It is what we Italians do."

Chapter 4

The West Kelowna Detachment of the RCMP sat at the edge of the downtown core where the main highway split into north and south lanes that had effectively killed the town's heart. Great streams of traffic drove the highway and had to stop at the town stoplights while belching out their gasoline and diesel exhaust. At the same time, the new police detachment was being touted as one of the most environmentally-friendly police buildings in the province. Built with massive glass skylights, the place was well-lit by natural light and was power friendly. The interior was built around a central rotunda, with elevated interior balcony corridors around the central space.

It was cool inside, but with the sun streaming in through all the glass, the air conditioning sent a constant thrum through the building that shivered up through the soles of Danny's soft-soled oxfords as he headed for his office.

That had been about the stupidest thing he'd ever done. When you were on surveillance, you didn't go and announce your presence to the person you were watching. Hell, if whatever the thing was had been keeping an eye on Victoria, he'd just announced that he was around to protect her. Just what the hell had he been thinking? It was like the thing that had been in his head back in June had eaten his common sense away.

Stupid. There was a certain part of his anatomy he'd been thinking with and it wasn't his head.

Shoulders hunched, he shoved into the office he shared with Jas Stone and collapsed in his chair, too aware of Jas facing him across the back-to-back desks that filled the center of the room. He was checking the clock on the wall.

"Before you say anything, yeah, I know I'm early," Danny said, to fill the uncomfortable silence. "There was nothing happening in Peachland and I thought that if I hung around there too much, there was a chance Lila and the others would catch on to what we're doing. With Victoria hanging with Lila and Lila aware of the danger, I don't think we have a lot to worry about in the daytime." So he lied. It was only a white lie at most.

Jas sipped his mug of detachment coffee and grimaced, but his gaze was steady on Danny. Too steady—as if he had something to say, but was holding back from saying it. Finally he set his cup down again and leaned back in his chair, his long legs up on his desk, his hands behind his head.

"You remember how you wouldn't let me catch a break when I was lusting after Chloe?"

"How can I forget?" Danny grinned and stood to pour himself a cup of coffee from the little drip coffeemaker they'd set up on top of the file cabinet to produce some good, strong, honest coffee— the kind he liked. Plain. Not all fancied up.

"I was on your ass all the time and loving it." He grinned over his shoulder. "Never seen a good man go down so far so fast. You were gone, man. Just gone."

Jas raised dark brows at him. "That right? You know, I just got off the phone with Chloe. She had a chat with Lila and Victoria when they came back from coffee."

An uncomfortable heat filled Danny's chest and spread up to his neck as Jas continued.

"Apparently Victoria is seriously exploring opening a 'design studio' with Lila." He hooked his fingers around design studio. "She said they had quite the coffee."

The bastard was actually gloating. Well, Danny wasn't coming clean until he knew he had to.

"Sounds like a big decision," said Danny. "Good for her. Last night she seemed kind of lost and worried." He settled back at his desk, the wheels of the chair protesting as he made a show of turning on his computer monitor so that it formed a nice little barrier between them. The RCMP logo swam onto the screen—*Maintiens le Droit,* Maintain the Right—as the motto surrounding the face-on buffalo head emblem with the British crown over top and maple leaves to either side.

He keyed in his password and the screen sprang to life. *Ignore Jas*, he told himself, but his damn partner wasn't about to be ignored. Jas swung his feet off the desk, stood, and came around to sling a hip casually over the corner of Danny's desk.

"So just what were you thinking, partner? Do I have any reason to be concerned?"

"What the hell's that supposed to mean?" Danny slid his squealing chair back so that he could face Jas. By the hard expression on Jas's face, the flipping man was serious. "So?"

Jas's dark gaze held as if he was eyeing a suspect. Did he think his partner was possessed again, or did he just not trust Danny's judgment? Finally Jas sighed and shook his head. "You broke surveillance protocol."

Busted. Danny rubbed his forehead—a worm of a headache forming.

"I had coffee with them and technically I didn't even have that. I saw them go into the coffee shop and thought I'd drop in, sort of casual like. It was harmless."

Jas eased himself up off the desk to peer down at him. "Was it? Because I'm thinking it's not like the Danny Forester I know to do something so stupid. The Danny Forester I know wouldn't be going into a coffee shop and specifically hitting on the person we're trying to protect *and* making a point of checking out the bracelet."

What the hell...?

Danny rubbed his eyes a moment. "Are you suggesting what I think you are?"

"A man who has done things the RCMP way all his life doesn't just stop following protocol for no reason. The last time you did that you disappeared, and when you finally showed up, you were spouting nonsense about aliens in your head. I gave you the benefit of the doubt then, because of all the shit that came down. Now I'm wondering whether it could happen again and whether I'd know the difference if it did."

Jas folded his arms across his chest, his expression hard. "What item did I lose on our last fishing trip together?"

The question was like a slap in the face, even though it was probably justified. It was mortifying that it was. "What the hell are you talking about? You hate fishing and I can think of about twenty ways I'd rather spend an afternoon."

Relief flooded Jas's face and all the tension flowed away. He slapped Danny in the shoulder before returning to slump in his chair.

"So it *is* you, not some alien. Okay. One suspicion dealt with." He leaned forward, braced with his elbows on the top of his desk. "So I'll ask the question again: What the hell were you thinking?"

Danny leaned back in his chair not knowing whether to feel pleased that he'd passed Jas's muster or like a fool because of what he'd done. Fool won. He shook his head. "Hell if I know. I saw 'em and it was like I just couldn't stay away. I really didn't have a purpose in mind and all of a sudden I was standing over their table and trying to make the best of an awkward situation. So I talked to her and Lila—well, to Victoria the most. And yeah, I checked out the bracelet. And no, it didn't come off when I tried it, so I'm not her true love or anything like that, so you can quit worrying."

"Jeezus." Jas shook his head.

"What? It was nothing."

Jas's head was still shaking. "You got it bad, man. Just listen to yourself. Babbling like a fool. You sound like I did when I fixated on Chloe."

"Like hell. She's a good-looking woman and all that, but I am not fixated on Victoria Angelucci. She's not my type. Not my type at all."

"And just what is your type, my friend?" Jas placed his hands palm down on the desktop. "I've seen you go after a lot of women— sort of like a fat man at a buffet."

Danny feigned injury. "Hey, I resemble that remark!" Then he grinned. "So I have a thing for the ladies. But Victoria's different. There's something about her that's a long way out of my league. She's nice enough when I got to talking to her, though. I guess that's what this morning was all about—get to know the person we're guarding."

"I think Chloe or Lila or Reggie could probably fill us in on everything we need to know."

Jas was probably right, but he still knew he'd done the right thing even if it felt like craziness. "Maybe. But I set the stage so that we can have a presence down there that our subject won't have a problem with. She already said she doesn't want anyone watching over her."

"You asked her on a date, Danny. Leastwise, you asked her for coffee—that's precursor to a date if ever there was one. So just how does that fit into your idea of good police procedure?"

To avoid answering, Danny ignored the man at the corner of his desk and pulled up his email. He made a show of scanning the screen. Bingo—something from Interpol. He opened the message and gave the message a quick run through. Whistled.

"Not to change the subject, but did you know that Abel Khan worked for a company called Elixir? It's apparently a company Interpol has had under observation for some time. They've linked it to a variety of criminal activities: money laundering, weapons trade, drugs, weapons for hire, mercenaries, and assassins." Abel Khan had tried to kill Lila Weber's friend Allison McVay when she wore the bracelet, before she reunited with her first love and they returned to Africa together.

"What?"

He looked up at Jas, thankful the topic had changed. "Says here there's been some indication that they have links to a whole stable of assassins."

"So Abel could have been hired to deal with Allison—instead of being taken over by whatever that thing is." Jas had come around the desks again to read over Danny's shoulder. "That's a different approach compared to what it's done before."

"Why different then? Why different again with Reggie? There's something going on here that we just aren't seeing." Jas went back to his chair. "An escalation?"

Danny unfolded his length and went to the white board on the wall behind him. Aside from a cork board of bulletins and a small photo of Jas and Danny doing their male bonding thing on a kayak trip to the Arctic, the white board was the room's only decoration.

"Let's look at this in progression." At the top of the board he wrote Kylee, Chloe, Allison, Reggie, and Victoria. "With Kylee it seemed to jump from place to place—the homeless man, the truck driver, me, and Tom Beaton." He listed each on the board under Kylee's name.

Jas nodded. "With Chloe it was only one guy, but it seemed to have held him for a very long time."

Danny wrote down Allan Green.

"Abel Khan was with Allison and he didn't seem to be possessed at all," Danny said, writing down Abel's name.

"And with Reggie it was the riding coach, but the guy had been around for awhile and then just suddenly struck as if luring them in."

"Yeah, but there was the whole theft of Reggie's files and the lawsuit, too," Danny said.

"All of which might have been planned to isolate her. So it was more devious."

Danny made a note under Reggie's name. Under Victoria, Danny drew a question mark and stood back from the board. "Looks more like a de-escalation than the reverse."

Jas leaned thoughtfully back in his chair. "You could be right. Clearly there've been different strategies tried each time—different levels of whatever-it-is's involvement. But what does that tell us?"

It was a puzzle, all right. It didn't make a lick of sense. Unless..."You know, it's almost like the first time, with Kylee, the thing was overconfident that it would get what it wanted without a problem. I remember the certainty I felt when it was inside me. There was no way it wasn't going to reclaim that bracelet."

"Reclaim. That's what Johan Fehr told Chloe, too," Jas said. "As a matter of fact, that's another thing about Kylee's case. Johan Fehr actually came here, to Peachland, to get it."

"So he was virtually certain he'd get it. Otherwise why expose himself? But that also suggests that that bracelet is damned important to him. Like mega important, given all the attempts he's made to get it since then. If we're right and it's him."

Jas nodded. "And if it's a matter of reclaiming the bracelet, then that makes it doubly important that we understand the bracelet's origins. We need the thing's motive."

"While we've been focused on the criminal side of the case, we've totally left that to Lila and the others." Danny thought a moment. "We need to spend some time with Lila and find out what they've learned. I mean, just why is that stupid bracelet enough to kill for? It's not like it's war time and it's got a secret message engraved on it or something."

"Lila it is, then. But in the meantime, if we're talking about Johan Fehr, maybe we need to know a little more about his origins, too. Do you think your pal at Interpol might be able to provide a little more? I know they've sent the recent info."

"I can send him the query. Worst he can do is say no." Danny turned back to the computer and typed in a message. Hit send. "Done. I asked him for information on Johan Fehr and family. Fehr did talk about the bracelet being a family heirloom. It might go back further than Johan himself."

He grinned up at Jas, thankful that the trajectory of their conversation had changed. "Doncha just love it when the brains start working on a case and you catch the scent?"

Jas nodded, leaned back in his chair, and replaced his hands behind his head. "I do. Now what's up with you and Victoria?"

Damn.

§

It took far less time than Victoria had imagined for Lila to arrange for them to see inside the possible shop space. She stood in the lavender bedroom above the *This and That* jewelry shop that she had stayed in since she first came to Peachland to work with Reggie on the designs for Milan. The collapse of the deal had left the dark-haired woman laboring in the workshop just out behind the store trying to recover from that debacle.

Victoria stood before the dresser mirror, twisting stray locks of her thick, honey-colored hair up onto her head to capture in a set of antique horn combs. The mirror was not too good—misty with age, but lovely for the ornate wooden scrollwork around the edge. She could understand why Lila had kept it. It gave a vintage feel to the room and the woman reflected in the glass. The scrollwork and the dresser the mirror stood upon had all been lovingly painted an antique chalk white, which matched the calming feel of the lavender walls and patchwork lavender-and-white bedspread. A huge bouquet of white lilies stood on the corner of the dresser, still filling the room with their heady sweet scent even after she had been here five days since her most recent trip back to Milan.

From the open window over the velvet, lavender, tufted chair came the sounds of laughter from the huge lake's shore and the grumble of boat motors. The day was in full swing, the parking along the water-edge promenade completely filled with day trippers looking for the cool of the water.

Satisfied that her curls were in place, she grabbed her purse and left the room wearing a simple, cream-colored dress that draped from the shoulders but was cinched in at the waist by a knotted belt of gold leather. With gold leather sandals that reached up over her ankles, she was good to go.

After the morning coffee's small embarrassing interlude with the handsome Daniel, she and Lila had had their talk about the business prospect of opening a store. Lila even had numbers to share, based on the five years *This and That* had been open. The numbers had shown the exponential growth in sales as the store became known for its quality. This summer the growth had been even greater once Kylee implemented the jewelry parties and the on-line sales. The jewelry store was making a decent living for the three owners and paying Kylee's wages handily. Lila's numbers suggested that even with more modest growth and the rental costs of the shop space, it was still possible to have a viable business—if Victoria was inclined to partner with Lila.

The woman had a very good mind for business. One even Victoria's father would admire if he could get past the fact that Lila was a woman.

"I am ready," she said, coming into the kitchen at the back of the house. It was a sunny place of white walls and cupboards yellow as the summer sun over the Tuscan hills. A bank of windows filled the back wall of the house over a long line of cupboards topped with a white marble kitchen counter—most likely Italian marble—and a comfortable eating nook in the corner that had bright yellow, tangerine, and turquoise cushions with a tropical feel. Altogether the room reminded her of St. Tropez. At least the colors did. So did the little tropical fish salt and pepper shakers and the turquoise clock on the wall.

Lila stood up from where she was reading a thick sheaf of papers at the kitchen table.

"Let's go then, shall we? The property manager should be at the shop at ten sharp." She was tall and model thin—a physique Victoria had envied through her adolescence until she embraced her curves. Lila wore a linen sheath that skimmed to her knees in a bronze color that brought out her hazel eyes. Black strappy sandals and a string of jet beads completed her ensemble.

"How do you do it—always look as if you are ready to step onto a runway?" Victoria held up her hand. "Do not tell me. You just reach into your closet and anything you put on makes you look fantastic. Some of us must work so much harder." She shook her head.

Lila just chuckled. "What you're forgetting, my Italian friend, is that I am *very* careful about what I put in my closet. Besides, what are you talking about? Someone could mistake you for a Roman goddess."

"Acha, Roma."She rolled the R in disdain. "Always dwelling on the past. Now, Milan—that is the future."

A little pang of regret filled her chest. Not for doing the right thing and recovering Reggie's stolen files, but for the loss of so much that she'd thought would be her future in the Milan fashion scene. She'd spent her life working to develop the skills to open her own fashion house, but instead of pursuing the dream, she'd let herself be trapped working for Erminio only to realize that he had been stealing her designs for years. She was so tired of her father paying people to help her. It was high time for her to do something on her own.

"And you'll be part of it." Lila laid a soft hand on her arm. "You will. Once people see what you can do, they will ask you back and you'll go—triumphantly."

Victoria shook her head. "I think—not. After all these years of Erminio using my designs in his line, everyone will claim that I am—what is the word?—derivative? But you are very kind."

Hiking her purse onto her shoulder, she smiled to hide the ache. "So let us go see this wonderful shop space so that I may see what my new life may bring." If *she* decided she wanted it. Not even Lila Weber was going to pressure her into it.

Lila led them out through the hallway, down through the beaded curtain, into the jewelry shop with its lavender-grey walls over dark wood wainscoting. A whiff of myrrh filled the air from the winding thread of incense rising from the stick in front of a little Buddha figure behind the cash register. The glass countertops gleamed, the display of Regulus designs now proudly back in place after Reggie's files had been safely deposited with Lila's lawyer. Reggie had finally been served the legal papers claiming that she had stolen her designs, but her lawyer, Cesare, had assured them the case was going to be dropped now that they had reclaimed Reggie's files pertaining to her most important designs. In addition, a groundswell of supporting documents from people who had known Reggie and bought her jewelry over the years had also been obtained.

At the cash counter, Chloe and Kylee were busily sorting through a new shipment of stones that Lila had bought at an auction. Chloe wore a long white caftan slit up the sides, with royal blue leggings. Her hair was restrained in a waist-long braid and she wore a mess of silver chains and ropes of beads around her neck. Her gaze settled on Victoria and she frowned, then she picked up something from amidst the mess of stones and left Kylee to come around the counter.

"Hey. You two are off to the store, I guess."

Lila nodded, but Chloe's regard never left Victoria. "For some reason this is important to give to you."

Chloe opened her palm and her hand held a small cabochon-shaped purple stone that almost matched the color Chloe's eyes had become. "I—I know it needs to be set, but I think you need to have this." Her gaze skittered to Lila. "We can just take it out of my part of the profits."

"Nonsense. You have good instincts. If it is to go to Victoria, then that is where it should go."

Chloe turned back to Victoria again. "This stone bears protection from danger and violent death. It also attracts justice and protects against thieves and homesickness. When I look at you, I get the words 'belief' and 'lonely.' Sorry. I know that makes no sense, but I get these impressions about people." She looked down at what she held. "Anyway, I would like you to take this as a gift once I have it set by Reggie, okay?" She looked almost sheepish.

Victoria didn't know quite what to say to a woman who claimed some sort of mystical message from beyond. Still, it was a kind gesture and the stone was—well—beautiful, like the deep purple water of a swiftly flowing river.

"I will be honored, Chloe. And I would be happy to pay for Reggie's design services. I know that it was Erminio and Milan that has caused all her problems. I feel partially responsible given it was me that brought her designs to Erminio's attention."

But Chloe shook her head. "Things like this are more powerful when given as gifts. As long as you're wearing that," she nodded at the bracelet, "I'd be happier if you wore the amethyst and this." She took a rope of black beads from around her neck that were similar to the ones Lila wore and placed them around Victoria's neck. "Please. Wear them in good health and always. When the bracelet comes off, you can return it to me."

"All this concern for a bracelet. I still do not understand. It sounds like such wildness."

Chloe nodded. "That's what we all thought. Believe me, it's not. The bruises have just finally cleared from around my neck. And you saw Cesare in the hospital."

"But surely that was only the work of a madman."

Chloe caught her hands. "Victoria. Listen to me. He was a madman, but he was mad because something took him over. There's something that wants this bracelet very badly. This chain will protect you—at least it helped me. If they burn, you're in danger. Understand?"

"Listen to her, Victoria. She's speaking the truth," Kylee said coming up beside Chloe. "I wish I'd had such good advice when I wore the bracelet, but we didn't know anything back then."

Chloe's violet eyes were so earnest a little shiver of unease ran through Victoria. But the stones were cool and comforting against her skin. She nodded at the two women. "Thank you."

But she had to get out of here because this was far too unnatural and these women far too intense. She looked to Lila.

"We should go, no?"

Lila gracefully checked her watch. "We should."

They went outside, escaping the incense for the clean scent of the lake. Victoria felt as if she had just escaped a grilling from her father. Down the porch stairs and through the gate and they followed the sidewalk the short distance northward.

"She is very intense, your Chloe." Victoria stroked the strange beads around her neck. They felt strangely weighty, and though the stones were all matching oblong beads, rather strange and unnatural around her neck. Certainly not something she would wear with haute couture such as she wore.

"You should have seen her when she was wearing the bracelet. She was a basket case because the darn thing seems to play with your emotions. It can make you throw caution to the wind and do very stupid things."

As if a bracelet could make her do anything. Still...

She glanced down at the bracelet and ran her fingers over the silver. From what they were saying, generations of women might have done just the same motion.

The building management company agent was waiting for them when they arrived before the stone and glass storefront.

"Morning, Lila." He was a tall man of middle age with a thin, runner's build—how did these North Americans grow so tall? He wore what seemed to be the uniform for men in these parts—khaki trousers and a polo shirt—this polo very white against the man's tan.

"Morning, Mark. I'd like to introduce you to Victoria Angelucci. Victoria, this is Mark Herman, who manages most of the commercial rental properties in town."

Victoria shook his hand—cool, dry, and firm.

"As you can see, the place has very good placement." Mark dropped into his sales pitch. "The bakery café draws many people to this area. It was a shame that the spa owner became so ill that she couldn't retain the business. But there is good window coverage for displays as well as large enough square footage that there's also room for nice internal displays. So just what would you be doing with the space?"

Victoria glanced at Lila.

"Victoria's from Milan. She's considering opening a small clothing shop of original and high-end designs here in Peachland—sort of cross promotion with *This and That*. A woman can come to Peachland for the most exquisite clothing and jewelry and leave fully outfitted. We thought this space might meet fit the bill."

His brows rose. "Don't tell my wife. She'd be here in a heartbeat. She's always saying there aren't any really good clothing stores in Kelowna—just the department stores and a few that focus on high-end casual goods."

So. What Lila had said was true. It should not surprise her given the woman impressed as a very good businesswoman.

Mark unlocked the door and held it open for them so that Victoria could almost imagine the little jiggle of bells above the door to announce a patron. The interior was painted gray, but lit by the golden Okanagan light through the windows. The floor was ceramic tile that had gaps where fixtures of some kind had been removed so it looked like a mouth with teeth knocked out.

"There used to be built-in manicure tables there and pedicure and wash tables there—she did hair, too. But there's more space than this." He showed them through a door to a hallway with a series of small rooms off the side. "These were for massage and wax treatments, I believe."

He led them into a large rear area that probably once held supplies, and that opened onto a rear lane behind the building. This space could work very nicely for construction and she could have a desk out front for design that might draw people in—a bit of an attraction beyond the usual. She mentioned it to Lila.

"It's a great idea. I know we've had a lot of requests from people wanting to watch Reggie work, and whenever she does a custom design to order, she sits with the person to do the sketch and there seems to always be a lot of people who like to watch the creative process."

If the small rooms were pulled out and replaced with a few change rooms, it would alter the store's shape so that there would be lots of room for displays and for good mirrors to allow the customer to view the garment from all sides. She could start with her own designs—she could return to her design school days and not only design, but sew the clothing herself to her standards.

But could she do it? Was her work fine enough? Was she fast enough? Were her designs good enough? It had been years since she went beyond design to creation with her own two hands.

While Mark and Lila talked, she stood in the center of the shop space, experiencing almost a double vision of the place as it could be layered above the vacant space it currently was.

"So have you seen enough?" Lila asked.

Victoria nodded. "It is a space to consider. Thank you for your time."

She nodded at Mark and he gave her his card and locked up behind them.

Lila went to leave, but Victoria stood there a moment longer, just considering the storefront. There would be large, concrete urns overflowing with flowers flanking her doors. In the winter she would have small topiary trees covered with lights at Christmas. Inside there would be cool spritzers for customers to enjoy in the summer and mulled wine in the winter. The paint would be a deep gray with white trim, and her beloved designs would be hung on the walls—both her inspiration and her own. There would be jewelry or scarves from *This and That* to complete the outfits and she would have a section of her own designs and a small section of couture fashion from other designers. Perhaps even a purse or two. And shoes! She had a designer friend in Milan who might be prepared to provide samples and perhaps even make custom-made Italian shoes to order.

Where had all of this come from? Her heart was beating so fast it felt like she had run a race, and Mark and Lila were standing there looking at her as if awaiting her response.

"I am sorry. I was lost for a moment."

"Mark just asked you if you were interested in the property."

"Interested?" The way her palms had gone sweaty and her heart beat like a drum she could sign the lease right now, but that was a fool's decision. No, she needed to think on this a while. "I think making a decision on the spot would be foolish. I must think on it."

"Then, Mark, we'll let you get on your way and Victoria and I are going to go have a coffee. If we're interested, I'll let you know."

Lila caught Victoria's arm and it felt like the auburn-haired shopkeeper ripped her away from her home. Victoria kept wanting to turn back one more time to see the shop and brand it indelibly on her mind, but Lila would have none of it. They joined the line in the bakery.

"So? What did you think?" Lila asked. Around them in the crowded wood-paneled bakery-café, people in shorts and halter tops still damp from the water bought iced lattes and Frappuccinos and muffins or cookies.

What could she say? That she had fallen in love today for the first time? No. She had to rein in her desire to just leap. She must look first.

"The shop would work well for me, I think. If I wished to open one."

Lila looked at her out of the tops of her eyes. "You aren't a very good liar, you know. You were positively vibrating with need by the time we got out of there."

Victoria looked at her, shocked.

"It was that obvious?" She swore to herself. She'd always prided herself on being in control of her emotions—not the caricature Italian.

Chuckling, Lila patted her arm. "I think whether it shows has something to do with its degree of importance. If I didn't know any better, I'd say this is *really* important."

A huge sigh escaped Victoria as they came up to the cashier and ordered their drinks—espresso and a decaf latte.

"I think—I think all my life I wanted the chance to grow a business from the beginning, but I listened to my father and accepted the position at Erminio's. It was so many steps up, my father said. It was no place for a daughter of Angelucci to be starting from nothing." Another huge sigh and she accepted her espresso cup from the barista and followed Lila to a table packed into the corner. "He will not be happy if I do this." She shook her head. "How can I even consider such a thing? I am an Italian citizen."

She settled at the table, her back to the wall.

"Seriously, Lila. Is this not just a *sogno impossibile*—a pipe dream?"

Lila caught her hands and looked her in the eye. "I am telling you as a friend and possible business partner—this is possible. After five years in business, I have a track record with the banks here in the Okanagan. Having to go through all my records to help Reggie with this copyright infringement case has made me realize just how broad and supportive my customer base is. Those same people are the people who would be very interested in designer clothing. Plus we have a lot of moneyed retirees in town and more coming all the time. Classic, beautiful clothes that look good on anyone—that's what I saw in those designs of yours. We could focus on your designs, but bring a few others—maybe some that you knew from Milan or other local designers—to fill up the corners that you don't want to tackle. It could have a special relationship with *This and That,* with all the benefits of cross promotion. And you could access Kylee's marketing smarts, too." She released Victoria's hands. "Go on. Drink your coffee and think about it. You know you want to."

Looking out at the so-blue-it-made-her-ache water, she did.

It made her smile.

Chapter 5

It was *pazzo*, crazy, and yet here she was—slightly more than two weeks later and she was wearing faded jeans, a sleeveless t-shirt, and running shoes, which she had sworn she would never wear again once she traded up for high heels at fifteen.

Victoria straightened from refilling the paint tray laid out on the drop sheet and shoved a blonde strand of hair that had escaped the careless ponytail she wore.

Just what was she doing? A week ago her father had said she was a fool—only in far less polite words—and had hung up on her when she told him what she was going to use her trust fund money for. It had sat in trust for the past fifteen years and never been touched. Just what was she waiting for?

At least that was what she'd told him. Not that it did any good.

Around her the shop was beginning to take shape. The massage rooms had been torn out and a bank of four change rooms placed against an inside wall. The flooring had been repaired and in the process she had had part of the tiles torn up and dark wood planking put in. It was amazing how much could be done quickly when one had some money to start with. Between her trust fund and the funds that Lila had contributed, the shop was going to start out in a healthy position financially.

The walls were of three shades of grey in long bands around the wall, with the darkest from floor to shoulder height, and the two lighter colors running in uneven bands above. The next step was small, lipstick-red circles at strategic locations on the walls. Together the effect was one of clouds lifting from dark water with the red as small hints of unexpected fun. With the black-and-pewter-colored fixtures she had ordered, the place would ooze cool sophistication. A few planters with topiary and orchids and the place would be beautiful and lived in.

She stood back and admired the smooth lines between the shades of grey, picking out the spots for the red highlights. She was just hammering the pale gray paint can shut and eyeing the small can of red when a knock came on the frame of the open front door that let in the daylight and the fresh air.

"Sì?" she said before the silhouette at the door defined itself in her mind.

A set of long, denim-covered legs; a faded t-shirt of green; red hair; and a too-big grin. Danny. Her chest tightened.

"Victoria. Hi," he said, his casual voice not quite casual enough to put her at ease—as if this was far more important to him than she could possibly know. "I just popped into *This and That* to see about taking you out for that coffee, but I heard you were here." Danny Forester stepped inside her shop with barely a hesitation though he had not been invited in. "So what's all this I hear about a new store?"

Frowning, she rose to face him and wondered at her irritation. It did not seem like him to just barge inside, given the hesitation he had shown the other times they had met. This disregard for boundaries simply was—well—unacceptable.

"Perhaps you can tell me what you have heard and I can tell you if it is true?" She faced him with her hands on her hips and his brows rose a little.

"Wellll. Rumor has it you and Lila have formed a partnership, sharing the costs, and you're going to design clothing to sell while Lila helps with the marketing and so on. Sounds like a big gamble." He shrugged. "Pretty brave of you both, I guess."

She knew he was trying to be complimentary, but it didn't hit her that way. She lifted her chin at him. "I guess it does not feel like a gamble when you believe in yourself. I know I have good designs. Why else would Erminio have stolen them all these years? Now it will be only me and I will succeed that way. But then, I do not expect you to believe in me. What do you know of women's fashion?"

She turned away to eye the wall again, trying to ignore the strong male presence behind her. Perhaps he would get the hint and leave. Yes, one circle of red would go there, on the far wall that had had time to dry, right where the bands of grey took an angled jog toward the ceiling. Another would go right around the corner there. She retrieved her stencil and started taping it on the wall.

"So what's the plan?" Danny said softly as he came up beside her and took the tape to feed her pieces.

She told him of the red circles and he frowned, considering.

"Let me guess—like lipstick prints, right? That's what you're going for?"

She looked back at the wall a little surprised that he had deduced her intentions so easily when she had wanted to be subtle.

"Perhaps you are right." But she didn't want him to know he'd surprised her. Perhaps there was more to this Danny Forester than she'd thought. It was odd that the possibility brought a smile to her face.

She went back to the paint and picked up the spray can of red. She shook the can and heard the little knock, knock, knock of the mixers inside.

"Maybe I can help with this." Danny eased the can out of her fingers and gave it a powerful one-two shake, then tried out a sample on the drop cloth. Nodding, he approached the wall like he knew what he was doing and carefully sprayed the circle full of red, with no sign of running. He stepped back and seemed to assess his work. Apparently satisfied, he turned back to her. "Something like that? Looks good."

She could see where it would, once the stencil was pulled off.

He moved to paint the second spot.

"I can take care of this myself. I do not need your help."

"Ah. A woman of independence as well as beauty, but you see, I was just doing this to help myself. I figured if I helped you finish, then I could take you for that coffee and you couldn't beg off."

That broad, handsome grin again that made him infuriatingly like Cesare had been through the years growing up together. Cesare had been everything she hated in a man, with his charming, handsome ways that had women swooning without him ever paying attention to the woman's brain. She was not going to be such a woman. She shook her head.

"I'm sorry. It was a kind thought, but I am too busy. The shop is due to open the end of the month and I have too much to do as it is. All the clothes must be cut and sewn and the fabric has not even arrived yet, even though Lila says she has seamstresses identified to help with the sewing. I must review their work and select those I can trust. I must choose the designs from the other designers. I was a fool to agree to try this in such a short time, but now I must make it happen."

"Then you work and I'll bring you that coffee."

She shook her head and took the can of red paint from him. "You are very kind, but I have no time. I told you. Now, be a good boy and leave me to work—please!" Though the offer was tempting.

She shushed him to the door as if he were a schoolboy and shut the door behind him, then sagged against it. What was there about the infuriating Mr. Forester that at the same time attracted her?

"You can't get rid of me that easily," he said cheerfully.

She almost leapt out of her skin and turned to the door. He stood close enough to the glass that his silhouette filled the paper she had taped to the door to stop lookiloos.

"Go away! I have no time."

"Right." A low chuckle came through the glass and she rolled her eyes at the ceiling. Then the silhouette faded away and the empty shop ticked around her. Funny how the space had seemed more lively with him in it. With the door closed and without air conditioning, the room was incredibly hot as the sun pressed more heat around the paper over the windows. Or maybe that was just her reaction to a certain visitor. Leastwise the silly bracelet felt warm on her wrist. She looked down at it and, *merda,* there was a fine spattering of grey paint on the doors and over her arms. That would not do. Lila and the others would likely kill her.

She hurried through the rear door of the shop to the sink and washed the paint off the silver links and off her forearms. Relieved that it had come off so easily, she returned to the shop area.

And found Danny Forester lounging, legs outstretched, on the floor. He had a napkin spread out on the wood floorboards like a picnic, with two cups of coffee and a couple of biscotti on their own napkin beside. By the scent of the coffee and the size of one of the cardboard cups, one was clearly espresso.

All the little hairs on her arms stood on end. This was not normal for a Canadian man, was it? Because she was not sure she liked it.

Danny grinned up at her like a boy pleased at a prank and she remembered what Cesare had been like. Her momentary concern faded.

"You didn't lock the door so I thought you wouldn't mind, given I was juggling hot coffee and all. Come. Sit. Drink. You have to wait for the other paint to dry anyway." He patted the dusty floor beside him. "Besides, I need to know whether you've heard anything back from that nanny of yours about the fairytale about the bracelet."

"You are a most frustrating man, Danny Forester. I said I have no time. And as for Maria, she is old—almost ninety. She remembers the story but said it will take some time to write it out for us. Now please. Leave me."

"Well, excuse me, Ma'am. I was just trying to be hospitable."

He tipped an imaginary cowboy hat at her and she rolled her eyes. "Fine. I will have a quick coffee and then you will go. Yes?"

"Absolutely." But the twinkle in his eyes said the truth of that was questionable.

She pointedly sank down cross-legged on the floor across from him and he made a show of handing her the espresso.

"Good and dark. I asked them to make it like Italians like it."

He was trying so hard she just had to smile. "And what are you drinking?"

"Plain coffee. Pretty good stuff, actually. You want to try it?"

He offered her the cup as if it was a dare. Did he think that she was some timid woman?

"I will, if you will try mine." She raised a brow at him.

"Deal."

She traded him cups and cautiously sipped—dark-smooth but just slightly insipid because it was not as infused as her espresso. She looked up at his waiting eyes. "*Comme ci commeça*. That is the expression, is it not? From the French? It has good flavor, but is too lacking in substance. Too much water, I think." She nodded at her coffee cup. "Now you."

He sipped and he looked momentarily surprised. "Wow. That could grow hair on your chest."

Color bloomed over his face as he realized what he had said. "I didn't mean..."

She held up a hand to stop his protests. "I know what you mean. It is strong—very close to the bean, with all the oils and flavors there to savor. It is what I prefer."

There. She had surely put him in his place. Not plain and simple. She preferred her complexity. She set down his cup and reached for hers, but Danny—what kind of a name was that, anyway? A child's name, and by the evil glint in his eye, this was no child—he sipped her espresso again. This time he was thoughtful.

"I can see what you mean. Never had an espresso before. It could really grow on a man."

He handed her cup back and reclaimed his own, leaning back on one arm, but his gaze never left her and she had the ridiculous need to finger her hair out of her face. Instead she sat on her hands and faced him matter of factually.

"So why are you so insistent on bothering me?"

He shrugged. "I could say because you're there, but the truth would be I'd like to get to know you better. I've never met someone from Milan." He looked away as if embarrassed.

She couldn't help herself and shook her head. "You men. Always want to get to know me better, when really you mean you would like to take me to bed."

His eyes widened a little in surprise—swiftly masked. That ability was far better than most men's. It must be a product of his police training. Then he relaxed.

"And there's a problem with that? You're a very attractive woman. I'm a man. We both like espresso." He waggled his brows at her and leered.

"*I* am not like that," she said and climbed to her feet. "I am not one to fall into bed with the first man who—who buys me a cup of coffee. Is that what you Americans think of Italian women?"

He burst out laughing, actually throwing his head back in spontaneous laughter that was most attractive—except that he was laughing at her. Then he stood to face her. "You're wrong on so many counts. First I'm Canadian, not American."

She shook her head. "No. You North Americans are all the same."

"No. We're not." He caught her shoulders and looked down at her. "Just like all Italian women are not the same—certainly I doubt anyone else could be like you."

His eyes had gone the palest green as if she could see through them to the man within.

"I think I'd like to get to know you, Victoria Angelucci. I think it would be a worthwhile thing to do."

He dipped his head as if it was the most natural thing to do and suddenly his lips were on hers—firm and insistent—and her senses filled with his scent of sun-warmed leather and man, and a flush of heat ran through her so her knees felt weak. Her hands came up to his waist and her awareness filled with the knit texture of his shirt, the leather of his belt, the feel of warm, hard muscle under the cloth, and she wondered what he would look like naked. For all his annoying qualities, Danny Forester was a good-looking man who would make a fine mannequin.

Too quickly he released her and stepped away. He checked his watch. "Guess I'd better be going."

"But…" She took a step toward him. "But we have not finished our coffee."

"Aren't you the woman who just kicked me out of her shop because she had too much to do?"

It was true. What had just happened? None of this was supposed to have happened. Her head was a jumble and she wasn't sure what she wanted. That unexpected kiss. The *infernale* man had proven to be a very good kisser. Her toes still tingled. So did her wrist under the bracelet.

"Then go." She flicked her hand at him. "I have no time for men who get in my way." She shushed him out the door one more time. "Now go and leave me in peace for my work."

He leaned down and planted a quick kiss on her lips. "Something to remember me by, in case you miss me."

"You!" she growled. "Get out of here."

He backed off as if threatened and then turned to walk away, chuckling all the while. The afternoon sunlight lit his hair aflame and placed burnished highlights on his fair skin. "Just remember that I'll be around. We haven't finished getting to know each other yet."

Then he shoved his hands in his pockets and set off whistling down the street. She could have stood there watching the nice V of his torso and the swing of those long legs under the tight package of his butt, but that would have shown more interest than she was prepared to admit to him—or herself.

She ducked back inside and pulled the door shut. But when she picked up the can of red paint, all she could think of were bight kisses on the walls.

§

Danny actually felt pretty proud of himself as he strode down the sidewalk to the brown police sedan he'd been driving since leaving the office this morning. The sky was blue, the lake was, too. Light waves and enough breeze that a white sailboat was floating by, far out on the lake. Closer in there was a bevy of beauties sunning themselves on the narrow beach so that he could understand why Brett, Kylee's beau, had spent time as a lifeguard when he was a teenager. Sometimes the perks were worth more than the poor pay. Of course, given the woman he'd just kissed, none of these babes were of much interest and neither was the spandex-clad jogger who gave him a saucy smile and a toss of her ponytail as she ran past him.

Damn. He had it bad for a woman and he'd seen what that could do to a man. Jas had been a basket case and not good for a whole heck of a lot when he'd been busy chasing after Chloe. 'Course, now that he'd caught her, he was never available for the camping trips or to just hang out in the evening. That wasn't going to happen to him. No way. No how. He was always going to be there for his bros. A woman was just a woman and they came and went like the seasons. Victoria Angelucci wasn't any different.

He reached the car and climbed in to lean back against the headrest.

For all it was a beautiful, late summer Okanagan day of blue water and sky, the gold light off the mountains was hard on his eyes and made his head ache. He'd been nursing the thing since he got up this morning—like a hammer tapping at the back of his eyes. It had gone still for a bit around Victoria, but had flared right back up once he'd left her. Another good reason to bug the magnificent Ms. Angelucci.

His phone buzzed and he dug it out of his pocket to stab it on. Jas, by the number.

"Hey Danny, where you at?"

"Down in Peachland. Doing surveillance." But he hadn't been, had he. Unless you wanted to call it up close and personal surveillance.

There was silence a moment. "I thought we'd agreed to meet at the office. I've been waiting all morning."

It was true and the realization was a like bolt through him. "Damn, Jas. I'm sorry. It just completely slipped my mind."

But had it? He remembered it clearly enough. In fact, it had been at his suggestion. So just what had gotten in the way of doing what he'd planned?

A sexy blonde visage floated into his mind. Had he been so determined to see Victoria that he'd dumped his plans?

But that wasn't like him either, and why didn't he remember?

Phone balanced against his ear, he dug his car keys from his pocket and started the car.

"I'm really sorry about that, buddy. I'll see you in fifteen, okay?"

There was a grumble of assent at the end of the line and the phone call ended. Danny dumped the phone on the seat beside him and pulled out from the curb to cruise past *This and That*, the little open sign gleaming in the front window. Out front a white Infiniti convertible was disgorging three windblown, attractive women in summer dresses. More piglets come to suck at the teat of Lila Weber.

What the hell? Where did that come from? Lila was a fine woman.

He came even with Victoria's shop and had the urge to pull into the curb again, but Jas was waiting so he pulled around the corner and out onto the highway to cruise up to West Kelowna.

He arrived back at the detachment still feeling guilty and a little confused. He climbed out of the car onto the hot pavement and jogged across to the glass front door of the detachment. Inside, the receptionist behind her glass wall buzzed him into the disinfectant-scented inner building. The place, as usual, seemed to echo with hushed voices like the recycled air was heavy with secrets. He took the stairs two at a time to the second floor and strode down the open walkway to the office door. Voices came from inside.

He stepped in and found himself facing Jas and Lila Weber, a stack of alligator-clipped volumes on the desk between them.

"Don't tell me. You forgot Lila was coming in this afternoon to show us what they've found so far."

Lila, who he'd just thought ill of in his car. Lila, who made his gut twist a little and there was clearly something not right about that given she smiled up at him with clear hazel eyes. The truth was he *had* forgotten.

He slid into his chair and hiked himself around the end of his desk, the wheels on the chair squealing in protest.

"So I'm here now. Where are we?"

"Lila was just going through the sections that Ally found about how Colonel George Bristol found the bracelet in North Africa during the war."

Jas picked up one of the volumes and turned it around so that Danny could read a highlighted passage. As he read, his gut twisted. When he was done, he shook his head and tossed the documents back to Jas. "Hidden in the wall. Who would have thought someone would take the time to do that—especially if they had not much time."

Jas frowned. So did Lila.

"What are you talking about?" Jas asked.

"Just that if the bodies in the back of the cave were killed and one of the bodies was protecting the others, it seems to indicate that whoever died was being pursued and had just been discovered. That wouldn't leave much time to hide the bracelet—and yet they did."

Where the hell he'd come up with that he wasn't sure, but it worked. *The mind works in mysterious ways, Danny-boy, and don't you forget it.*

"Earth to Danny? You all right, man?"

Jas and Lila were looking at him strangely.

"Sorry." He rubbed his eyes. "I've got a heck of headache that's been bird-dogging me all day. Must have zoned out for a moment." Like he'd zoned out earlier and suddenly found himself in Peachland?

Victoria *had* been on his mind a lot. And he had been keeping watch when his job and time permitted.

"So what did Victoria have to say?" Jas asked.

"Victoria?" How the heck did they know he's spoken to her? Was Jas keeping tabs, now?

More expectant regards and Jas and Lila looked at each other.

"I called back to the store because I'd forgotten to tell Chloe about another shipment of stones that were coming for Reggie. She mentioned that you'd been in."

Innocent enough, but something about it made him uneasy. He massaged his temples, but still didn't feel right.

Lila looked from him to Jas. "Have you two got her under surveillance?"

The dead silence in the room magnified the white noise of the air conditioning. Danny studied his hands and apparently Jas looked away, too. The next thing he knew, Lila's long slim arms were around him and her lips were cool on his cheek.

"Thank you." She repeated the embrace with Jas. "I've been so worried about her because she's just as bad as Chloe was about going out alone. The only good thing is she's staying with me, so I at least know where she is when she's home and when she goes out. She just doesn't seem to believe in the danger at all."

"We figured we'd better keep an eye, given what's happened to the rest of you. It's only been good luck that no one's died," Danny said.

"Abel Khan, and the German," Jas murmured, a reminder that people had.

"So what did Victoria have to say?" Lila asked.

Danny shrugged. No way in hell was he going to tell them about the little verbal repartee, or the lovely little kiss that only left him wanting more. Or the expression of desire that flared so briefly in Victoria's eyes she might not have even been aware of it herself.

"Not much. She's excited about the shop and in a bit of a panic about all the work she has to do. She had the painting just about finished. I gave her a hand for bit—until she kicked me out."

"Bad luck, dude," Jas deadpanned.

Lila's eyes narrowed at him.

"You making a move on my girl?"

Danny sighed. "I might if she'd let me. She's pretty good at telling a fella to piss off. If I wasn't such a stubborn cuss, I might be offended."

"You mean if you weren't such a thick-skinned, won't take no for an answer kinda guy. He's a lady killer, Lila, don't worry about his feelings. And yeah, he's making a move, such as it is.

He's always been a little slow on the moves department and he's always had delusions of grandeur, even though he can be a bit of a klutz."

"Hey! I do just fine with the ladies."

Jas tipped back in his chair, clearly enjoying Danny being the center of the teasing.

"So did this lady have any news from her nanny about that folk tale about a bracelet?"

"She said the old lady was ninety and had forgotten." Not quite the truth and why wasn't he telling them that there might be something more to come? He still held his tongue.

"That's too bad. I was hoping the story might give us some hints about what we might be dealing with," Lila said.

"I still don't get how a story like that is going to help," Danny said.

"Origins, Danny. Remember? The story might be a fairytale, but it might hold a grain of truth. Something we can grab hold of to tell us what we're dealing with."

"You mean witch or demon or what? How the hell do we put something like that in a police report?"

Jas shook his head. "Short answer: we don't. But we use the information as something to aid in the investigation, just like wiretap information. It might not be admissible but it might give us clues about what areas and who to investigate."

"Well, Victoria didn't have anything to say. What have you two found out?"

Lila flipped through dog-eared pages, found what she was looking for, and opened the tome. "There's this: apparently when he got back into Cairo, not only did he seek help identifying the bracelet through the Egyptian Museum, he tried taking it into the markets as well to see if anyone recognized its style. No one did. But he did meet an old woman who said she could help him. With much trepidation, he went with her and found himself in what he first thought was a brothel because of the lurid curtains and fringe and incense. Turns out it wasn't—it was an Egyptian psychic's place. Unlike the crone who had brought him, the woman was young. She claimed all sorts of crazy things, not the least of which was that she was the last surviving descendent of the high priest of the Pharaohs and blessed with the all-seeing eye.

"He'd come that far and frankly he was a little discouraged, so he agreed to a psychometric reading. He laid the bracelet out for her and was surprised when she took one look and immediately asked him to leave. He refused and forced her to sit down and speak to him."

Lila shook her head. "Here's where the story gets even weirder. "She told him that the bracelet was never meant to be found. That the touch of a female hand would awaken something dark and that six doors must be opened so that the seventh can be made free and the evil slain."

"The psychic allegedly collapsed then and started crying, so Bristol took his leave and that was all he said about it except that it was a whole lotta codswallop."

She turned the book toward him so he could read, but he didn't. The words were somehow familiar. They made too much sense.

"Nothing about how to get rid of the thing, huh? How to destroy it?"

Lila's auburn curls bounced as she shook her head. "Nothing about destruction—just the admonishment to keep it safe and keep it secret. I guess he took her word for it."

"All to have his precautions undone after his death," Danny mused.

All to something evil's advantage.

"Kylee must have woken something when she touched the bracelet," Lila said.

Jas nodded behind her. "Or the estate agent. You know, the internet holds a lot of folk stories. I'm going to do some research and see what I can find. Is there a geographic area that the story would have come from?"

Lila shook her head. "You know as much as I do. If Victoria's nanny knew a story, surely it was from Italy, so I'd start there."

"Italy it is, then."

Danny rubbed his head again. His skin felt clammy.

"Are you all right, partner?" Jas asked. "You're about as white as a sheet, and that ain't pretty."

Lila laid a slim palm on his forehead. "You're hot, Danny. Fever. Maybe you'd be better off at home in bed."

"Nah. I'm fine. It's just the heat from outside, I'm thinking. So how are plans for the store going? Victoria was saying how she couldn't even begin to get it done without your help. Are you really going to get it open so soon?"

Lila checked her watch. "That's a good reminder that I need to get going. Things are manic as heck, but I think we can make it happen. I've already been showing customers of *This and That* the kinds of clothes that Victoria designs and there seems to be a lot of interest. I think we're going to open with a bang. The challenge will be to keep 'em coming back. Brand loyalty is one thing, but we need to stay current, too. And unique. That's the big seller these days—to be unique enough, but still recognizably within norms. Victoria's designs do that, from what I've seen, and she's been in touch with other designers who are a little edgier. It should make for a nice mix." She stood up. "I hope that's been some help for your investigation. I'll leave the diaries with you, if you like."

Jas walked her out of the office and the secure part of the building. While the office was empty Danny almost put his head down. A damned jackhammer inhabited his brain and was proceeding to blast his gray matter apart. It was a wonder it wasn't oozing out his nose the way he felt.

"Danny, you really do look like hell. I think you should take Lila's advice and get some shut-eye."

Danny lifted a bleary eye to his partner. "I really must look like hell for you to be so serious."

"Like death, partner. Not even warmed over." He nodded to the door. "Get outta here. I'll do the internet research this afternoon and if you feel better we can meet up at my place this evening. All right?"

"What about Chloe?"

"Chloe's got inventory this evening."

It was so hard to think with his brains running out his eyes. The office had gone shimmery shot through with silver spikes that hurt his eyes.

"I think—I think I'm going to take you up on your offer."

He headed out, barely made it to his car and home to his house in West Kelowna after losing his stomach contents along the highway. The darkness of his bedroom was cut with bars of light leaking through the closed venetian blinds. He collapsed face first on the bed and just before he lost consciousness, he got the weirdest sensation that he wasn't alone.

Chapter 6

Two days after Danny Forester had disturbed the quiet of her shop, Victoria was going slowly crazy with everything she had to do. That and the fact she felt terminally distracted by the ghost sensation of lips on hers that she just could not rid herself of. And then there was the fact that she wasn't sleeping properly. Each of the last two night she'd been plagued by dreams that jerked her awake and yet she couldn't remember them, just the shadowy traces of fear.

She looked around the shop. It was coming together. A shipment of clothing had arrived yesterday from her friend Annalise in Milan, so she had spent the morning carefully steaming out the wrinkles from the luxurious, hand-painted, raw silk kimonos in colors of cream and vivid paprika, amber, and teal. She and Annalise had agreed on a price and Annalise was trying to scrounge the money to come over for the store opening.

Victoria hung the pieces on a display rack, then chose one to drape over the shoulders of a black velvet mannequin with its back turned to the shop so that it allowed the customer to see not just the vivid color, but the artwork of an Italian garden on the back. Luxurious and gorgeous and with a significant price point, but Lila kept insisting that there was money in the Okanagan. Victoria supposed that she would find out.

From the rear of the shop came the rumble of sewing machines as the two meticulous seamstresses she had hired busily transformed fabric into finished garments. Mostly they were making samples in a variety of sizes, but from these, women could select what they liked and Victoria and her seamstresses would take measurements for custom-made clothing. After getting a sense of what sizes sold best, she could then have a few ready-made pieces on hand.

At least, that was the plan.

She sipped the espresso she had brought from the bakery café—the baristas had begun to start her order as soon as they saw her enter the shop—and settled in her chair behind a drafting table that she had set up to display the design process. She picked up her sketchbook. After staying in Peachland these past weeks, she'd begun to get a feel for the place and was thinking about a line of summer wear for the summer crowd next year. The rest of her clothing would have the simple but elegant label, "*Angelucci,*" but these summer pieces would have a lower price point and would be "*Angelucci Peaches*" for the luscious grapefruit-sized fruit that Lila brought home from one of the local orchards.

The sketch pad's thick white paper was empty and aching to be filled. She needed to get the designs for the *Peaches* line to the seamstresses. With the concepts in mind, she'd already received a rush order of fabric. Now to take those hazy ideas and make them whole.

The fabrics she had bought included a soft, gauzy cream and gray, as well as a thicker fabric of the same shades and a lightweight, crisp cloth that would be good for trousers. Her charcoal pencil swiftly drew the lean limbs of a model clothed in a mid-length shorts and a gauzy, sleeveless tunic top that covered the hips and was caught below the waist with a slouchy belt. Strappy legionnaire sandals wrapped up her ankles. With the slight gathers at the shoulders and the plain front, the piece screamed for one of Reggie's necklaces. Maybe even one of the pieces she'd made for Milan. On a whim, she sketched in a hammered silver disc set with a single pearl and the outfit came alive.

Smiling, she flipped to the next page and was sketching a model in narrow-legged cropped trousers with a short, boat-necked top of the heavier knit fabric when her door rattled. She paused at her sketching and looked toward the door. Tall silhouette. Male.

Danny?

For all she'd rejected him and sent him on his way, that kiss of his had left her wanting more.

She set the sketch pad down and slid off her stool.

The door rattled again, more insistently this time. Not a knock, but an impolite rattle as if whoever it was just expected the door to be waiting open for them.

She headed across to the door thinking up a quip she could tease him with, but two steps from the door she stopped.

Something wasn't right. The silhouette seemed to shift as if the edges weren't quite complete. A whiff of smoke caught her nose and a chill ran through her so that all the little hairs on her body stood on end.

Whoever was out there, she did not want to see. More *importante,* she did not want whoever it was to see her. Slowly, so her footsteps could not be heard, her presence not sensed, she eased back from the door. Backed across the room to the short hallway that led to the workshop at the rear and turned and ran. Scrambled through the workshop door and slammed it behind her to stand there in the concrete-walled workspace, her pulse thundering in her ears.

Emma Scott and Birdy Phillips, the two women she had hired as seamstresses, looked up from the industrial machines she had rented until the ones she had purchased arrived. Emma was a woman of about forty, with red-blonde hair and a worn look around her brown eyes as if she had seen too much of the world. A single mother, perhaps she had. She had told Victoria about how she had kept her family off welfare doing alterations for local dress shops and sewing for a few clients, including Lila. Once she had dreamed of being a designer herself.

Birdy Phillips was in her fifties and had never sewn for anyone other than her family, but what a seamstress she was. With steel-gray hair and thick, wire-rimmed glasses on a bird-boned frame, she could sew and serge one of Victoria's designs in under an hour, including the hand sewing.

"Are you all right?" Birdy asked, standing from behind her machine. She came around it to Victoria and led her to her chair. When Victoria tried to wave her away, Birdy insisted, "You look like you could use this seat more than me. Emma, get Victoria a glass of water, would you?"

Birdy bent down to look Victoria in the eye. "Hon, you look like you've seen a ghost or something."

Victoria shook her head. What could she say? Even thinking about it, she felt foolish for her reaction. More so as the sounds of a normal afternoon in Peachland wafted through the open receiving door where they received shipments. The open door allowed in the sounds of lawnmowers and people's voices from the café that was just around the corner and traffic sound from the highway that ran along the hills behind the town. With the sound came the scent of the lake, cut grass, and coffee.

"*Io sono stupid*! I don't know what happened. Someone came to the door of the shop. I thought it—I thought it was someone I knew, but then—it was not." She shook her head, feeling a cold sweat on the back of her neck and between her breasts. Whatever it was, it had affected her worse than she'd thought and she was not a weak-kneed woman.

She shoved herself to her feet. "I am sorry. I did not mean to interrupt your work. Please, do what you are here to do. I am just going to step outside for some air."

Feeling shaky, she stepped outside into the shady loading bay that served her store and the stores beside it. It was a simple place, shaded by the condominiums above, allowing space for trucks to back in with their cargo to unload into the stores and for shared black and blue garbage and recycling containers in the corner. She inhaled deeply. No smoke. Not even the smoke from the fires that the news said burned in the forested mountains above North Kelowna. So how did she smell smoke in the store? Imagination? Was something wrong with the air conditioning? That must be it, and the silhouette must have just been someone seeing if the shop was open yet.

But even as she made those excuses, she could not find it in her heart to believe them.

She leaned back against the concrete wall and closed her eyes against the view of the low bungalow houses that lined the other side of the street behind the shop and the bakery. They were simply homes mostly owned by seniors and were kept up with perfect lawns and small gardens. She inhaled the fragrance of flowers and willed her pounding heart to settle.

The rumbled of a car engine disturbed the hum of the day as a car—probably one of the neighbors or one of their friends—cruised past toward their house, but instead of passing by, this rumble paused in the street in front of her. "Hey, stranger. How's the shop-keep business?"

She opened her eyes to see an ice-blue Corvette convertible idling in front of her, a welcome red-haired driver grinning at her.

"Danny! *Ciao*! How good it is to see you!"

She stumbled away from the cool concrete wall and into the blinding sunlight to stand on the sidewalk next to his car, and the odd thing was, she really *was* happy to see him.

She scanned the impressive car and back to Danny's face. If anything, his grin had broadened. "Is this your car?"

He nodded, clearly proud as a new father.

"She's vintage. I restored her."

"She?"

He shrugged. "Something as sleek and beautiful as this has to be female. Would you like a ride?"

Would she? It was the type of thing she would have done as a girl—leaping into the beautiful cars of the sons of her father's business associates.

Instead she pursed her lips and looked up and down the street. No one was here, though there was traffic at the end of the block. "Is it safe with you at the wheel?"

"Madam, I am a police officer. They train us to be safe drivers." He looked vaguely hurt, but the grin said it was an act. "Besides, would I risk the two most beautiful beings in Peachland?"

He opened his door and climbed out to catch her hand and pull her around the car to the passenger side where he opened the door for her, but before she could slide inside, he stopped her. Holding her shoulders, he leaned down to place the lightest of kisses on her lips. So light that she caught his waist and leaned up to prolong the sensual touch.

When she stepped back, there was a flare of desire in Danny's gray-green eyes that lit a core of heat inside her.

"I think that was a proper kiss "hello," but in Italy it is done like this." She stood on tiptoe to buss his cheeks left-right, then lightly kissed his lips again.

For a moment Danny looked dumbfounded. Then he shook his head as if his thoughts finally fell back in place like the pleats of a gown. "A man could really get to like saying hello the Italian way."

But he helped her into her seat, then closed the door carefully behind her with barely a solid thunk of metal on metal and came around the car to settle beside her. He looked strong and confident with the sun catching on his pale lashes and the golden hairs on the backs of his hands. He truly was a good looking man—just very different from the dark-haired, olive-skinned men of her country. Danny was all sun-faded red hair and freckles on the most golden of pale tans, but the bone structure was there and the handsome features. With the breadth of his shoulders and the taut muscle she'd sensed when she held his waist, she could imagine him taking the modeling runways by storm because of his unique combination of policeman's world-weary gaze and seemingly unstrained good humor. Other people would certainly see what she saw in him.

The ice-blue car pulled out from the curb and they turned onto Beach Avenue away from her fledgling store and *This and That*, the only two places that she really knew in Canada. For a moment she felt lost, but the lake was blue and Danny glanced over at her with his full-force, delighted smile and then caught her hand. Squeezed.

"I'm really glad you let yourself be stolen away for a while."

"Stolen! Oh my goodness. I did not tell Birdy that I was going! We have to go back."

Shaking his head, Danny fished in a pocket. "I let you go back and you might not get in the car again. How about you phone her."

She did as they cruised through Peachland's downtown of a few one and two-story buildings housing a pharmacy, an old general store that looked like it has been there for years, a few restaurants with crowded umbrella-table-strewn terraces out front, and the town's green complete with a dock for the local boaters to tie up to while they shopped. She hung up just as they passed an odd, old, red-and-white building with eight sides and what looked like a steeple sat at one end of the town.

"Is that a church?"

Danny nodded. "It was built as one. Now it's the town museum." His expression clouded a moment.

"What is it?" she asked.

Danny shook his head, the wind catching in his hair as he slowed the car before turning southward onto the highway.

"Just that that is where Kylee was held prisoner when she was abducted. We were really lucky to get her back."

Victoria glanced back over her shoulder and a little shiver ran through her. Seeing a place where one of those so-wild stories had taken place brought back all the ill-ease she had felt this morning at her shop's front door. Maybe it had not been entirely foolishness that had made her back away from the door. Her hand found the bracelet around her wrist and twisted. She wished she'd seen the face of whoever it was that had made her so nervous.

§

There was something about beautiful women who didn't seem to know just how beautiful they were. Maybe it was a glow, or maybe it was just a presence, but women like that seemed to fill up the space around Danny with a beauty like the scent of roses from a garden on a still, dark night. You wanted to stand there and just close your eyes and inhale in hopes that your body would always remember just what it was like at that magic moment.

Having Victoria in his car traveling south along the broad, four lane highway was like that. Every time he glanced her it was like that garden, and every time he looked back to the sun-heated gray pavement strung along the hills above the lake it was like he was starving and needed to return to that magical place.

And that was a bit of mush he was not going to put into words any time soon. Jas would be all over him with the teasing.

"So where are you taking me?" Victoria asked, as the lakeshore rushed past and the highway followed the edge of a cliff.

"I thought you might be interested in seeing more of the Okanagan. From what I hear, you've stuck pretty close to Peachland since you got here." He grinned and expertly guided the Corvette through the curves of Summerland, the next town southward on the lake from Peachland. Orchards grew thick right up to the road, the blue lake glittered beyond them, and the gray-green hills rose above them.

"My business is in Peachland. The store—I need to finish what I am doing." She glanced over her shoulder as if willing herself back to the place.

"Didja ever think that maybe a little time off might refuel you—give you more energy and all that. It might even spark new ideas. Now come on. A little drive and some ice cream. That's what the doctor ordered."

"And what doctor would that be, Daniel?"

She arched a sculpted brow at him and his heart did a quick thud-thud.

"What? What is it?"

"Nothing. It's just that no one's ever called me Daniel. Except maybe my mom when I was bad."

She frowned. "I know Danny is how everyone calls you, but Daniel seemed to fit you this morning." A lovely blush lightly touched her cheeks. "You prefer Danny, then?"

"No. As a matter of fact, exactly the opposite." Because in Victoria's deep Italian accent, Daniel came out like music. He wanted to hear it spoken that way often and would prefer to never have Danny pass her lips again. Danny was Jas Stone's partner. Daniel was someone that this goddess might find time for.

"Then I shall call you Daniel. It is a good name." Her gaze sized him up. "I think it suits you far better than Danny."

"Chloe tells me I'm all about finding the humor in situations." Why he was telling her that, he didn't know. She was going to think him frivolous as hell.

She eyed him again, then shook her head. "Humor, perhaps, but there is a serious core to you, I think." She turned forward, the wind streaming her golden hair back from her face. "She told me that the word she gets about me is lonely, though that is hard to believe with all the people around me."

"Maybe you just haven't found the right people," Danny murmured and turned away to face the highway. Penticton came up with Victoria oohing at the old Fintry Queen paddlewheel boat tied up at one end of a golden beach, and at the slow-moving river that formed the perfect inner tube journey for a lazy afternoon ride from Okanagan Lake to Skaha Lake, the next lake south. He explained how the Okanagan Valley was filled with a long string of lakes all the way down and across the US/Canada border, and each lake had its own little community. He almost thought he caught her looking at the brightly colored inflatable rafts and tubes in longing, but then she seemed to shove it away and sit stoically in her seat. That was the trouble with Victoria Angelucci, she just needed to learn how to have fun—and he could definitely do something about that.

He accelerated up out of Penticton with Victoria marveling at the golden sand beaches that rimmed Skaha Lake. Then they were driving through more orchards and dry ranching country before curving down to the far end of the turquoise waters of Skaha Lake. He turned off the highway then.

"Where are we going?" Victoria asked, almost in alarm.

"There's a little winery up in the hills. I thought we might try a tasting and maybe grab some lunch."

"But the lunch hour is past already." Her hands gripped the edge of her seat.

"Then we'll have a snack. Think tapas or something. And a glass of wine."

But the worried expression on her face said something wasn't quite right. He slowed the car on the very windy road to look at her.

"What's the matter, Victoria? It's just you and me and a glass of wine. I mean, if that's so unpleasant a prospect, I can turn the car around." Waiting for her reply was like waiting for a death knell.

Victoria seemed tense as if she would leap out of the car, but then she slumped in her seat. "I am sorry," she said with a shake of her head. "I think I am—how do you say it? Spooked? Just before you arrived, someone came to the shop and rattled the door. I know it sounds silly, but it terrified me. There was something not right about the silhouette. It made all the hairs on my arms stand on end. Even thinking about it now..."

She held up her arm and fine golden hairs and gooseflesh decorated her forearm.

Danny swept her hand into his and held on. "Let's warm you up."

He drove one-handed and soon they were at the top of the steep road and turning into a gravel parking lot surrounded by vineyards and a low-slung, vine-covered, single-story building with a verandah built out over the slope to enjoy the view of the lakes northward.

When he turned the car engine off, the afternoon was heavy with the hum of insects, the clack of grasshoppers, and the scent of dusty vines ripening in the hot sun. Sparrows fluttered and tweeted in the grapevines around the restaurant/tasting lounge, and a couple of crows hopped around the almost empty parking lot. Danny went around the car to open the door and offered a hand to help Victoria out. Then he stopped her by pulling her into him and running his hands up and down her arms.

The kiss came easily—as natural as if it was meant to be. He lowered his head. She tilted hers and their lips met in what could have been a quick peck, but became a slow, languorous exploration of her lips, her eyes, the lightly perfumed shadows under her hair.

It was with a groan that he lifted his lips from her neck, kissed her lips one more time, and caught her hand.

"Come on," he said, his voice rougher than he wanted. He led Victoria, still looking a trifle glazed, up the small stone stairs to the building.

"Better than wine," she said, her fingers tracing the line of his lips as he held the door for her.

He hoped he understood what she meant.

They dallied in the tasting room and then were shown to a table on the verandah that held a cluster of small, white-table-clothed tables and wrought iron chairs. They were the only ones there. They ordered a fruit and cheese plate from the menu and the best wine they'd sampled—a lovely unoaked chardonnay. Danny described what they were seeing below them—the green bottomland of Okanagan Falls that became the waterfowl refuge and slough that then became shallow Vaseux Lake, the tiny hamlet of Okanagan Falls, and the string of expensive houses along the old road that ran the eastern side of the lake.

"The place has changed a lot, I hear, but it's still got a small town feel in most of the Okanagan, except maybe Kelowna."

She nodded as she nibbled on a slice of ripe pear and brie cheese. "It is all very small town after Milan."

For a moment he thought it was said in disapproval, but then she sighed and leaned her elbows on the table to cradle her chin in her hands.

"I feel like it has been a very long time since I stopped to smell the roses." She smiled up at him. "That is the saying, is it not? To smell the roses?"

He nodded. "But I thought all you Italians knew how to enjoy life—the food, the wine...the love."

She shrugged very prettily. "Many do, but if you want to succeed in business or in design, it is another life completely. You are always running after the next design concept, the next fabric, trying to keep your designs secret from the competition.

It is very dog-eat-dog. Another of your expressions, I believe? A very good one.”

“And you seem to have collected them.” He caught her hands. “They sound like new in your accent.”

She tilted her brow at him. “You mock me because I talk funny?”

“God, no! You make everything sound fresh and exotic—sort of like you, I guess.”

God, he was a dolt—sounded like a love-sick puppy, and wasn't he the one who wanted to love 'em and leave 'em and not settle down? It was certainly what he'd told Jas.

She placed a soft palm against his cheek, her gaze searching deep into his. “Why are you so kind to me? You barely know me.”

“Because you're new to the Okanagan and because I want to get to know you.” *And hopefully catch you before all the handsome men of the Okanagan discover your presence.*

God, she was beautiful, with those rich brown eyes of hers, like looking into deep woods or the heart of a tree or a vat of the very best chocolate in the world. But there was so much seriousness there. He inhaled and glanced away to the valley.

“Look! An osprey!”

She followed his finger to where an eagle soared on grey-black wings over the valley. “It looks very wild and free. To dance on the wind must be marvelous.”

He nodded. “I took glider lessons when I was a kid in Air Cadets. Being up there is the closest thing to what a bird must feel like. It's so silent with just the wind rushing past, and the glider can positively dance. It's wonderful and terrifying, but the wonder makes you forget the terror.”

“You are very brave. I would not climb in any plane that has no motor.”

“Not so brave.” Because, if he was truly brave, he'd have already swept her away and found a time and a place to make love to her. He grinned at her and poured the last of the wine into her glass.

“Drinking wine with a view must be nothing to you, what with living in Italy. I've got something else to show you.”

Just what the heck he was doing, he didn't know. Why bring a woman of the world like Victoria Angelucci to some backwoods winery like this, even if it happened to be one of his favorite places? He'd come down here for a couple of bottles and just to get his 'Vette out for a drive. And his other plan—to take her to his favorite ice cream parlor, now seemed like the stupidest thing he'd ever come up with. What the hell was wrong with him? Victoria wasn't some high school girl to be impressed by a flashy car.

He met her gaze. "But maybe this was a stupid idea. Maybe I should just get you back to the store. You said you had a lot to do."

Victoria frowned. "I thought you had something else to show me."

Feeling like an idiot, he shrugged. "Nothing you probably haven't got bigger and better in Italy."

He shoved away from the table and stood. "Come on. Let's get you home."

He paid the tab and left a handsome tip, then ushered her out to the car. The sun was warm on his shoulders and the sparrows were peck-peck-pecking in the dust. Insects hummed in the heated afternoon air and the ranks of grape arbors rose up the steep slope behind him.

Victoria caught his arm. "It truly is beautiful here. At home the wineries may look out on the next hill and its vineyard and the Lombardy poplar. We do not have rugged mountains like this and the eagles flying. It is wild here, and much more free. Sometimes I feel that wildness stirring in me."

She did? He was still pondering her statement when she stood up on tiptoe to plant a kiss on his lips.

She tasted of the citrus of a good Chardonnay and smelled of heat and the perfume of oleander and felt so warm and real and wonderful that his arms came around her and he pulled her into him. The kiss that might have been intended as a light brush of the lips became something else entirely as her arms stretched up to encircle his neck and he pulled her closer. By the way her body yielded, perhaps she felt the same as he did; and the smooth curves of her body under her clothes made him want to take her somewhere private. Oh, yeah. This was a woman—not one of those emaciated girl-women the media seemed to think was what men wanted.

Swallowing back his desire, he set her away and opened the car door for her. "All right. I'll show you my other little secret pleasure, but first a drive to see the country."

He took her through paved country roads up through the dry hills, discovering homes set amongst the ponderosa pine and small lakes somnolent in the sun. Horses loafed in paddocks. They counted seven deer grazing on the heavy, ripe, Saskatoon berry bushes along the road and fifteen marmot, scurrying to hide in tree stumps. Then the road turned down to join the main highway in the midst of peach and cherry and apple orchards.

He turned north through the small town of Oliver and then kept going up past Vaseux Lake toward Okanagan Falls. Before he hit the town, he turned off into a gravel parking lot that encircled a low-slung, ramshackle building that looked like it had been added onto many times. Picnic tables sat in the shade of a line of trees and more sat under an awning at one end of the building. He parked near the awning and came around the car with a grin.

"I hope you like ice cream, because Circus Ice Cream is the best in the Okanagan."

She arched a perfect brow in question. "Ice cream?"

He waved a hand at her. "I know, I know. Italy invented gelato. How can this possibly compare? But this is delicious, creamy ice cream in a gajillion flavors and they do it best. They've been bringing in flavors for years, but now they are making their own, as well. Come on. You'll see."

He led her past the murals of giraffes and pandas hosting a carnival and through the red door. Inside the place was festooned with circus-themed doodads and doohickeys and thingamabobs. Inspirational signs with a circus theme covered an area of the wall. Stuffed animals with top hats overflowed wire displays. Jams and jellies with names like *Big Top Brambleberry* and *Strawberry Show Stopper* filled shelves along with knickknacks of elephants and slim girls doing tricks on horseback. Mobiles of trapeze artists and wind chimes of small glass elephants hung from the ceiling. Images of Barnum & Bailey circus tents were scattered throughout. The cooked sugar scent of homemade fudge and cotton candy filled the air.

On one wall, a long glass ice cream case extended the length of the building with young servers busily filling handmade sugar cones for a line of people. Danny led Victoria into line.

"Don't worry. They've got a system and they're fast. The flavors are written on the white board up top. The specialty handmade flavors are over there." He gestured to a dark green chalk board. "What appeals to you?"

She eyed the towers of ice cream that were leaving the shop in happy customers' hands. "That is far too much! In Italy we are satisfied with a single scoop of excellent gelato."

He grinned and pulled her into his side, enjoying the way she fit and the way her eyes shone. "Well, you're in Canada now. I suggest you choose two flavors."

She settled on a compromise that included the tried-and-true chocolate for one scoop and a bold, handmade ice cream of merlot, chocolate, and red current. Danny had royal cherry and a handmade flavor of ice wine with peach and apricot.

They sat outside under the awning amidst a gathering of families with small children and had to race the heat that melted their ice cream. All conversation ceased as Victoria delicately sampled the Merlot ice cream. Her eyes widened.

"This is so good!"

Danny nodded, his mouth full of the ripe sweet taste of ice wine, apricot, and peach. "So's this. Want to try?"

He held out his cone and she eyed it and him with suspicion for moment, but then leaned in and daintily took a bite of his ice cream.

"Oh, my! That is good, too! Who would have thought to put wine in ice cream?"

"Well...ice wine is a BC specialty. They harvest the grapes just after the first frost to heighten their sweetness."

She nodded and tucked into her ice cream so that it didn't run down over her fingers and somehow managed to finish the complete ice cream cone.

"See?" Danny said. "I knew you could do it."

"If I ate that way every day, I would soon need to buy new clothes."

Danny chuckled and caught her hand. "I always say that it's a good thing the place is so far away or I'd be in serious trouble. Now come on—I know I've stolen too much of your time and you need to get back to that store of yours."

With regret he climbed back in the car after settling Victoria in shotgun and they headed for the highway north. Soon they were in Peachland cruising Beach Avenue.

"You know, I'm always mystified the way that a trip can seem so long going and so short coming back. It's like the world rearranges itself to let us get home sooner. Almost as if it didn't want us to leave."

He glanced at Victoria and found her studying him as they pulled up in front of her shop. He turned the car engine off and the air filled with the sounds of voices from the beach and coffee shop. The scents of suntan lotion and coffee filled the air, but somehow couldn't mask the scent of Victoria's oleander. She made no move to climb out, so he sat there beside her. They'd been gone four hours and the afternoon was almost gone, the sunlight angling from the westward mountains.

"I'm sorry I kept you away so long." But the time had passed too quickly.

She shook her head. "I will get an early start tomorrow to make up for it. But thank you, it was an unexpected pleasure." Her long, tapered fingers played with the edge of the upholstery along the window edge.

"Victoria..."

"Daniel..."

They spoke in unison, then smiled at each other.

"You go," he said.

"No. You. Please."

"No. You."

She eyed the store and sighed deeply, then looked at her hands. "I must thank you for taking me away today, for truly I do not know how much work I would get done. You see, when you saw me, I was escaping."

"Escaping?" He turned in his seat to face her.

She nodded. "From the figure at the door that I told you about. I remembered all those stories from Lila and the others. My heart pounded so hard and I was so afraid. That was when you appeared on this lovely metal charger of yours." She smiled up at him. "A knight to rescue me, yes?"

"Obviously." He caught her perfectly manicured hand, so soft, so small in his. "Listen. I don't want you to be afraid. If anything like that happens again, you call me and I'll come a-running. Whatever this thing is, it's not getting to you. I'm going to make sure of it. Okay?"

She leaned over the console and gave him a light kiss. "Okay."

"That's what I'm here for, ma'am," he said in his best mock TV cop voice. He tipped a pretend hat and then climbed out of the car and rounded it to hold the door for her.

Victoria climbed out of the low-slung vehicle and stood before him. "I feel safer knowing you will be around."

"Then around is what I'll be." Okay, Forester, take the chance now. He inhaled. "On that note, I was wondering if you'd like to have dinner with me tonight." He held his breath as she considered, but then she smiled and the sunlight netted in her hair like gold.

"That would be very nice."

"Perfect. We'll go down to the Blue Hills Restaurant. Nothing fancy—just good food and better company. How about I pick you up at six thirty?"

When she nodded he felt like clicking his heels, but instead he walked her to the shop door, waited until she opened it and then checked inside. There was no one there, the two she had told him about having apparently left their finished garments for Victoria's inspection. At first glance he could see her pleasure at the flow of fabric and color—they looked like clothes to him. Nice clothes, but clothes.

"These women. They are wonderful! They have captured my designs perfectly!" Like a schoolgirl, she grabbed the nearest garment and twirled. When she stopped he steadied her, then leaned down for one last kiss.

She still tasted of merlot and chocolate and her kiss was sweet and wanting. Gently he took the garment from her and set it aside, then he caught her mouth again and the kiss deepened to one of longing.

He smoothed the bright strands of her hair from her silken cheek and smiled. "Dinner feels a long way away."

She nodded, a brightness catching in her gaze as she looked up at him. "Sometimes wanting something is half the pleasure."

He leaned in to touch his forehead to hers. "Then this afternoon will be an eternal wanting."

One last kiss and he left her there, let himself out to his car, and sat there inhaling the lake-scented air.

It had gone well—better than he'd expected—perhaps as good as he'd dreamed it might. But still, a cold edge of fear cut the heat of the afternoon, because the scary thing was he could not remember much of the day—not getting up and dressed, not stepping out of his house, and certainly not driving his baby out of the garage. As hard as he tried, there was nothing until he pulled up behind Victoria Angelucci's shop.

Almost as if he'd known she'd been running scared.

Chapter 7

The door clicked shut behind Daniel, and Victoria sagged against the sewing table where he had cast the flowing tunic that Birdy had finished. The room ticked around her, though from outside came the sounds of the highway and voices that could only be people leaving the bakery café. The room smelled of sewing machine oil and the chemicals of fabric sizing, but most of all came the faint, clean-leather scent of Daniel.

She pulled the soft fabric up into her hands and rubbed it along her face. Soft, as opposed to the rough feel of Daniel's hint of red, five o'clock shadow. That grizzle had felt sensual as he ran his jaw along her cheek seeking the soft places under her hair.

Shivering at the memory, she returned the new tunic to its place, hung on the wall. The workmanship was as immaculate as she had envisioned so she'd definitely chosen rightly in her seamstresses. The second garment was as well made, but examining the seaming didn't help her shake the feelings Daniel had raised in her.

It made no sense. He was not her type at all—frivolous, if anything. Going for lunch and ice cream when she should be working here. She was not a child pining for gelato and yet here she was, tasting the apricot, peach, and ice wine of Daniel's lips. Her failure to focus on the task at hand had cost her more time that she did not have. An entire line of Peaches to design so that Birdy and Emma could get them made.

She should not be going out for dinner. She should be spending the evening in her room at *This and That* with a glass of wine and her sketch book. That was what a person dedicated to her business would do. Not fly off with a man to dinner. Not even a very handsome man, even a man who seemed to have the ability to smile at just about anything and whose smile was increasingly infectious.

That blue car of his fit him perfectly—a little bit showy, a lot of power. His body was powerful, too, and a little frisson of heat ran through her. Broad shoulders. Lean torso. Strong legs as if he was a runner. He must be fit to be in the police.

It had been a long time since she had contemplated being with a man, but Daniel the policeman had her considering that long lean body beside her.

Totally impractical, and standing here mooning about the man was not going to help her, either. In a flurry of movement, she reclaimed her purse from under the store counter and left through the front door. This close to Labor Day, the beach had emptied early as if, instead of coming to the late evening meal al fresco, the people were already preparing for hibernation from the freezing climate of Canada.

Late afternoon sunlight filled the street as she turned toward the jewelry store, but a shiver ran through her and she checked up and down the street for someone who would match the silhouette she had seen on her front door. No one was there who remotely fit the description. Still, she felt like a heroine in a thriller movie as she hurried down the street and in through the gate to *This and That* and around to the back door.

The scent of roasted chicken met her nose as she came around the house. The barbecue was in action and through the broad bank of windows she could see Lila and Chloe busily making a salad inside the kitchen.

"Victoria," Lila looked up as Victoria came through the back door. "We were just about to send out a search party. Reggie's just gone home to get Thalia and we were going to all have dinner together given the guys have made plans to watch a football game or something."

Victoria paused. Had Daniel forgotten? Was he going to phone and cancel their dinner arrangements? No. There had been a look in his eyes that said that would not happen.

She shook her head. "I am sorry. I should have called. I have an invitation to dinner."

Lila straightened, surprised. Chloe swung round to face Victoria.

"You mean like a date?" Chloe said, her dark braid swinging around her blue caftaned shoulders. This afternoon her string of black beads was interspersed with intricate silver beads.

What could she say? The look in Daniel's eyes had said it was definitely a date, but she did not want to tell all about what was developing between Daniel and herself until she was sure. It could be no more than a brief infatuation.

"It is dinner with a friend."

Chloe raised one brow. "And just what friend might that be? Anyone we know? Perhaps a certain redhead?"

A flush ran up Victoria's shoulders and neck. Had it all been that obvious?

"It is dinner with Daniel, yes. He took me for a drive today and asked me for dinner."

"Well, that's too bad. We were looking forward to hearing about how the shop's going," Lila said as she chopped celery for the salad. As usual, Victoria's hostess looked model cool and reserved, this time in a simple, oversized, short-sleeved, buttoned-up, white shirt and Bermuda shorts with red espadrille shoes and her array of silver rings.

"It is going well. The seamstresses are doing well. The first garments were finished today and the shipment from Milan arrived and is steamed and hung—some beautiful, hand-painted kimonos that you will love along with some simple dresses to go under them." The clock on the wall said five p.m. She really needed to get up to her room to get ready.

Lila must have read her need because she glanced up from her chopping and smiled. "Before you get ready, there's a message for you by the phone in the corner. I think it might be your old nanny because I could barely understand the Italian accent."

"Maria? Oh! And I missed her!" And Milan was nine hours ahead, which meant it was two in the morning. Not the time to call an aging woman. "*Chepalle!* I shall call her first thing tomorrow and catch her in the middle of her day."

She went to leave, but Chloe held up her hand. "Hold on a moment. I've got something for you."

She went over to her purse—a large crocheted bag in tan, with a flap over the drawstring top, and dug inside to come up with a box with the silver embossed *This and That* logo on the top. "Here."

Victoria accepted it and opened the top.

At first she didn't understand what she was looking at. Snugged in the cotton batting was a silver pendant on a silver chain. The pendant was the amethyst cabochon stone, the setting fashioned to look like two half-furled wings tucked tightly into the side. As if the stone was the breast of the bird and the bird was diving. Beautiful, sleek, and detailed so she could see the tiny feathers. She picked it up, marveling at the shine, at the balance of the piece that could only be a Regulus.

"Chloe, it is beautiful—far more beautiful than I imagined. And so quickly. You must chain poor Reggie to her workshop for her to have this so soon."

"Nope." Chloe shook her head. "Reggie knew how important protection was. She set her other work aside to get this done."

Victoria looked from Chloe's almost violet gaze to Lila's hazel eyes and read the worry.

"You truly fear for me. You think this will help." She looked down at the pendant and then at the bracelet on her wrist. It weighed heavy at the moment, and was cool, the links thick. Her fingers strayed to the tiny Dutch door. She seemed to toy with the thing a lot—as if it was a magnet for her free hand.

"Like I said—amethyst is protection from burglars and thieves and wards off danger and violent death. With the black beads I gave you, they should help keep you safe."

And she was wearing neither because the black beads had not fit in with her vision of the outfit she wore today. And there had been that silhouette at the door to her shop. A shiver ran up her back and she gave a little shudder.

"What is it?" Lila asked, concern on her face. "Something's happened."

Victoria shook her head. "Most likely nothing. I reacted like a foolish schoolgirl after watching too many—how do you call them?—the slasher movies."

"Something *did* happen!" Chloe caught her hands and went to pull her to the nook at one end of the sunny yellow, white, and turquoise kitchen.

Victoria pulled away and held up her hands to fend off the others. "I said it was most likely nothing. A silhouette on the front door and someone rattling it as if to get in. It rattled me, more like after all the tales you tell me, so I went out back and that is when I ran into Daniel. He was kind and took me for ice cream." She couldn't help her smile.

Then she caught Chloe giving a meaningful brow-tilt to Lila.

"It is nothing. Nothing at all. Just he is helpful being there when I needed a break. And now he offers me dinner and I must get ready."

She escaped past Chloe down the hall to the stairs but not before she heard Chloe's snort of laughter. "She calls him Daniel."

Lila's soft response was indecipherable.

In her room she changed to a simple, scoop-necked cream dress that hung to her ankles but clung to all the right places. It was sleeveless so she grabbed a pale pink pashmina in case the wind off the lake was too cool. She pulled out the pins that held her hair up because the time spent in the car had destroyed the smooth lines of her hair. The blonde mane of her hair fell onto her shoulders and for a moment she considered simply wearing it down this evening.

But no. She was not a schoolgirl. She was a woman and she looked more mature with her tangle of wavy curls contained in a chignon. She brushed out her hair, then swiftly coiled it up on the crown of her head, bobby pinning the stray ends in place. Satisfied, she reapplied her makeup, intensifying the eyeliner and shadow around her eyes and added dangling silver hoop earrings. That was all she needed.

But her gaze fell on the silver, embossed box with the amethyst pendant and the tangle of jet beads she had eschewed today. Would wearing them have protected her? Would they protect her tonight? But she would be with Daniel. Wasn't that enough to keep her safe?

But her dress was plain enough, she could get away with wearing one of the necklaces.

She pulled the amethyst pendant from the box and over her head. The chain was long enough the pendant hung fashionably right above the décolletage of her breasts. The silver was cool on her skin and in the mirror the pendant drew the eye and the décolletage held it.

She smiled in satisfaction. Yes, this was a look that Daniel would like or he was a blind man, and judging by the heated way his gaze had touched her skin, he was anything but.

She checked her watch and it was almost six o'clock. She would wait up here until he came calling because it was far better to keep a man waiting. She settled in the lavender tufted chair under the window and found her fingers stroking the bracelet once again.

No. She would not focus on the bracelet. She turned her attention to the view out the window. The shadows of the mountains were lengthening across the lake, the beach had emptied out, and there was a lineup of boats waiting to be brought to shore at the boat launch. Far out on the water, a few white cruisers and houseboats sought the sun across the lake.

It was so strange here—strangely like Lake Como, and yet most assuredly not. Too dry, too sparse in vegetation compared to the lush grounds of the villas and towns around the northern Italian lake. The way the road separated the buildings from the lake was also strange, but there was something else about Peachland—a friendly, small town feel that she had not felt in Como for a very long time. Como had become too much about the tourist dollar, while Peachland was still first and foremost a home to those who lived here.

Her consideration was broken when a silver-blue Corvette cruised into the curb out front of *This and That*. She almost leapt up, but remembered her resolve. She was *not* the woman who rushed into a man's arms as if she could not live without him. She had lived on her own for too long—much to her father's disgust.

Babies, he had told her. Babies are what you should be concerned with, not designing clothes and certainly not the family business. He would have her designs focused on baby diapers instead of high fashion.

Seeing her now, designing for the women of the Okanagan—well, she could imagine her father belly-laughing out loud. That her stomach fluttered about a man—he would find that doubly hilarious—until he began pushing for marriage and again for—babies. Of course, then he would demand to meet the man and it would be her turn to laugh because her father would never approve of a simple policeman. Not that she cared about his approval.

"Victoria! Danny's here!"

Lila's voice floated up through the door and Victoria stood and smoothed her dress one more time before heading sedately down the stairs.

He stood talking with Lila and Chloe as they set the small, glass-topped table on the back patio. He looked handsome and cool in brown trousers and a green, short-sleeved shirt that brought out the color of his eyes and emphasized the breadth of his shoulders and his narrow hips. His red hair was combed neatly, the red curls just covering the top of his collar, and his face looked newly shaved, the red of his beard almost invisible.

When she stepped outside, all conversation stopped and everyone turned to her. Lila smiled. Chloe's eyes widened a little, while Daniel just looked dazed. Then he shook himself and crossed to her.

"Wow. You're a knockout in that dress."

"This dress? It is a very simple design."

Daniel leaned down to lightly kiss her lips, but the heat flared inside her at the touch of his fingers on her shoulders. "It's not the dress. It's the woman wearing it."

He glanced back at Lila and Chloe. "We'd better be going. Reservations and all that."

He led her around the house and blew out a deep breath. "I don't know about you, but that was like running the gauntlet. I feel like I had to face your father, and they're just your friends."

"They are very protective, yes?"

Daniel shook his head. "That ain't the half of it. They're downright scared for you, Victoria. I am, too. That's why I'll be sticking close to you."

He slipped an arm around her back to hook her into his side and she went willingly. Out the front gate the car waited, but he paused. "We can take the car, but we can also walk. Your choice."

"Do we have time before our reservations?"

"If we don't, does it matter? We'll still get seated."

He caught her hand in his and led her across the street to the promenade along the water that was separated from the road by lovely plantings of lavender and tall, tasseled grasses that were golden from the sun. The breeze was soft off the lake and the air was warm, but Daniel still placed his arm around her shoulders and it felt good—right—as if they were meant to be like this on endless nights together.

For a moment the evening shimmered around her and instead of paved promenade and lake front, she had an image of a long dusty road that shimmered in heat and seemed to lead into forever. She was scared, but her beloved was beside her and if they could just go far enough, perhaps they would be safe.

Gasping for air, she came back to herself, Daniel holding her shoulders and looking worriedly in her eyes.

"Victoria? Victoria?"

He spoke her name as if he'd been speaking it a long time and getting no response.

"I—I am here." She stepped back from him and nearly collapsed on weak legs. Would have if he hadn't caught her again. She rubbed her forehead trying to fathom how her head could ache so suddenly. She inhaled deeply of the lake-scented air and Daniel pulled her into his warm scent of leather and soap and water.

"Maybe we should cancel tonight. Maybe you should just be home in bed."

His voice rumbled nicely in his chest and she liked the sound. Shaking her head, she looked up at him.

"I am fine. Truly, I am. I just had this strange sensation that we had done this before, except it was not walking by a lakeshore, but down a dry desert road. Very odd, I think. But the headache is fading."

It was, too, as quickly as it had come, though Daniel did not look like he believed her. To prove it, she tugged away from his strong hands and the steady beat of his heart and started walking in the direction he'd been taking her. Finally she stopped and looked back at him.

"Are you coming?" She held out her hand, and in three long strides, he caught it and his large hand enveloped hers and side-by-side they walked down to the restaurant.

She had spotted the structure on their drive through town. It was built of logs, large ones fitted together tongue-in-groove to create a two-story structure unlike anything she would find in Milan. A great stone courtyard was built on three levels and crowded with tables with umbrellas and filled with patrons.

"Do we eat outside tonight, then?" She was glad that she had brought her pashmina, for already the lake breeze was cooling.

"We can, but I reserved a table for us inside. Right there, to the right, is a more formal dining room and behind the courtyard is a pub/restaurant. I made reservations in the dining room, but if you'd rather not..."

He looked suddenly uncomfortable. "I know it's not some fancy place like you'd get back home, but this place is written up all over the Okanagan. Even tours come down here for the food."

"Daniel." His name got his attention. "It is fine. Better than fine. Perfect, even." She stood on tiptoe and kissed him until the hostess interrupted.

Daniel mentioned the reservations and they were ushered inside into a quaint log building with windows on three sides looking out at the lake. The place was small and crowded with tables and decorated with homey touches of butter churns, old milk jugs, antique tea and biscuit tins, and blue-colored bottles. The smell of the food was, well, to die for. She hadn't realized she was hungry, but then her lunch of fruit, cheese, and wine—*and let us not forget the ice cream*—was a long time ago now.

"I just realized that I am famished," she said as they were ushered to their table overlooking the lake.

He held her chair like a perfect gentleman and then slid in across from her.

"I was remiss. I should have bought you lunch. My mistake."

"Not a mistake. It was a lovely afternoon. Now it will be a lovely evening."

He caught her hand and squeezed. "Anyone ever tell you that you are a very easy person to be around?"

She had to chuckle. "Never. Cesare would tell you I am difficult. So would Erminio. As for my father—he raised us to be driven by what we could accomplish, but then did not appreciate such a trait in a girl."

Daniel shook his head. "Sounds awfully exhausting. Everyone needs to relax a little sometime."

She shook her head. "Not in the Angelucci family. Success is everything. That is why Cesare disappointed my father so much."

"And yet now he has his partnership in the winery and is working his heart out to open a restaurant—but he still finds time for Reggie."

She cocked her head to study him. "Love can do strange things, can it not?"

"Some people would call if finding balance."

Danny grinned at her and her heart did a little flip-flop.

"Are you saying I am unbalanced?"

He shook his hand. "It's not my place to say one way or the other, but today—eating ice cream—was the first time I've actually seen you smile, and I don't think I've ever seen you laugh."

Could it be true? "I laugh."

"You work. You eat. You sleep. You talk with people you know. You smile at ice cream, and a wonderful smile it is, but you've never laughed where I can see you. But I'm putting you on notice that I've made it my goal to make you laugh. Now before I get to work, perhaps we should look at the menu."

He picked up the leather-bound document and then paused, waiting for her to do the same.

It was an impressive menu, leaning toward German schnitzels and roulade, but also with a healthy dose of northern Italian cuisine and a few seafood dishes that were west coast fusion. She chose a pesto-crusted halibut with a medley of vegetables and baby potatoes, while Daniel ordered a schnitzel with mushroom sauce and red cabbage. By agreement they ordered a bottle of Elkhart Chardonnay that the waiter recommended for its pairing with both fish and schnitzel.

When it came, she tasted with caution, though her experience with BC wines to date had pleasantly surprised her. She hadn't expected good wines in Canada. But the baked apple and butterscotch flavors won her over. She sipped the wine and eyed Daniel.

"You know such an amount about me, but I know nothing of you except you are a policeman."

"An RCMP officer. Sure." He shrugged. "What's there to know? I was born in what used to be BC's third largest city called Prince George. It's smack-dab in the center of British Columbia but everyone considers it the north. I grew up playing hockey and cross-country skiing because the winters were long. My parents had ten acres out on the Buckhorn south of town and when you live out in the sticks like that, you learn to amuse yourself. I've got a brother and a sister and we used to ride our horses in the hills and go swimming in the lake and generally cause trouble with the other kids in the neighborhood. I was lucky. I never got caught for half the things we did or I probably wouldn't be sitting here."

He shrugged.

"So you are the black sheep of your family?"

"Maybe." He thought about it a moment and grinned. "Now that I think about it, I probably am. My sister's a veterinarian. My brother's a pediatric surgeon. I'm just a lowly plainclothes cop, but I'm mostly happy."

"And what makes you happy, Mr. Plain-Clothed Policeman?" She sipped her wine and rested her chin in the palm of her hand.

"Happy. Hmm." He frowned as if it was a difficult question. "Well, for one thing, having dinner with you. I like camping for the quiet and the getting in touch with nature."

Camping? She had to fight to conceal her revulsion—dirt and insects and sleeping on the ground...

"I like putting my feet up at the end of the day and looking out at the lake; a barbecue with friends. Laughter. Simple things. Like when you smile." He raised his russet brows at her.

She smiled. "A good list."

"So what about you? What makes Victoria Angelucci happy?"

It was a harder question than she'd thought it would be. Happy? When was the last time she had thought about being happy? She removed her elbows from the table and looked down at her hands. Her fingers fidgeted with the bracelet links, seeking and finding that locked Dutch door again.

"I do not know if I ever think about being happy. There is happiness in a good design, I suppose."

"That sounds more like satisfaction."

"That is a kind of happiness. And there is more happiness in watching a sketch on paper come to life in cloth. It is a wondrous thing."

Daniel nodded. "I'm sure it is—like watching a child blossom or a garden you've planted bloom in the spring."

"Yes. That is my happiness." But it didn't sound like much. She was happy when Erminio approved one of her designs—before she realized he was stealing them. She was happy having a glass of wine at a café, until she realized now that she was usually alone, the glass consumed on a quick break from the studio so that she could gain inspiration from the sea of fashionable Milanese women.

She frowned and almost felt like crying. How had she not realized how narrow her life had become? Yes, she had dated, but it had felt like an obligation to her friends and her father. Until now. Friends and family had not entered into her decision to have dinner with Daniel. That had been her decision based upon a lovely afternoon.

"This afternoon made me happy. So is this dinner with you." She felt mildly surprised as she said it, but she couldn't help but smile at Daniel's self-satisfied grin.

"Well, that is a happy piece of news. I was wondering if I was just bothering you."

"Oh, you bother me, but I put up with it." She flicked her fingers at him and made a show of studying the antiques in the room.

Daniel looked at her out of the tops of his eyes. "I do believe the lady just made a joke."

"You will never know."

He sat back in his chair. "You wait. I'll figure you out and enjoy doing so."

Dinner came and they savored their food. The halibut was moist and light, the pesto bright flavored against the delicate fish, the vegetables were cooked but still crunchy. Daniel devoured the rich brown sauce over the crunchy schnitzel that looked as well made as anything she had seen in Europe. He let her taste and the meat was tender, its crunchy coating redolent with butter.

Outside the light was fading, the mountains across the lake turned apricot and amber, the sky fuchsia pink. The lake water had gone dark, the surface troubled by wind so that the last few boats were forced to plow through spray for harbor. Inside the restaurant it was warm and snug, old-fashioned hurricane lantern-style chandeliers and small candles on the table placing a golden glow on Daniel's face. Or perhaps it was the wine.

She could feel its heat in her cheeks as they shared a decadent wedge of peach cheesecake baked in-house this afternoon, and Daniel shared a silly story about a woman who had phoned the police for help because she had lost files on her computer—stolen, she had claimed.

She was laughing by the time he was finished and sat there looking at her. He shook his head. "It's what I was afraid of."

"Pardon me?"

He shook his head again. "It's like I feared. You're even more beautiful when you laugh, and you should laugh all the time."

He scanned her empty espresso cup and the decimated desert plate and held out his hand. "What do you say we get out of here and take a spin?"

Accepting his proffered hand, she stood and swayed a moment—surely from the wine. Daniel gently took her pashmina from her to drape around her shoulders. He left money on the table for the bill, thanked their waitress, and led Victoria outside.

The wind was cool, but Daniel pulled her into his side, the warmth of his arm across her shoulders better than any pashmina could ever be. They strolled down the promenade, the wind tugging at her hair and the ends of her pashmina. By the time they reached Daniel's car, she was shivering until Daniel grasped her shoulders and dipped his head to her.

She tasted the warm, sherry mushroom sauce on his lips and the hint of sweet cheesecake. Most of all she inhaled his scent of sweet, sun-warmed leather as his firm lips found hers and parted. His hands slipped down to the small of her back and pulled her into his lean muscle.

Then he pulled back and looked in her eyes. "You're cold: too cold to go for a drive, so I have another option for you. We could just call it a night and you could go inside and be with your friends, or you could brave the cold for a bit longer and we could go to my place and continue this lesson in laughter."

His thumbs stroked her cheeks as he looked down at her so seriously she almost felt nervous. She wasn't sure—did she want the night to end? Daniel clearly did not want it to and her body responded to him—not just her body—her. He was different than anyone she had met before and he had made her laugh. It had felt like something loosened in her chest that had been wound up tightly all her life. She was not sure what it was, but she wanted to explore it. To see what would happen with this very different and most interesting man.

"I think—I think I will go with you on an adventure."

The wondrous smile that blossomed on his face was worth it. He kissed her again—harder, if that was possible—so her toes positively curled in her gold-and-cream Manolo Blahnik shoes.

He handed her into his car, pulled a blanket from the back for her and then swiftly climbed behind the wheel to start the car. He pulled a U-turn and then quickly guided them back onto the highway, this time northbound.

The evening air caught in her hair and she pulled the blanket and her pashmina more tightly around her.

"Are you okay? Maybe I should have put the top up."

"No. I am fine." She held her face up to the wind, inhaling the clean scent of the air. Traffic might move around them, but they were all a mirage. There was only the silver-blue car moving through the dusk and Daniel beside her. His large hand released the gear shift and caught her hand so she twined her fingers in his.

"In fact, I am better than fine. I feel safe with you." She told him how her chest felt and he squeezed her hand as they cruised up the long hill out of Peachland and around the curves toward West Kelowna. Instead of entering the town, he turned off by a sawmill and aimed uphill past a housing development. Then he turned left into the trees again and they passed through shadows until the driveway came out beside a log house that reminded her of the restaurant for its structure.

"This is your house?" she asked. The place wasn't large, but was shaped like an A-frame with huge front windows that faced out toward the lake.

He pulled the Corvette into a two-car garage behind it where he turned off the engine. "Mine and the bank's. Come on. I'll give you the grand tour."

He held the car door for her again and held her hand across the gravel driveway to the house to let them into a small kitchen.

The place smelled of—Daniel. Clean leather and sunshine. The kitchen was plain and utilitarian, with white cupboards and stainless steel appliances forming an ell at the rear of the house. A counter of black marble separated the kitchen from the front of the house, where a great room held—not much.

A low black leather couch and ottoman. A big screen TV. A real wood fireplace with a river stone chimney that flowed up two stories to the ceiling.

"The kitchen," Danny said, flicking on lights. "I know it's not much, but I don't spend a lot of time here—I seem to spend it at the office, or as Jas's place. His is just down the hill on the other side of the highway."

He led her past the counter. "There's space for a dining room table, but I haven't got one yet." He motioned at an empty space next to the kitchen and then led her out from under what must be the upstairs floor and into the living room with its floor-to-ceiling windows. Through them, the lights of the valley were coming on. Kelowna, the area across the lake that Lila had said was called the Mission, the homes of West Kelowna tumbling down the hillsides toward the lake, the dark spaces of the orchards and vineyards.

He flicked a switch and soft music filled the room.

"Jazz?" she asked.

Daniel nodded. "I like jazz and blues and Celtic music. I'm pretty eclectic."

Eclectic. A word she would need to look up, but she believed she got the sense of it through the wine that sang in her veins. "So you like many kinds of music."

He nodded and she placed her hands on his chest and looked up at him. "Many kinds of women?"

"Nah. I'm more of a one-woman kinda guy." His fingers brushed hair out of her face and then smoothed across her shoulders. "Your kinda guy, I'm thinkin'. Would you like another glass of wine?"

She agreed and he left her then, to fuss in the kitchen. She wandered around the room. The floors were solid hardwood, varnished to a shine. The log walls were rich with natural color, and over the fireplace Daniel had hung a painting of what looked like rugged coastline with wind-twisted trees and wild waves on ocean.

"This is not here," she said and Daniel glanced back at her as he poured two glasses of wine.

"It's the west coast of Vancouver Island. Tofino."

"It looks very wild."

"It is." He brought her a glass and stood beside her to consider the picture. "I never buy art, but for some reason, this picture I had to have."

"You like it there."

He nodded. "I thought that someday I might retire there. It's a good place. A place to raise a family where children can roam."

"Such wildness. I would think I would be scared, but with you, perhaps not."

He turned to her and tinked her glass with his. "Perhaps we can visit together sometime. I can show you the things that captured me."

His eyes were so green—as deep as the sea, as shifting as the flow of a gossamer gown—and she could drown in them.

"I—I think I would like that. So far, what you have shown me I have enjoyed."

"Tofino sits on the open ocean with nothing but water between us and Japan. The ocean's a force that can't be tamed. I like that. I can try my own prowess against it. Surfing. Kayaking. It's the challenge of man against nature."

So different than she expected. The Daniel she knew seemed so humbly humorous and yet now she sensed an unmasked danger about him and a glow in his gaze to match. "I thought you were content here—in this house—in this town."

"I am, but there are other ways to live my life and I want to try them before I'm too old to." He grinned like a schoolboy and the Daniel she knew was back.

"Let me guess: you were the boy who took every dare at school."

At that his grin broadened. "You caught me."

"And now you dare to date me—the foreigner." From the stereo speakers blared an old Big Band standard by the Benny Goodman Orchestra that stirred her blood.

"Nope. Now I dare to make the foreigner laugh."

With that, he caught her and swung around in a two-step. "Come on. With this music, you can't help but dance and laugh."

And maybe she could. The tight feeling she'd had in her chest since she put the bracelet on her wrist seemed to ease a little and she let Daniel lead her around the room, swinging her to music her parents might have danced to. Her dress belled out around her legs and Daniel looked dashing and handsome in the reflected blush from the mountains. Then the song ended and he dipped her back, finishing up with a deep, lingering kiss.

When he pulled back, his gaze found hers and held, his pupils so large and dark she saw herself deep inside.

"I think I should be truthful: I brought you here for entirely nefarious reasons." His voice had gone deep and rough with need and heat flushed though her in answer.

"I think I was hoping that was the case." She stepped up to him. He was so different than anyone that she knew—charming and serious and boyish and dangerous all at once, and yet she felt safer with him than she ever had. She hadn't realized how important that was. Swallowing, she ran her hands down his face to his solidly muscled chest and felt a frisson of need that she had not felt for too long. "I think I knew this would happen from the first time we met."

She caught his chin with her hand and stood on tiptoe to reach him. Then she whispered in his ear. "Keep me safe. Teach me to laugh. Take me places I have never been before."

§

The soft warmth of her breath on his neck was an aphrodisiac. Danny could take her right here and now, but instead he reached for her hand and pulled her into him to dance her across the floor like the guy and the girl in that *Dirty Dancing* movie. At the bottom of the stairs, he paused for one more kiss and let the heat surge through him. Victoria's face was flushed and her brown eyes wide as he paused to nibble the side of her neck.

"Are you sure?" he asked.

In answer, she stepped up on the first stair riser and hooked a perfectly manicured finger at him. Then she turned and sashayed up the stairs, her hips softly swaying. Ye gods, if she was just leading him on, the woman must have the most wicked sense of humor in the world.

Halfway up the stairs, she paused and fluttered her eyelashes at him and he felt like one of those romantic leads in the old romantic comedies of the fifties and sixties, stumbling up the stairs after her.

At the top she waited for him in that splendid cream dress that was blessed with her curves, hiding and yet hinting at a bountiful array hidden beneath the cloth. Behind her lay the loft area of the house. It had held two small bedrooms and a small loft, but he had changed that, opening up the rooms to create a single massive bedroom loft with a bathroom and large closet at the back. Log rails separated the loft from the floor below. His king-sized bed was set under the slope of the wood-paneled ceiling and a large, white, sheepskin carpet covered most of the open hardwood floor.

"You did not mention that you had an entire floor of the house as a bedroom," she said, looking at him askance. "It suggests a different side of you, no?" she asked sultry-voiced.

His blood pulsed a little faster in embarrassed arousal as he caught her hands and led her into the room.

"I wanted the view from the front window and, given no one else lives here, I could do what I want."

"Do you always get what you want?"

He turned back to Victoria, who almost purred at his glance. Was this some game she played or was this sex kitten really her?

"No. I don't. I live on my own, mostly because I haven't met a woman willing to put up with me." He didn't quite know why he'd said it, but it hung there between them.

"Well, then. I think you relate to me very well. Let us see if I'm willing to put up with you." Her lips curved in a smile as she spoke.

"My God, the woman made a joke." He caught her in his arms and she met his need, her arms encircling his neck as she pressed her curves into him.

Lush was the word that came to his mind. Lush mouth, lush hair when his fingers found the pins and pulled it down. Lush scent of oleander. Lush softness of skin.

He picked her up by the waist and swung her around so she stood by the bed. Gently he went to ease her down, but she stopped him with a shake of the head. She caught the sides of her dress and shimmied it up over her head. He helped her get it off and she stood there in only amazing high heels shaped like golden leaves, and a delicate lace bra and panties that only highlighted all that he'd suspected waited under her clothing. Miles of tawny, golden, voluptuous skin with a silver necklace that drew his eye to her breasts.

In answer he unbuttoned his shirt, but she stilled his fingers and did the task for him, sliding her electric-warm palms over his pecs when she was done. He shivered and traced a finger down the shoulder strap of her bra to the top of her breast, then flicked the strap off her shoulder and leaned in to kiss where it had been. He followed the faint mark down to her now half exposed breast and felt her shiver in return.

Pulling back, he smiled down at her expectant gaze, then eased her onto the bed and stretched himself beside her to run a palm light-as-a-feather down her side.

She shivered and reached for him, to kiss him again. Kisses on her brow, her eyes, and her mouth. They drank deeply of each other, then he buried his face in the tumble of her hair, nibbling at her earlobe, at the dark place underneath, and followed the cords of her neck down to her shoulder and lower, down to tongue the taut nipple through the lace. His fingers caught the second bra strap and slipped it off Victoria's shoulder, then slipped the bra lower. Her breasts sprang free, lush like the rest of her, broad brown nipples tight and puckered. He caught one in his mouth and she moaned and moved against him, one long, tawny leg hooking over his hips.

He smoothed his hands up over her, one palm finding her other breast, the other finding her face, her hair as he played with her there, suckling, teasing, so she thrust against him and groaned.

"*Capisco.* I see you are a man who gets what he wants." Her brown eyes flashed open and he kissed her again. Her hands came between them as they worked at his belt.

"You will not keep these between us and what we want."

In answer he rolled off of her and swiftly undressed. Naked and oh-so-ready, he lay next to her, discarding her bra and then hooking his fingers in the sides of her panties.

"Time for these to go, too, lovely though they are." He slipped down to kiss her belly, then lower to tongue her through the lace until she lifted her hips and he slipped the cloth off, returning to his task in the welcoming juncture of her legs.

She was already moist amid the tight blonde curls. His teeth found the small button of paradise and she shuddered under him. His tongue tasted her salt and a rush of heat ran through her, her belly spasmed, and he lifted his head, trailed kisses up her luxurious body, and found her gaze startled, dark, and lust filled.

"My turn," she murmured and squirmed out from under him so her breasts hung tantalizingly over him, nipples skimming his chest so he throbbed under her, caught her, and raised himself up to tongue her nipples again.

"No. You lie back."

She trailed her mane of hair over his chest to hide her movements, but her fingers were busy, then her mouth was, too, and all the air left his chest. Golden hair splayed across his belly as she nuzzled his length. Golden hair rippling as she took him in and her tongue worked its magic. He caught her hair in his fists as she straddled him and worked along his length, made her pause to lie beside him so they could pleasure each other at the same time.

Oleander and sex perfumed the air as he tongued the soft core of her. She whimpered as she suckled him and his world contracted to the woman who took him to the edge of explosion as she trembled and spasmed once more.

He pulled back then, and drew her up to him, scenting his sex on her, drawn to the flush of her skin, the wide darkness of her eyes, and the tangle of her hair. He twisted his fists in it as he rolled her below him. Gently he kissed her. Then he grinned.

"Now you'll really see how I get what I want. Do you want that?"

Wide-eyed, she nodded and raised her knees around him.

Swiftly, he rolled a condom on and then it was the long, slow pleasure that could never be compared as he pressed into the soft folds of her welcoming flesh. She hooked her legs farther up his back to ease his entry and she was slick and waiting. He slid inside and met her gaze, aroused at the unexpected depth of her pleasure. They sighed together, her back arched, and she shimmied under him to take him deeper.

Then he began to move.

Chapter 8

Blurred shadows cast by dusk's dimmed light filled the open sleeping area of Daniel's house. They crept from the corners to loom around the broad bed with its rumpled white cotton sheets and seemed to loom over Daniel's shoulders as he knelt above her. The warm air shifted around them, stirred by a ceiling fan that limped round and round the peaked ceiling, and the scent of fire filled her nose along with the scent of sunburnt leather.

Daniel's scent.

She accepted his slow easy thrusts, feeling like she was melting as she tilted her pelvis to meet him. This easiness was new, a languorous enjoyment as if reaching climax was the last thing they wished. As if being caught in the moment was everything and she had to let her shop, her problems, her life fall away to focus on this man.

His green gaze held her and demanded her attention. So intense because emotions she was not sure she wanted rose up in her chest.

She slid her hands up his solid back to his shoulders, his head, ran her fingers through his silky, russet hair and down to his jaw. Lifted her head and kissed him—small string of kisses like seed pearls across his lips. More down his jaw line, his neck. He tasted sweetly of salt sweat. Her hands slid down his back to his butt, rock hard with each thrust, and the feel of his muscles, of him moving inside her, made her lift her legs higher around his waist.

"Harder," she said, almost unable to meet his gaze. Then she did and the desire there broke through her hesitation. She cupped his ass with her hands. "I want all of you inside me. I will not break."

Daniel smiled down at her, his eyes half-mast and sexy. He caught her legs and pushed them forward, baring her fully to him, and rose above her to gaze down at their joining as he slicked in and out of her. The flush of desire bloomed darker on his skin and he held her legs splayed and thrust once-twice-three times, hard inside her.

Her back arched and for a moment she could not breathe, the pleasure robbing her of everything but sensation.

"Is that what you want?"

Gasping, she nodded.

His hands smoothed down her thighs and found her nubbin, thrummed her like a magician and then he caught her hips and pulled her half onto his lap as he thrust home.

Where the slow, languorous strokes had gradually built her fire, this was a flood of sensation too much to examine. There was only the long hot rod of him inside her and she wanted all of him. *Madre di Dio* she wanted more. Wanted him fully inside her skin.

She caught his shoulders and shoved him to the side, stayed wed to him physically and ended up straddling him, still impaled. Her fingernails raked his chest and caught on his nipples. He held her hips and she plunged over him, sending him as deep as their bodies allowed and still it was not enough.

She arched her back and raised her hands above her head, his hands a steadying force on her hips or fire on her breasts. She gasped at each thrust. Moaned, as his hips thrust to meet her and as he buried himself deep like a buried treasure, as she ground her pelvis onto the rock of his hips, as his head twisted back and his hands slid up to twist in her hair. The bracelet burned on her wrist.

"Victoria!" he shouted and sat bolt upright before her, holding her hips as he thrust once-twice-thrice deep inside her, pulsing, and her body answered, bolts of lightning blazing through her flesh, through her skull so she fell blind as his arms came around her, trapping her against him.

He rocked her there for a long time as their hearts pounded together, as their gasps and the shudders slowly waned, but she was still hungry, already wanting this man again. She wrapped her legs around his waist, refusing to let him go.

"Hey," he said, and chucked her chin.

She looked up at him, feeling like a wanton as she rubbed her aroused nipples against him. "How can it be that I have just met you? I do not come to men with such abandon."

At least, she had not done it before. Sex, yes, but not the desire to flaunt herself to a man. To tease him and give him as much pleasure as she could. Always it had been what she could get for herself—because that was how her partners had been—take pleasure. If they gave it in return, it was by chance, not design.

He cupped her head and pulled her into his shoulder. "I think...I think we fit together. Like maybe we were meant to be." His hands slid down her shoulder and brought her wrist with the bracelet up between them. For a moment he looked disappointed.

"What is the matter?" she stroked his sweat-damp hair back from his face.

He shook his head. "Nothing, I guess. This bracelet—it's been known to come off when two soul mates make love."

"And you think we are soul mates?" She pulled back to look at him, but still kept their bodies connected.

"I thought it might be a possibility." He gave her an aw-shucks grin and collapsed back on the bed, dragging her with him.

He held up her wrist to admire the bracelet. "Of course, there were others who had mad passionate sex and the bracelet stayed on until something else was resolved." He eyed her speculatively. "I wonder..."

"You wonder if we have other things to resolve?" she asked.

"Well, we have figured out that we're good in bed. That means that it has to be something else, doesn't it?"

"No." She shook her head. "It may just mean that we were not that good in bed. If this thing has a spirit, perhaps it was not satisfied with our effort."

"Not satisfied, huh." He rolled her over on her back. "Are you saying you weren't satisfied?"

"Meh." She shrugged her shoulders. "How do you say? It was okay."

"Okay! Them's fighting words!"

Suddenly Daniel was a mass of teasing fingers that tweaked her breasts and found the most ticklish parts of her body. She shrieked and rolled away but couldn't escape him, gasping as laughter rippled out of her, as he straddled her to trap her and tickled her some more until she was almost begging for air.

Then he stopped to peer down at her, his laughter suddenly stilled.

"I thought you were beautiful when I first met you, but seeing you like this, wanton and with laughter in your eyes—now you're the most beautiful woman in the world."

Freed of her, in their squirming altercation he'd grown aroused again. She eyed him and scrambled up to sitting, caressing him.

"I still want you. If anything, I want you more. I could stay here forever, just making love."

He stretched himself on the bed and pulled her down beside him, spooning her. "We have all night," he whispered to her, his breath heated against her ear.

His hands came around her to fondle her breasts and then one slid lower, fingering her to arousal as he slid into her from behind. Pleasure like this—she was glad they had all night.

§

He woke in the half-light of morning with an absolute sense of contentment and relaxation. His arm draped around smooth shoulders, his hand cupped a full, too-tempting breast, and a warm derriere tucked seductively against his groin so that he could not help himself. His body roused as he woke and kissed a shoulder, tweaked a still-taut nipple.

Victoria sighed the most contented of sighs and he rolled on a condom and then slipped inside her from behind and they slowly, slowly, greeted the day with the most sensual of waking. Then they lay together, her head cupped under his chin, a sheet thrown over them as, through the ceiling-high windows of the A-frame log house, they watched the sun rise over the mountains beyond the lake.

First came the pink blush of the clouds and then spires of golden light that imparted color into the world. The gray mountains turned green, the still water of the eighty-mile-long lake shimmered waveless in the breathless air of the morning. Then the sun hefted his head over the hills and light turned the water deepest blue, the hillsides verdant green with orchards and vineyards. Closer in, the trees around his house released the birds, and the twitter and call of sparrow, jay, grosbeak, and oriole filled the morning.

Usually at this time he was up and out the door for a run. Today, however, he felt like staying where he was. Hadn't he burned enough calories overnight and this morning? He felt satiated—for the moment—and thirsty and hungry, but not enough to leave the warmth of the woman beside him.

"You snore, you know." He murmured it into her ear and felt her stiffen. God, she was so easy to tease.

"Never! You speak lies!" She squirmed around to face him and saw his grin. She swatted his face. "You tease me again." Disgust.

"Anything to see that beauty I saw last night. I love your laughter." And your naked form like a goddess.

He wiggled his fingers in threat of tickling and she shrieked and rolled off the bed laughing, pulling the covers with her. Raising himself on one elbow, he considered her. "You look like a Greek goddess after a slightly debauched bacchanal."

Tossing her hair, she tugged the sheet into a more chaste form and wagged a finger at him. "You are a very bad man."

He crawled naked across the bed toward her and snagged the sheet before she could retreat. "Only where you're concerned."

He used the sheet to haul her back on the bed and kissed her deeply. She answered fully, willing in his arms. But he had work and she had her shop, and the cares of another day impinged. Smoothing the mass of blonde hair back from her face, he looked down at her.

"There is nothing I would like better than to spend today exactly as we spent last night, but I fear that there are other people who have a claim on our time. My bosses. You've got the shop and Lila to deal with." He leaned down to kiss her pout of disappointment. "How about if we shower together and then catch a bit of breakfast before I drop you off at *This and That?*"

She nodded and ran her fingers through his hair. "You realize that I am going to undergo questioning."

"You and me both." He swung up to sitting, sheet-swathed Victoria in his lap. "My partner's as bad as your friends at the store. I think he's taking great pleasure in getting some of his own back after all the ribbing I gave him when he was chasing Chloe. So shower first?"

When she nodded, he tumbled her to the floor, sans sheet, and chased a delicious golden derriere into the marble-tiled bathroom. A few minutes later and they were in the glassed-in shower stall, warm water blasting down their bodies.

He used the soap on her smooth flesh, and felt himself immediately harden at the sensual silk of her. Then she stole the soap from him and scrubbed his chest as she rubbed her sudsy stomach against him. He took her then, forgetting the condom, lifting her up until her legs wrapped around him and holding her ass as he pumped into her, only her silver necklace between them. The water sluiced around them, sluiced between them in a sensual downpour until she shuddered around him and he came in response. He slumped against the shower's tiles and let her slip down in front of him, cursing himself as a fool for not using protection; and damnation, he was still aroused, still wanted her again.

He'd wanted women before, but never like this. Never like he was ravenous for her every moment.

He pulled her into him and held on and she clung to his shoulders.

"This is crazy," he whispered over the pounding of the water.

She nodded into his shoulder.

"We should turn off the water and get dressed and go," he said.

Neither of them moved.

It was only when the water started to cool that they broke apart and he turned off the shower to hand Victoria a thick, red, plush towel. He grabbed its mate and scrubbed himself off, then patted her dry while she toweled her hair. She used a slim palm on the mirror over the gray marble counter to remove the steam and looked into the glass, clearly disgusted at what she saw.

"My hair is a matted mess. Everyone will know what I have been doing! I do not even have a brush."

He snagged an arm around her and pulled her into a hug. "I hate to break it to you, but you walk in this morning and they're going to know anyway."

She looked up at him, a lovely crimson flooding up her chest and shoulders to her face.

"Does it matter that they know?" He nibbled her neck, inhaling the oleander fragrance that seemed part of her skin.

She looked up at him with a troubled expression. "I do not like people knowing my business."

But she caught his gaze and smiled as she ran a palm down his cheek. "It does not matter, does it? What does is that we are together." She kissed his jaw.

"You've got that right. They'll just be jealous." He ran water in one of the sinks and proceeded to shave, while Victoria tried to make some order out of her hair using a comb Danny provided. She padded naked out of the bathroom and it was all he could do not to follow after that delicious derriere and call in sick for the day.

Smooth cheeked except for a nick where he'd rushed the shave next to his jaw, he went out to the bedroom and found her stripping the bed, dressed in only her panties, bra and the silver and amethyst necklace that she had never removed. Her demure cream dress hung on a hanger. He swallowed at the sway of her breasts, and the pert point of her nipples, and the way her hips sashayed. When she noticed him, she smiled and pulled the dress over her shoulders. Okay, not quite as demure as he remembered. It was more like a curtain that barely hid the wonders within it. Sexy as all hell when you knew what was there, and he sure as hell had every curve and dimple branded on his brain.

He pulled on jeans and a dress shirt and led her down to the kitchen where his coffee machine had chugged on automatically.

"Eggs," he said, suddenly nervous. "I'll make us eggs." It wasn't often that a woman remained at his house for breakfast. What did you talk about? Was she as uneasy as he was? Well, maybe not uneasy—as desperate for the whole affair not to end?

She poured coffee while he rushed to get eggs and milk out of the fridge, grated cheese, and pulled some paprika out of the cupboard. He broke eggs quickly into a bowl, added milk, whisked them and then added the cheese. All he needed was a hot skillet; and of course, like a nimrod, he'd forgotten to get the frying pan out.

He turned on the burner and placed the skillet with a dollop of butter on the stove. Victoria moved like a model, somehow finding his cutlery and salt and pepper to place on the counter, while he opened the top of the back door to let in the fresh morning sunshine.

The clatter of silverware on the floor turned him around. Victoria stood with her hand to her mouth, a shocked expression on her face.

"What is it? What's the matter?" He went to her, but she avoided him.

"What is this?" she asked, her eyes huge and dark with shock.

He scanned the room. What the hell was she on about?

"The door. It is a Dutch door, correct?"

He looked back at the open top of the door that he'd hooked back against the side of the house. Outside the ponderosa pine spread their long dark needles and a Steller's jay squawked somewhere amid their branches.

"Uh, yeah. It was here when I bought the place. I like to open it in the mornings during warm weather. Sort of let in the fresh air and the nature. What of it?"

By the way she had her fingers clasped over the bracelet, he knew. His gut twisted. Fear? Excitement? He wasn't sure which it was.

Instead he crossed to her and gently unclasped her fingers. He twisted the silver around her wrist until he saw it. A miniature representation of the door, down to the padlock that had been on the door when he bought the place. An electric tingle ran up his arms. He looked from the bracelet up into Victoria's terrified gaze.

"Well, that's something to think about, isn't it?"

She said nothing, just barely nodded her head. Make a fuss, because this must mean that they were meant for each other, or run like hell? He wasn't looking for permanent, was he? Was he? If he was, there was no way in hell that a woman like Victoria Angelucci was going to stay with someone like him—not even if they were very good for each other in the sack.

It sucked, but it was true.

To hide the hurt, he patted the back of her hand and placed a kiss on her cheek. "It doesn't mean anything. Now—given I don't have a dining room table, why don't we just use the ottoman?" he grimaced. "Sorry. This place is a bit of a work in progress."

Victoria shook her head as if clearing out the daze that had filled her face. Her tangle of damp hair was somehow even more erotic as she shifted around the room. But she didn't say anything further about them or the bracelet.

That hurt, too.

Shutting the feeling away, he swiftly whisked the egg mixture one more time and poured it into the frying pan, then stirred in the grated cheese and sprinkled paprika liberally.

He stuffed bread into the toaster and stirred the eggs with a spatula into a frothy, sun-yellow scramble streaked with cheese. Two plates out of the cupboard and the toast and eggs divided and then he balanced them into the living room where they settled side-by-side on the ottoman. He took a long pull of coffee and that seemed to settle whatever had been going on in his head, but he didn't know what to say. All the easy banter seemed to have evaporated like liquid evidence at a crime scene.

Victoria sampled the eggs. "Mmm. Good. At home we would serve them with potatoes in a frittata. If you like, I will make you one sometime."

Her smile was shy as if she was embarrassed that she'd spoken.

Pointing at his plate with his fork, he tried to find the energy to talk. "That'd be nice." Not that it was likely to happen. "This—this is just camp food. I make 'em when I'm out in the bush. That's when they taste their absolute best. Maybe you can come with me sometime and try them." He could have kicked himself—this beautiful woman was from one of the largest, most cosmopolitan cities in Italy. She wasn't likely to be found huddled by a campfire. Hell, she was a fashion designer. *Get real, Forester!*

"Maybe I would," she said with soft hesitation. "They are so good here, maybe I would try camping."

She cocked her head. "If you love it so much, can it be so bad?"

His fork clinked loudly against his plate. "Really? You'd really try it?"

Against all odds, Victoria's dark eyes met his. "You tell me that I take no chances of finding laughter. Maybe I will find it camping with you?" She cocked her head. "You make me laugh. You work very hard at it, no?"

Her slim hand ran up the back of his forearm and his mouth went dry. There wasn't much about the prospect of getting Victoria alone in a tent that didn't appeal to him. Even if this was just a fling, after last night there was no way in hell he was turning this opportunity down.

"You—me—camping. You've got a deal."

Chapter 9

It was almost nine thirty when Daniel dropped her off at *This and That*. Victoria stood on the sidewalk across from the deep blue lake and knew that she was going to have to face Lila and Kylee—both early risers—and likely Chloe as well, given her crystal healing business was filling up her schedule. Reggie was a given with the woman driven by her designs and creation in order to make up for the disgusting lawsuit that that had ended her planned debut on the Milan fall fashion runways.

The morning was bright with the sun still low over the mountains, but filling the Okanagan valley with light so that the red-and-white house glowed. It was a different light than in her native Milano, not so hazy, the rough mountainsides across the lake etched clearly with morning sunlight and shadow. There was none of the mystical layering of hillside upon hillside upon hillside one got in Italy, where each hillside was topped with a small town or villa. No, in Canada, from what she had seen, there was either wilderness or sprawl. Small towns like Peachland were becoming part of the sprawl, but you did not have to go far to return to wilderness. The thought of camping in the wilds was scary, and yet the thought of camping with Daniel was not. For some reason, the man not only filled her belly with a sweet fire that so far might have been many times satiated, but still was hungry for more, but he also made her feel cherished, desired, and, oddly, safe.

Extremely odd given the bracelet. She rubbed its cool, silver links.

She couldn't remember the last time someone had made her feel safe or cherished. Desired, yes. But cherished rarely. Not even her father had shown her that kind of caring. And safe?

Just when had she ever felt safe unless she locked the doors and windows behind her?

With a last wave at Daniel looking *molto bene*—very fine—in his silver-blue Corvette as he pulled a U-turn and headed back to his office, she pushed through the front gate and looked up at the front door and porch. The 'open' sign flashed discreetly in the window, but she wasn't going to parade her evening's activities before anyone if she could help it. She ducked around the side of the house to the rear patio and was just about to the kitchen door when she heard movement behind her.

"Well, well, well, if this isn't a walk of shame, I don't know what is."

Victoria whirled to face her accuser and found a bemused Reggie Lewis leaning crossed-armed on the door to her workshop. She was a stunning woman of raven-black hair that she wore like Cleopatra, but instead of Egyptian robes, Reggie could usually be found dressed as she was now, in a pair of old fatigue camo pants and a black singlet t-shirt that showed off the Celtic knot tattoos that looped her upper biceps. So not what you expected when you came looking for the maker of the exquisite line of Regulus jewelry.

Victoria had to quell the need to simply bolt through the door and ignore her. But this was Reggie—the woman who was sleeping with Victoria's brother.

"Let me guess—Daniel?"

She nodded, suddenly uncertain. Had she really felt more than just a sexual heat? Was the fact that his scent of sun-warmed leather filled her head more than simple infatuation? "I did not intend it to happen. He is not my usual kind of man."

Reggie shook her head and straightened. "You're singing to the choir, sister. Cesare wasn't exactly the kind of guy I had in my scrapbook, either. Or at least I didn't think so. Turns out I knew nothing. He's a pretty great guy."

"But Daniel is *polizia*—and he...he likes camping!" Victoria scrubbed her fingers back through her hair and realized she probably looked exactly like someone who had just rolled out of bed after a very good roll in the hay.

"To heck with a box of chocolates: Life and love can be bitches, sometimes. You never get what you're expecting." Reggie came over to her and slung an arm around her shoulders. "Tell you what. How about we go inside and enlist Chloe's help to make one of those little Italian espressos you so like so much while you go get ready to face today. Then we can drink coffee and have a talk."

Reggie shepherded Victoria into the sunny yellow-and-white kitchen where the air carried the hint of early morning coffee and faint patchouli incense from the shop, and then pointed her in the direction of the stairs.

"Hey, Chloe! If you're not busy, we've got a coffee emergency out here," Reggie called when Victoria was half way up the stairs.

Bless Reggie, because having to deal with Chloe's teasing, too, would have been just a little too much when she was feeling a little bumped and bruised in the confidence department. Yes, she was confident Daniel was infatuated with her right now, but whether it was the right thing to do and whether it would last were other things entirely. And the fact that he had a door at his house that matched the charming silver link of the bracelet—that was just too—too—too bizarre!

She might not want to admit it, but the thought of ending what they had started made her throat close up so she felt like crying. Maybe there was more to this bracelet thing than she had thought possible.

"We will have no crying," she muttered to herself as she stood in her room. The lavender chair looked like the perfect place to collapse and feel sorry for herself. Clothes. She needed to change clothes and get her face on. Then she would feel better. Stronger. The lilies on the dresser filled the misty room with their sweetness.

She stripped off her dress, bra, and panties, wadded them up and shoved them in the laundry. She left the necklace on. Then she pulled on plain silk underwear and bra and stood looking at herself in the mirror. Not sexy at all, they looked like old lady panties and bra after what she'd been wearing. The problem was, she *felt* sexy as heck. She stripped them off and pulled on another lace bra and panties, her hands lingering over her breasts and the sensitive places between her legs. Daniel had touched her there, like this.

The memory of his hands, his body, had her nipples tighten, her body spasm with pleasure.

No! She was not even sure whether she should regret last night. She should not already be looking forward to another night of pleasure.

She pulled on plain white Bermuda shorts and a long crisp blouse that looked more like something Lila or Chloe would wear because the neckline sat demurely at the collarbone. She opened the collar to expose the necklace and décolletage, then tugged the collar closed again and pulled the necklace over the collar. She did not need to show off her body to be a sexual being.

It took longer to brush the mats out of her hair, so that she was teary eyed as she did her eyeliner and mascara. She eschewed any foundation, for her skin was smooth and this morning she just wanted to feel clean. Yes, clean and crisp and very well screwed— if she let herself think about it.

Her feet in white espadrille sandals, she went down the stairs again to the powerful aroma of fresh coffee. Someone had ground fresh beans and brewed real espresso.

She found Chloe waiting in the kitchen with Reggie, both of them sipping from small espresso cups. Chloe handed Victoria a third cup, dark-swirled with crema on the top.

"You are a goddess," Victoria said as she sampled the coffee. "Very strong. Very bold. Just the right nose. Perfect."

Chloe shrugged. "I prefer lattes, but a good espresso can go a long ways to curing what ails you after a long night. I make 'em regularly for Jas and me."

Her blue eyes had gone almost violet and she eyed Victoria up and down. "Not your usual style, my dear. Did old Danny boy have an effect on you?"

"Chloe! I told you to be nice. She's feeling a little confused right now. She needs our support, not our teasing."

"Says the woman who did nothing but laugh at me when I was going through my own hell." Chloe set her cup down and crossed her arms over her chest. Then she grinned. "All right, so I wasn't exactly being fair to friend Victoria, here. What happened, kiddo? A night of good sex shouldn't leave a woman looking so down in the dumps."

Feeling slightly mortified that everyone knew her business, Victoria allowed Chloe to herd her into the nook with Reggie. They settled themselves on the bright turquoise, yellow, and mandarin cushions and then eyed each other as if unsure where to begin.

Victoria looked at her hands and shook her head. "It was a very good night. Very. We—fit. We had a nice dinner and then he took me to his place."

"The cad," Reggie muttered in humor.

"He was not a cad. We—we both wanted it to happen, I think."

"There goes the bracelet again. What did we tell you? The darn thing makes you do things against your better judgment. Apparently it knows what's good for you," Chloe said and grabbed Victoria's hand. "Still on, I see. So just what is it that you have to work out?"

"Darn it, Chloe! Give the poor woman a break. Have you forgotten how messed up you were? It was only a month ago, for goodness' sake." Reggie drank back the last of her espresso as if it were a shooter and slammed the cup down in its saucer. She turned to Victoria.

"So you slept with the man. I'm sensing our Danny didn't let you down, so what's the problem?"

Victoria shook her head. "That is it! I don't know. Perhaps it is too much, too sudden. There is a door...the back door to his house..."

"Whoa," Reggie said. "He's got the matching door and you feel something for him and are afraid."

Was that it? She met Reggie's almost black gaze. "Perhaps that is it. I don't know if I can accept feeling so much so quickly. What do we have in common? A *poliziotto*, a designer? Pah—there is nothing!"

"Well, the flush on your face and the little mark I see there on your neck suggest otherwise," Chloe said, sitting back in her seat. "Jas and I were like fire and water. I mean, I'm a psychic and he's a realist—a cop like Danny. But he respects me and I respect him. That's what counts. If you like Danny, then isn't it worth it?"

Nodding, Victoria sipped her coffee. Then she sighed. "I guess—I guess this means I'm going to try camping."

Through the kitchen window, Victoria saw Lila cross the patio from the carport to the house, her arms full of grocery bags, and scrambled up to get the door for her.

Lila breezed inside with a thank you and plunked the bags on the counter. She looked jaunty today in cropped, rust-colored trousers and a long, cotton Nehru-style tunic in the same shade that brought out the copper in her long auburn curls. A set of oversized brass beads graced her neck and a brown leather purse was slung across her chest.

She turned back to them. "So what brings this meeting together in my kitchen?" Her assessment settled on Victoria. "I didn't hear you come in last night."

"That's 'cause she didn't," Reggie chortled. "I caught her doing the walk of shame at nine thirty this morning."

Lila's hazel eyes turned back to Victoria. "With Danny?"

"Of course with Danny," Chloe said before Victoria could answer. "Who else has been hanging around her like a bad smell?"

Enough of this! She did not like them talking as if she wasn't even here. "Daniel. I was with Daniel. It was a good night. Very good, in fact. I do not think I have ever met someone who makes me feel as he does."

"There's the good ol' Canadian male for you. They go unsung in the romance novels, but you gotta give 'em credit for honing their skills on all those cold Canadian winter nights." Chloe giggled.

"You're not helping," Lila said and brought Victoria back to the table. She slipped into the nook bench next to Reggie and motioned Victoria to the chair at the end of the table.

Oddly, Lila's expression was deadly serious. None of the kidding of Chloe or Reggie. There was concern.

"Did something happen last night?" Lila asked.

"She got home at nine thirty this morning. Something definitely happened." Reggie smirked.

Lila waved her away. "Other than sex."

"How about he has a door that matches one of the doors on the bracelet?" Chloe said.

Lila's look of concern grew.

Victoria sighed. "We had dinner. We had breakfast. Daniel was gentle—a gentleman. He—he wants to take me camping." The last part came out more as a whimper than a complaint.

"Oh, my goodness," Lila caught her hands. "And you're considering going, aren't you? You really like him."

"He—is so different." How could she explain everything he made her feel? "I feel safe with him."

Lila's grip tightened on her hands. She shook her head and the friendly humor had drained from her face. "I'm happy for you. Really, I am, but I'm not sure you should go. There's something you should know about Danny."

"Lila?" Chloe stopped her. "Is this necessary? He's been fine all summer."

Victoria looked from one to the other, all three of them suddenly deadly serious.

"What is it? Something about Daniel I should know?"

"But he wasn't fine in June," Lila said with finality. "Victoria, we've told you all about the bracelet, but the piece that's usually left out is Danny's part in it. I think you need to know it if you are going whole heart into a relationship—especially when you're wearing that bracelet."

It sounded so ominous, so like something one would see in a melodramatic movie, but all three of the women looked seriously worried and would not meet her eye.

"What is it, then? What is this deep, dark secret?"

"It's not something to joke about, hon," Chloe said.

Lila nodded and tightened her grip on Victoria's hands. The warm light of the kitchen turned suddenly cold. "You see, back at the beginning, when the bracelet first came to us, there was already someone or something looking for it. It had been at the estate sale where I bought the box of jewelry. It killed the woman who ran the sale."

At that news, the room went a little colder. Victoria sat up straighter. Someone had died? Why had no one told her sooner?

"It killed the woman and then leapt to another person—a homeless man, who was then interrogated by a Royal Canadian Mounted Police officer who was called in to assist in the investigation. The thing—whatever it is—leapt then to the police officer, who pursued the bracelet out of Kelowna to us."

"Daniel. It was Daniel." Victoria's heart hurt because she did not want it to be true. Her stomach shrank to a little knot of fear. But this was Daniel—Daniel of the soft green eyes, whose one ambition was to make her laugh. There was nothing dangerous in that.

Lila nodded. "That's right. The thing rode him right into the store, asking about Moira, the woman who died, and to see the things we had bought at the sale. At that moment the bracelet was already gone from the package and was safely on Kylee's wrist. But Danny kept watch on our place until he spotted the bracelet. Then something happened—whatever it was left him and he was confused and didn't know how he even got to Peachland. It was Jas who helped put him back together, and the two of them and Chloe's brother Brett rescued Kylee when the thing tried to abduct her."

"So he was a good guy—did nothing truly bad."

"Honey, you have to listen," Chloe leaned in to take over the story. "He was taken over and did that other creature's bidding."

"You do not know that. He got free. Did those other people get free?"

Lila shook her head. "No. No, they did not. Some went crazy.

One took his own life. Danny's the only one that walked away with his mind intact."

No. She would not listen to this wild story. She pulled loose from Lila and pushed away from the table. "His mind is intact. He is not a risk—at least, not to me." She stood and Lila gracefully unfolded from the nook bench to block Victoria's path.

"I don't get any pleasure out of telling you this. I just worry and I want you to be safe. It's not that Danny's bad. I'd swear my life that he isn't, but we don't know what's been inside his head and whether it will come back again. Think about it, Victoria. What if whatever it was came back and took him over again? You'd be in grave danger."

"And I say it cannot be true, no matter what you say. I was with Daniel almost the whole day yesterday and much of that time was in private. We drove out into the country. Last night we were alone in his house. He could have done anything to me and yet I stand safe and sound before you." She shook her head. "No. You are wrong in this, friend Lila, though I know your heart is in the right place."

She spun on her heel and marched out of the room. She needed to move, to work out her feelings, but all this talk of abduction and death made her hesitate to leave the house for the promenade along the lake. Instead she mounted the stairs to her room and closed the door behind her. She slumped into the lavender tufted chair by the window and all her stiff resolve fled.

How could this happen, just when she had found someone she cared about? Yes, she cared for Daniel—more than she wanted to admit. Her body still shivered at the thought of the two of them together. The thought of his teasing still made her smile.

No, Lila had to be wrong. Daniel was good and strong and that was why he won free of this thing—this demon that had possessed him. They'd need a better story than that to make her believe that Daniel Forester still had a demon inside him.

Story.

"Maria!" She leapt out of her chair. She'd forgotten to call back her old nanny about that childhood fairytale that everyone had been so excited about—something about lovers and a bracelet.

She would not have remembered it, but Cesare had.

She checked her watch. It was nearing eleven o'clock in the morning, which meant that it was about eight o'clock in the evening in Milan. Still early enough to call. She pulled her cell phone out of her purse and dialed the number, listening to the rough burr of the international line.

From far away in Milan she heard the click and *"Ciao?"* in the beloved voice of Maria—her Maria.

"Ciao, Maria. È Victoria."

"Victoria. Il mio piccolo angelo! Come stai?"

The old woman, who had to be in her late eighties, still sounded vibrant and filled with life. Victoria's throat filled with emotion. She had missed the old woman and not even known it. But that was how her father had raised her—emotional connections were something to be let go of. Certainly she didn't have a close relationship with her father, and even with Cesare it was only now that they were developing some closeness.

"Sto bene. E tu?"

The old woman rattled off a list of ailments and then burst into a hearty cackle. "They are the badges of age," she said in Italian. "You wait. You will earn them, too. So what adventure has Cesare dragged you on?" More cackling. "That boy. Do you know that he phoned me to tell me that he was in love?"

Victoria had to smile. That *was* something. Maria had been the mother to them that neither of them had ever had. For Cesare to say such a thing to Maria meant he was serious. Good news for Reggie.

"I didn't know he had phoned, but I knew that this time it was serious. He has met a fine lady named Reggie Lewis."

There was a pause on the phone. "Reggie does not sound like a girl's name."

"I think it is a nickname, Maria. I think her real name is Regina—like a queen. Cesare is very happy."

She could hear Maria nod across the miles. "He was a good boy at his heart. I always knew that. His father just chased him away. But you—you refused to be chased. You ate up your father's demands and went beyond."

It was true and it had hurt so much over the years that her father had barely noticed. "It is strange, Maria. I have reached a place where I don't care what he thinks anymore. I am free."

And like that, a small twist of pain that she had carried for so many years uncurled in her chest. With it went the resentment that she had felt toward Cesare, who was always their father's focus. None of her father's expectations mattered anymore. What mattered was sorting this thing out with Daniel and proving to Lila he was beyond reproach—no matter what had happened to him in the past.

"Maria, you called me, remember? We were asking after an old fairytale you told me and Cesare as children. It was about lovers who were beset by a demon, but a bracelet was involved. Have you remembered the tale? Was that why you called?" She held up her wrist, the bracelet glimmering innocently in the sunlight.

"*Si .Si.* The story. It is very old. It involves a tinsmith and a woman with a heart of gold. I remember it now and will tell it to you."

"Hold on a minute. Let me turn my tape recorder on." Victoria pulled the phone away from her ear and tapped the record icon. "Go ahead," she said.

Maria began talking.

Twenty minutes later Maria had finished her story and the cadence of her voice had transported Victoria back to the nursery in the house her father kept in Lake Como. She had loved that place, the nursery looking out over the lake. Maria would sit beside Victoria on the edge of her bed and tell her tales like this as her eyelids grew heavier. But this time she was not left ready for sleep. This time she felt her blood rush in her veins. This story made sense. It fit too well with the bracelet as it was known. Her fingers came around her wrist and absently rubbed the small Dutch door. The upper half felt loose, as if it would open even though the lower portion was still locked shut with the padlock.

"That is the story as well as an old woman can recall."

Maria's voice crackled over the phone line, disturbing Victoria's thoughts.

"That is the story. I remember it now. Thank you, Maria. Thank you so much. When I am in Milan next, I will come for a visit. Cesare says the same."

"Aacha. You children are too young for an old woman like me. You have your lives to live. If I see you, it will be a wonderful thing. If I do not, it will be what life brings."

"I will visit, but now I must go and share the story. Love you, Maria. I have missed you."

The old woman said her goodbyes and Victoria hung up and considered the phone in her hands. She hit playback and Maria's crackling voice filled the room. Lila and the others needed to hear this. She saved the recording and was just leaving the room when her phone rang.

"Hello?" she answered.

"Hey, beautiful."

Daniel's deep husky voice. All her muscles loosened and the room went up a few degrees in heat.

"Daniel. Hi. I have been thinking of you."

"Same here. I can't get you out of my head. Listen, it's Thursday today and I know you've got a lot to do at the store, and I know this thing between us is still new, but I was wondering whether you might want to try out camping this weekend. I know this great little place in the hills. When I go, it's usually just me and maybe a few fishermen."

"I would love to go. When would we leave?" Just hearing his voice, she wanted to be with him; and the prospect of being with him for a whole weekend—well, that was even better—even if it was camping.

"I thought I'd take a day off tomorrow and maybe we could pack up and be gone before noon. We'd come back Sunday if you can stand camping that long."

She swallowed. Not only had she never been camping, she barely knew Daniel. Well, she knew things about him that she liked, but there were all those things that Lila had said. No. Lila was just trying to scare her with ancient history. "I suppose only time will tell whether I am a camper."

"We'll consider this trial by fire. You survive, you get automatic camper status."

"That does not bode well, Daniel. You make this sound like hard work."

"Hard work, but worth it. Have I got you scared yet?"

She could hear the smile in his voice. He was trying to scare her! She started to laugh. "If you think that your scare tactics can keep me from this experience, you must think again. I am Italian. We are known for doing crazy, wonderful things."

"Well, crazy wonderful is what I'm going for. So break out your flannel and denim and we'll do this. I'll pick you up tomorrow at eleven. Or might talk to you beforehand."

"I would like that." Actually she'd like him right here, right now in her bedroom, and she really did need to get a place of her own. She could not impose on Lila any longer.

He signed off and she stood there a moment, remembering his hands ghosting over her flesh. The sensations flared as if they were real and she wanted to lie back on the bed and welcome him in.

But Daniel wasn't here right now and the tape recording from Maria was. She struck out into the hall to play the tape for Lila.

§

Danny set down the office phone and tapped his fingers on his desktop, then held them to his nose. Yup, even here in the sterile RCMP General Investigation Office, his hands still carried the scent of Victoria's oleander. Hell, maybe his clothes did too. Maybe he reeked of it, given the way Jas had smirked at him when he first put in an appearance after dropping Victoria off at the store. He looked back at the computer screen on his desk. He'd been writing a report about a home invasion file and he'd been working on the same section for the past three hours. Same section? More like the same paragraph.

"Shit." He didn't need Jas Stone to tell him he had it bad. Victoria might be an exotic Italian, but what he was feeling was way more than physical attraction, though that was part of it. Every time he thought of her—which was pretty damn often—just the memory of how her skin felt, of how they fit together, aroused him so that he was sitting here with a half-formed erection. That was no way to focus on words on paper.

The sense of being watched brought his head up and he found his illustrious partner leaning on the doorframe, considering him, a mug of office coffee in his hand held as if he didn't trust it. They'd run out of their own coffee this morning. Point of fact was that Jas actually hated what he called the swill at the office. The natural light of the green-built RCMP building caught on Jas's black hair and his dark, bemused gaze.

"How long have you been standing there?" Danny asked.

"Long enough to see your eyes go glassy when you hung up the phone." Jas hiked himself into the white-painted room and slouched over to his desk that backed onto Danny's. Jas slumped in his chair and swung his long legs up onto the desk, then gave Danny the once-over.

"Let me guess. Victoria?"

Danny nodded.

"If I didn't know better, I'd say you were smitten, my friend."

"What d'you mean, if you didn't know better?"

"Because the Danny Forester I know laughed when I decided to settle down. He crowed that getting me off the market left all the women for him. But I have to say that tales of your exploits seem to have totally dried up around the office. No nightclubbing, Danny? No time at the bars?"

"I've been busy doing surveillance." Danny hooked his notebook toward him and made a show of reviewing his notes before entering a bit more into the report.

Damn, Jas just sat there.

Danny sipped his coffee and grimaced. Then he leaned back in his chair because the sour scent of the coffee just made him think of the 'picnic' he'd had with Victoria in her store. Not that the espresso had smelled anywhere like the office's vile concoction—and where was this coming from? He *liked* the office coffee. It was Jas who was all up on lattes and Americanos and other concoctions.

Slamming his notebook shut, he stood. "Feel like going for a real coffee? I could really get out of here." And maybe Jas and discussion of other cases would help him get a certain woman out of his head.

Jas just raised his brows and looked up from reading a file. "I thought you were the one who liked plain office swill." He hooked his fingers around swill.

"Not this morning, I don't. Stuff stinks big time and one of your Americanos sounds good."

Shrugging, Jas climbed to his feet and together they followed the open balcony walkways to the stairs and down to the security door. They buzzed through and stepped out of the air conditioning into the sweltering parking lot.

Danny ducked his head from the sun and started walking up the street toward the small strip mall that housed their favorite restaurant. West Kelowna was a small town that the provincial government had done a disservice to when it built the north-south highway. Instead of routing the highway around the town's center, the provincial government had driven it, like a stake, right through the town's heart. The two lanes of northbound traffic formed a steady stream of one-way traffic down one main thoroughfare, and the two lanes of southbound traffic did the same one block over. The result had been a burgeoning of shopping malls just outside the town center and the ongoing decline of the town itself. Now West Kelowna's heart was a small cluster of shops and restaurants that were constantly fighting the traffic's carbon dust.

One of the small restaurants to survive was Betty's, run by Elizabetta di Maria, who had once been Miss Westbank before the newcomer population changed the name of the town to West Kelowna. It was as if everything that had been Westbank was being erased. Perhaps its name was the last to go, though a few hardy souls still had Welcome to Westbank signs on their lawns. But pushing into Betty's was like pushing into the town that had been. Small, cast-iron tables with uncomfortable cast-iron chairs filled the small space, and the luscious scent of fresh Italian tomato sauce filled the air. From the kitchen came a sense of bustle and a clatter and clang along with a raspy voice singing something in Italian. Then a head of iron-gray curls popped up through the window into the kitchen and Betty's narrow face split into a grin. She was the daughter of Italian immigrants who had had an orchard here in Westbank. Betty had grown up amid the peach, cherry, and apple trees, becoming Miss Westbank along the way. She'd married and raised her own family, but when her husband died prematurely, against her children's advice she'd opened her little restaurant named after herself. *A simple name for simple food* she always said. It specialized in delicious homemade pasta and, according to Jas, some of the best Italian coffee in the valley. You couldn't prove the latter by Danny, but darn it, he should have brought Victoria here!

"Boys! You are early, the ziti Bolognese and the cannoli will not be ready until noon."

"Hey, Betty, that's okay. My friend here was just needing good coffee for a change. Could you bring me my usual and bring Danny a single shot Americano?" Jas called.

"Nope!" Danny held up his hand. "Changed my mind. Make mine espresso, please." He hadn't minded the one he'd shared with Victoria.

"Holy cow, Victoria's converted you." Jas whistled and ushered them to their usual table in the back corner. He slipped into one of the small, cast-iron chairs and Danny slumped on his chair beside him.

Betty bustled around the kitchen to the chugging of the espresso machine, but Danny felt the weight of her glances and Jas's full-on consideration.

"So? What gives?"

Danny sighed and shook his head. "You know I've been keeping an eye on Victoria."

A knowing smirk filled Jas's face. "I think the word you used was surveillance." He held up his hand when Danny went to protest. "Before you say anything, I totally concur that we need to keep an eye on her. There've been too many attempts on the bracelet wearers. Not that the RCMP brass would, but I get it. But something's going on beyond that, I'm betting. You were all goo-goo eyes for her at Lila's party."

"Goo-goo eyes? Who is goo-goo eyes?" Betty arrived from the kitchen, her black eyes bright. She wore a blue floral dress and white apron and placed two white espresso cups and saucers on the table before them.

"This one." Jas tipped his head sideways at Danny. "Contrary to popular myth, he is no longer cutting a swath through Kelowna's women."

"Daniel? Have you met someone?"

Her use of 'Daniel' only brought Victoria's sultry voice more vividly to him.

The tiny, bird-boned woman grabbed his hand and squeezed. "Tell me. Is she a nice girl? Is she from around here?"

"She's from about as far from here as you can get," Jas chuckled. "You'll be happy to hear that Danny seems to have met his match in a good Italian girl."

Betty's brown eyes widened. "Daniel? Is this possible?"

He sighed and nodded. "She's from Milan. Name's Victoria Angelucci. A fashion designer, but her dad's someone important."

Now she frowned. "Angelucci. I know that name. A ruthless financier if I remember. This girl—she is not like her father?"

Danny had to smile at that. "About as far from it as possible. She's lovely and she's trying to get out from under her father's scrutiny."

But Betty still shook her head and patted his cheek. "You be careful, young Daniel. A woman raised in that family could only be difficult for a normal man. Too used to luxury and leisure. I ask you, can you see her here cooking at five in the morning so that the restaurant is ready? Or for her children?"

In all honesty, he couldn't. Victoria was far too exotic for something so mundane. "She's up early to get her store opened..."

"Pssht. A store. It is not the same as food. Can she even cook? A girl from such a family would have servants for that. You be careful, Daniel. Perhaps she needs you for something. A visa, perhaps?" She turned to Jas. "You watch his back, Jasper.

Otherwise I shall have to refuse to serve one of my favorite customers.”

Shaking a finger at the two of them, she headed back to the kitchen, leaving them to their coffees. Danny added two sugars and sipped. It was a lot like the coffee from the café in Peachland, but this was far, far better—so rich and creamy he really didn’t need the sugar.

“So how does she do this? This has got to be the best coffee ever.”

“Uses the best beans and the right water. Betty tells me she filters all her water,” Jas said.

Danny took another sip. “I think I may be ruined for the office coffee. Hell, my home brew, too.”

Jas took another appreciative sip and then looked at him again. “So how *is* it going with Victoria?”

“Surveillance wise? All good, though there was that incident a few days ago. Nothing serious.” Danny eyed his partner. Tell him about the concern he had? The blank spaces in his day that he couldn’t account for? Jas had put his own career on the line when he covered for Danny after the initial event that Danny had come to call his alien possession because it had felt like something else had shoved him aside to inhabit his head.

But there was no way in hell it was happening again. He was in control.

He came to himself with Jas studying him. Jas raised his brows in question.

“Sorry. Just cogitating. Victoria and I—we sort of took it to the next level.” He felt the warmth come seeping up past his collar.

Jas’s mouth quirked. “That color looks good on you, my red-haired friend. So what happened?”

Danny sipped his coffee. He wasn’t the kind to kiss and tell. “Let’s just say I took her for dinner last night and things went well.”

“By the gleam in your eye, I’d say that’s an understatement. I remember, with Chloe, I felt like I actually couldn’t breathe with the need to be near her. Stupid. Had to be the pheromones.”

God, he could relate, but he was *not* giving Jas more ammunition. For some reason, he wasn't going to mention the door-thing, either. Jas was bad enough teasing as it was, without getting him going on this soul mate thing.

"So has anything come back from our queries about *Schwarzenacht Corporation*?"

Jas shook his head, but didn't comment on the change of subject. "Not much. The corporate crime group sent me a bit of a dossier. *Schwarzenacht* has been cited a lot for environmental infractions, which is consistent with what happened with Ally McVay's Pemba Island project. But we're not getting anything much on Johan Fehr. Went to Oxford, took over the business from his father when he was thirty. His father was institutionalized at about the same time."

"Institutionalized?" Danny asked. "What for?"

"Apparently it was quite the thing in business circles. The guy suddenly went off his rocker. One day he was king pin of the boardroom and feared by most, even though he was an old man by then. The next he was crazy. He eventually killed himself."

The restaurant disappeared for a moment and a shiver ran through Danny. Then he looked at Jas. "Doesn't that sound awfully familiar? I mean, we've got how many people in the psych ward right now and the driver of the pickup that killed that estate agent killed himself."

Jas straightened in his chair. "Now that you point it out, yeah."

"And all of them claimed there were aliens in their heads."

"Damn, Danny, are you suggesting that this thing, whatever it is, had control of Fehr's father?"

He nodded. "And Fehr. What if Fehr is the body that the thing always goes back to?"

"That would make sense." Jas knocked the rest of his espresso back and stood. "Betty. That Ziti Bolognese smells delicious. I'll be back for lunch." He turned back to Danny. "You coming? We've got some digging to do into the Fehr family."

"I wonder if they ever spent time in North Africa," Danny said as he drained his coffee and stood.

"It would explain a lot, wouldn't it? 'Course, it still doesn't give us the evidence we'd need to pin Kylee's abduction on Fehr, or all the other attacks, either. No one would believe us if we told them what we knew."

"Heck," Danny said. "Even Victoria's skeptical. Betty, I'll be back for lunch, too," Danny called when they reached the door.

Her narrow, high cheek-boned face appeared in the kitchen pass-through. "You be careful, Daniel. Don't you go giving your heart to a girl who will stomp all over it."

"Don't you worry, Betty," Jas called over Danny's shoulder. "He's going to scare her off first—he's taking her camping!"

The little woman's eyes rounded in horror as Jas, laughing, tugged him out the door. The damn man and his eavesdropping. He'd heard more than he should.

Chapter 10

Victoria hung up her cell and carried it and its recording with her as she went in search of Lila. Outside of her misty-grey and lavender bedroom, the hallway through the center of the upstairs of the house was filled with shadows. She felt a little shadowy herself after seeing the matching door on Daniel's house and having agreed to the camping trip with him. She was pretty sure that Lila would not approve, but it was not Lila's heart that was involved.

She held her hand up to eye the bracelet. "You will not misbehave, do you understand?"

She jingled the bracelet links and peeked in Lila's open office door. Lila sat in her computer chair eying spreadsheets on her computer screen, but looked up when Victoria looked in. "Victoria, hi! Listen, I'm sorry I spooked you downstairs. I'm just concerned is all."

Victoria raised a hand. "It is no matter."

"So we're good?" Lila asked, her auburn hair a lovely cloud around her fine features.

"We are perfect." Victoria stepped inside the room, but there was no other chair inside. "I called my Maria and this time she remembered the story."

"Wonderful! What did she have to say?"

"I recorded her." Victoria held up the phone. "Lila, just so you know, I am going camping with Daniel this weekend." Said in a firm voice that would brook no protest.

Lila bit back whatever she was going to say and stood. "We should play the tape where we all can hear it. Kylee should be in, and Reggie we can pull in from the back."

Together they went down the stairs. Lila called Kylee and Chloe from the front and then went out to Reggie's workshop. Reggie followed Lila back to the house. Inside, Reggie went to the kitchen sink to wash grime from her hands and face while the others crowded into the kitchen nook. It was a tight fit with the four of them around the table on the bench. Reggie took the chair at the table end.

"So Victoria's nanny remembered the fairytale that seemed to be relevant to our bracelet," Lila said. She caught Victoria's hands and placed her wrist and the bracelet in the midst of the table. The silver gleamed dully in the indirect late morning sunlight through the bank of windows.

Victoria set her phone on the table by her wrist and hit the replay button. From the speaker came the raspy voice of Maria.

"It's in Italian," Kylee said quietly.

"*Sono così stupido!*" Victoria used the heel of her hand on her forehead. "I will play it and translate for us."

Everyone went silent and then she stopped the recording.

"Once upon a time there lived a tinsmith in a small Italian town. He was a very talented tinsmith and the noble families from all around the country used him to mend their pots. But this tinsmith wanted to be more than a tinsmith. He wanted to make the jewelry that would grace the heads and necks and wrists of the great people, so he gave up his tinsmith work and sought through the world for the greatest silversmith in the land. This silversmith lived in a palace in a distant land. It stood on a rocky cliff overlooking the ocean. Behind it was desert for miles in every direction."

"That fits," Kylee interrupted. "The Colonel's diary said the bracelet was found in the desert."

"But not in a palace—in a cave," Reggie said, shoving her dark hair behind her ears. "I'm thirsty. Anyone mind me getting a glass of water? Anyone want anything?"

When everyone shook their heads 'no,' she went to the fridge and found a cold pitcher of lemon water and poured herself a glass. This she brought back to the table and settled herself again.

Victoria waited until she'd drained the glass before playing a bit more tape and continuing the story. "The tinsmith begged the silversmith to teach him and finally the great man took the tinsmith on as his servant. The silversmith was a very jealous man who had gathered great treasure over a very long life. He guarded his skills, his secrets, and his money. Most of all he guarded a woman who he intended to marry. She was, according to the few other palace servants, a great beauty out of a far country that their master had brought away with him to this outpost. She was kept in a tower of the palace and her food was sent up to her every meal in a bucket that the tinsmith raised and lowered on a rope.

"The silversmith was a hard taskmaster, but he taught the tinsmith very little. It came to be that after a year laboring in the palace, the tinsmith came to regard his time raising and lowering the bucket with the woman's meals as the best time of his days, for when he did so, the woman often peered out the window of her tower and everything said about her was true. She was a beauty with long, sweeping black curls and eyes that blazed right into the tinsmith's heart, even over the distance to the top of the tower.

"He became infatuated with her and called her his Beauty, while the silversmith he named the Beast. He became determined to free her and have her for his own. He began to send messages to her in her meals. You can imagine his surprise and pleasure when one day he found a note from her that said she gave her heart to him.

"He began to plot their escape. Unbeknownst to the silversmith, the tinsmith had snuck into the silversmith's workshop and by espying his equipment, the tinsmith had determined how the silversmith's work was done. In secret the tinsmith designed a bracelet that was different than anything anyone had ever seen. He planned it to look like all the doors of the palace, for the palace was a wondrous place, with rooms that held the beauty of the world's marvelous places in their palm trees and water canals and white sand.

"The tinsmith labored in secret and one night, with the aid of the cooks who placed a sleeping drought in the silversmith's wine, he stole into the silversmith's room and made a cast of the key that the silversmith wore around his neck. This was the only key to the woman's room.

"It took a few more weeks, but he finished his project using silver he had brought with him as a torque around his neck. He made a bracelet of silver doors with the key to the woman's freedom as the clasp."

Victoria paused to listen to more of Maria's recording and Reggie brought her a glass of the chilled lemon water. Victoria downed it in a few gulps, for telling the tale was thirsty work and she remembered how Maria had always sipped from a glass she brought with her into the nursery when she told her bedtime stories.

"It fits so far. It fits the bracelet and the diary," Chloe said and ran her fingers over the bracelet on Victoria's wrist.

Fortified, Victoria once more started the recording and continued translation.

"On the night he finished the bracelet, he stole up the stairs to the woman's room and released her. Together the two escaped the palace and took ship across the ocean. They thought themselves free, so in love were they, but the silversmith was not truly a man. Instead he was a creature far older than men. Of smokeless fire he was, and he took flight and followed them. By sea he attacked them, raising great waves, but they made it to shore and hid in the hills. For months they hid until finally they reached the tinsmith's home. There they wed and began their home in a walled villa."

Chloe looked up, startled, and shivered. "My visions: they were of a villa and a man and a woman frightened because someone evil came for them."

A chill ran down Victoria's back as she listened to the tape of her nursery story. As a child she had probably listened, rapt, but now the story took on deeper meaning because the terrible things might really have happened.

"It was in the third year after they thought they had reached safety that their peace was disturbed. In the middle of the night, the silversmith came with soldiers. They surrounded the villa and tore down the door. The woman wished to return to the silversmith to save her beloved, but the tinsmith would not be protected. He was a man. He would protect his wife and he had hatched a plan.

"It was then that the silversmith revealed his true self—of great power and smokeless fire, he rose up and up and yet the tinsmith still defied him, for the tinsmith had studied the great man closely and wished to rid the world of him. In answer, the silversmith stole the tinsmith's bracelet. He told the tinsmith that he would always be a little man—too paltry to ever amount to anything. The silversmith struck the tinsmith down and stole his essence to be trapped inside the silver bracelet for a thousand years.

"But as the silversmith struck, the woman screamed and ran. She so distracted the silversmith that the tinsmith was able to fight back and draw much of the silversmith's power to him, so though he was trapped, he was also able to curse much of the silversmith's power and draw it with him inside the bracelet.

"In fury the silversmith pursued the woman, for he knew she had posed a distraction. In the disruption, the silversmith forgot the bracelet for he did not yet realize what the tinsmith had done. A serving girl took the bracelet and ran. But the tinsmith's wife was caught. In vengeance the silversmith turned her into a door in his palace—to exist there until the palace was destroyed. When he realized what the tinsmith had done to his power, he pursued the bracelet, but the maid had by then crossed many countries. To this day the bracelet has never been found and though the palace of the silversmith has long ago blown away to dust, the Beauty still wanders the world as a ghost until she reunites with the man she loved."

The recording ended with Maria's voice saying that was the story as she remembered it and Victoria's own husky voice telling her thank you. She clicked the cell phone recorder off and looked at each of them.

"Does this help? You must remember that my Nana is older now—close to ninety—and though she is still sharp, age dulls some of her memories."

Four sets of eyes looked at her. Four heads nodded.

"I think we should have you write it down with all the nuances of the translation. It isn't like the teaching tales of many fairytales and parables or fables. It's a story, a tragedy, really," Lila said.

"But it all fits with what we know or suspected from the Colonel's journal and Chloe's visions. The silversmith must have found the maid. I'll bet one of those bodies in that cave the Colonel found in the desert was the maid who stole the bracelet. It was lucky that they'd hidden the bracelet when he found them."

"But what are we facing?" Chloe asked. "It's pretty clear that it's something powerful. There's no mention in the story of the thing jumping bodies. What did Maria call it—smokeless fire? That would explain the scent of burning I had in my apartment when the thing attacked me, but what is it?"

"Something considered old and powerful even in the time of the story," Victoria said, all the little hair on her body on end. She didn't want to think what it could be. Such things belonged in nightmares or bad movies, and she had enough to concern her in real life with trying to get the store open and the new relationship she'd started. Yes, it *was* a relationship—she was sure it could be if she wanted it, just as she was sure a certain fabric could make the perfect garment.

"I think we're going to have to do some research. Maybe look for other fairytales."

"Seems to me that if we're talking about old desert stories, maybe we should start with the *Thousand and One Nights*." Reggie said, looking thoughtful. "There's something about this story that reminds me of it. Mind you, I was just reading the children's version to Thalia."

"Reggie's right," Lila said with a shake of her head. "Publishers changed most of the Brothers Grimm stories because they were so gruesome. Not what we consider children's tales at all in their original form. They were intended to teach children the rules—or scare them. The *Thousand and One Nights* might be the same."

"Plus, *Thousand and One Nights* is middle eastern. That fits with the desert and all," Kylee said.

The clock on the wall said noon and Victoria leapt to her feet. "I am sorry, but I really must get to the store. Hopefully Birdy's key worked so they could get in and keep sewing."

But Lila caught her wrist before she could leave. "Do you understand now why we're concerned?"

It was a double question and one that she was not fully prepared to answer about Daniel. "About the bracelet, yes. I will be careful."

She slipped her wrist free and hurriedly left the room.

§

It was a long afternoon in the quiet of the General Investigations squad office of the RCMP detachment, with only the general hush of the building backed by the hum of the air conditioning. Across from Danny, Jas studied the computer screen on his desk, having agreed to do research on the web. Which left Danny to do his own research.

Sure, the espresso from Betty's kept Danny's blood circulating, but it also made it nigh on impossible for him to drink the swill from the office machine. So, while he scanned the electronic files sent over by the Commercial Crime section, he kept endlessly picking up his mug out of habit. It was unappetizing as hell, with a sludge of cold coffee on the bottom.

The influence of Victoria, no doubt. How the woman had impacted him so much in such a short time was inconceivable. It couldn't just be the bracelet, could it?

For the millionth time, he glanced up at the round-faced clock on the white wall and swore God or his crony had played the supreme joke and slowed down time.

He wanted to see Victoria more than he had wanted to see anyone. Just thinking of her had him half out of his chair or his hand reaching for the phone. Stupid. Idiotic. A swooning fool. What was he—some cliché out of a romance novel?

Sighing, he scrolled the page on another PDF file, this one tracing the history of the *Schwarzenacht* dynasty.

The company began between World Wars One and Two during the time the German economy was at its worst. Heinrich Fehr had been a young soldier who had gotten separated from his unit in North Africa. They had counted him amongst the lost until he turned up at the end of the war, but he had rejected all contact with old family and friends, and from somewhere came up with the funds to purchase a small factory. The company flourished when his competitors did not. He bought them out and the company grew, becoming an international force in automotives, communications, high tech, and engineering, with subsidiaries in areas like entertainment and tourism.

Danny sat back in his chair, the wheels squealing. The clock on the wall had moved another ten minutes. Two thirty and this afternoon was never going to end.

"So what'd'ja find?" he asked Jas when Jas when looked at him.

"Not a lot. A lot of stories about Johan Fehr and his father Heinrich. Apparently the transition from one man to the next was almost seamless. That surprised a lot of the pundits, given Johan Fehr had a rep as not much more than a playboy scoundrel before he took over. But when he did, his approach was exactly the same as his father's—to the point where the joke was his father controlled the company from the grave."

Jas scrubbed his fingers through his hair. "It almost fits too well, doesn't it?"

Danny nodded and told him the history of the corporation. "Most Germans had nothing after the war, but this guy turns up when everyone thought he was dead and he had money—enough to suddenly become a businessman, when his family were simple German peasants before the war."

"What kind of company was it he bought? Jas asked.

"A foundry of some sort. Silver, copper, tin. That sort of thing. They made teapots and kettles and pots and pans, but they also had a division that made jewelry. The corporation is also the benefactor of a museum that houses antique jewelry from around the globe. They have the largest collection of Mediterranean items in the world."

"Now that is interesting." Jas came around the desk to read over Danny's shoulder. "Do you think this is a cover for trying to find the bracelet?"

"What else? Apparently they're well enough funded to pay top dollar for pieces, no questions asked. A few foreign governments are after them to return items stolen from museums during local conflicts. A lot of Afghani gold pieces stolen by the Taliban ended up in the Fehr museum."

"So he has friends in low places."

"Commercial Crime seems to think so. They've also suggested that international intelligence agencies have him on a watch list for a variety of activities including human trafficking and arms deals."

"Nice guy! He doesn't miss a trick if it has potential to make money." Jas hooked a leg over the side of Danny's desk and continued reading.

"The net has more rumors or things that could lead to rumors—like Fehr's friendship with a Berlin nightclub owner who's thought to have connections to high-end brothels. There are even reports of investigative journalism stories that had to be removed because of threatened lawsuits. Apparently someone tried to sue for patent infringement on some process used in putting a patina on copper and the corporation rained all over him until the guy lost everything. Then *Schwarzenacht* offered him a pittance—enough to keep his home—and the guy caved.

Danny met Jas's gaze. "Reggie," they said in unison.

"Not to mention Lila and Chloe and the others. They've all stood firm on this lawsuit thing when most people would have pulled back and gone into hiding so they wouldn't be a target."

"And the guy is just as ruthless today as his father was when he first came back from the war. If he wants that bracelet, he'll stop at nothing."

Nothing at all. Danny stood up.

"I think I'm going to go check on Victoria."

Chapter 11

The inside of the shop called *The Next Thing* had taken shape nicely. The shop would soon be ready to open at this rate. She'd been thrilled when she arrived at the shop to find Birdy and Emma fully involved in making a series of long, slim sheaths that would pair beautifully with the stunning kimonos Victoria's friend had sent. There were also draped, high-waisted trousers *àla* 1940s ready for pressing and a few pull-over, hip-length, simple tops of fine cotton that had been inspired by Chloe's caftans. In pure white, they caught the eye and should swing around the body as either a cover-up or a top for jeans or shorts. Perfect for a beach town.

The shop itself was filling up. The displays of kimonos still held pride of place, but also many of her own pieces in banks of softly compatible creams and tans, gray and black and white. She would stick to two palettes and have accessories that set each off. Jewelry displays from *This and That,* a few purses brought in from Milan. It was digging deep into her trust fund, but she had faith that she could make this happen. If Cesare had found his dream here, why couldn't she?

She sat on her stool out front with her phone and tablet, transcribing Maria's story as Lila had requested. She'd also already downloaded the *Thousand and One Nights* to start reading—she just needed to find the time. Maybe camping with Danny this weekend?

The shop's air conditioner quietly churned out cool air. From the rear of the shop came the whir of sewing machines and the music preferred by the two women—country, which wasn't exactly to Victoria's taste but was beginning to grow on her.

The view from out front was still blocked by the paper covering the windows, but she could hear the traffic and the voices from Taste Café and the shouts and laughter of the beach goers. She really was in a perfect location. She went back to her transcribing, but a sense of being watched brought her head up. Not Birdy or Emma. She could still hear their voices.

A shadow on the paper over the windows caught her attention. Male figure. Broad shouldered. Clearly standing there looking at the paper covering the windows, but it felt like he was looking right through the paper at her.

The air conditioner felt like it blew hot and muddy air so sweat claimed her skin. The bracelet pulsed so piercing hot around her wrist that she expected it to glow. It didn't, but the air smelled of smoke. Was there a fire in the building? There was no alarm. No screaming.

No smoke.

Smokeless fire, Maria had called it. If it was more than a fairytale.

Whatever it was, she was not going to sit here waiting. She slid down off her stool, grabbed her tablet and phone. Phone. Phone someone. She hefted it in her hands. Who should she call? Lila? She was close by, but what could she do against a stalker or the mythical creature they described? Daniel, then.

She stabbed his number and waited for it to ring. One. Two. Three.

"Hello. This is Corporal Danny Forester with the West Kelowna RCMP. I can't take your call right now. Please leave a message after the beep. If your matter is urgent, please call 911. *Beeep.*

"Daniel. It's me. Please come."

She hung up the phone. The scent of burning filled the room and the figure still stood silhouetted on the window. She edged toward the hall to the rear of the store, but suddenly found herself standing by the front door. Something in her pocket pulsed hot against her hip.

Che Cosa? How could this be?

She tried to turn around, but her legs would not work. Her hand, however, snaked toward the front door handle and something in her pocket felt like it burned through her jeans and into her flesh. Then she remembered the amethyst necklace that Chloe had given her. She had stuck it in her pocket, not quite believing Chloe's promise that the necklace would provide protection. Or, for that matter, that she needed protection.

She tried to pull her hand back to her side, but it was no use. Her fingers shook with effort, but her hand would not move. She would unlock the door and step outside and whoever it was out there would take her away and do whatever he wanted.

Her heart beat harder than it ever had during one of Erminio's fashion shows. Her body was hot, then cold. Her palm closed on the cool of the door handle. Just a twist and a flick of the lock and the door would open.

She wanted to scream, but her throat closed on all sound. A strangled moan came from deep in her chest.

"Victoria? A word? Emma and I have a couple of questions."

Whatever had seized her fell away with the voice. Victoria spun on her heel and staggered against the door to face the slight form of Birdy. The door rattled in its frame.

Finding strength she didn't think she had, Victoria scrambled across the room, grabbed the older woman's arm and dragged her down the hall.

"Victoria? Is something wrong?"

In the production room, Victoria slumped against a table strewn with fabric and patterns and waited for her breath to even out before talking. Her heart still thundered in her ears when she turned to Birdy.

"Did you see it? The silhouette on the window? Smell the fire, the heat?"

Emma and Birdy looked at each other and then at her as if she had lost her mind. Birdy shook her gray head 'no.'

"Surely you must have smelled it, though—the smoky smell like a fire…"

Another no.

Victoria scrubbed at her face. Her skin was clammy. Was it all her imagination? What was the matter with her?

Her fingers found the bracelet and the comforting link of the small Dutch door. She smoothed her finger pads across it over and over. Stay calm. Just breathe, and soon it would all be over. What was happening to her that this occurred in the store—two times now?

The sweet-acrid smell of the fabric sizing used in manufacturing to strengthen and smooth the cloth filled the room and clogged her lungs. She needed air—needed something.

Straightening, she faced the two women. "What was it you needed?"

The two women looked at each other again. Birdy checked her watch. "It's almost four thirty. It can wait until morning."

Victoria fought the need to run for the back door. Just be normal. Just deal with normal problems and everything will *be* normal.

"Tell me now. I may be away tomorrow."

They were mundane queries about the flow of a dress, the pleat of a trouser. Birdy had an eye that would have done her well in a design house. With each problem she also brought a solution, and each of them Victoria agreed with. By the time she was done, her heartbeat was normal and the women no longer looked at her as if she was about to fall apart before them.

She excused herself and pushed through the rear door to the loading area to lean against the stucco wall in the shadows. Eyes closed, she inhaled the lake air. It was filled with the sour scent of roasting coffee and something that had burned. Not what she was going for when her lungs felt closed up to begin with.

Had it all been her imagination? Was it just Lila's concerns that had her so jumpy? Or was it the fact the door on her wrist matched Daniel's door? Somehow that fact made the danger she had felt more real.

But it was such a wild story—linked to a children's fairy tale.

The first time she'd seen the silhouette in the door she'd been scared and that had been before Lila came on so strong. So just what was happening? She liked Peachland. She liked the store. In fact, she loved it. In Milan she would have been relegated to a tiny shop no more than a single room in size. At best she would contract out her pieces for sewing to one of the large cadre of producers that had developed just to help the newcomer designers. At worst she would be sewing the clothing herself in her apartment. The former would lead to less than perfectly made clothing. The latter would take far too much time. No, Peachland had been good to her, and if she could get her visa so she could stay, things would be even better—unless things kept spooking her as they had.

Sighing, she opened her eyes and almost screamed at the figure silhouetted against the somnolent bungalows and church across the street in the sunlight. Broad-shouldered as the figure on her window, but this one carried the scent of leather and sunshine. He stepped forward and transformed from threat to Daniel, a look of concern on his face.

"Victoria? What's happened?" His hands warmed her shoulders and pulled her into him.

Safety. That was truly what Daniel felt like. Except—except the last time she'd been scared in her shop Daniel had appeared back here, too. She looked up at him. "Were you...were you standing out front of the store five minutes ago?"

"No. But if you thought it was me, why are you hiding out here?"

Swallowing, she shook her head. "It—it felt wrong." She told him about what had happened and leaned her forehead against his chest. "It was only Birdy coming to ask a question that saved me. It was like the—the *costrizione*, the compulsion, broke then."

He folded her into his chest and kissed her hair. "I'm sorry," he whispered into her hair. "I just got here."

§

In the shade of the loading dock, Danny ran his palm over Victoria's hair. She pulled back from him trying to be strong, but he shook his head and held her tighter.

"I'm here for you. I'll always be here for you."

She smelled of oleander and rich red wine, like the kind Cesare, her brother, had brought to dinner one night. She shivered in his arms. Still scared, and his muscles tightened. Anyone who would purposely try to scare this woman would answer to him. Yes, she was strong and beautiful and people might think she had it all from the lovely face she showed to the world, but he'd come to realize that there was another side to Victoria—the sensitive, creative artist designer who had obviously been injured at some time in the past so she did not fully trust herself—or those around her.

But she had when they had been together. She had trusted him enough to make love to him completely and had allowed herself laughter. He liked it when she laughed. Liked it better when they laughed and loved together.

The trouble was, at the moment he remembered his urgent departure from the office this afternoon and he remembered standing beside his car just outside the loading dock. He wasn't exactly sure he remembered the drive or his arrival. How long had he been standing there before a motion in the loading dock attracted his attention and he spotted Victoria? He wasn't exactly sure. What he was sure of was the fact his car keys were in his pocket and he had the taste of strong coffee in his mouth. Not the coffee from Betty's because that was hours ago. No, this was the coffee from Taste Bakery.

He was tempted to go into the café and ask them if they'd served him, just to confirm his suspicions. But with Victoria in his arms, did he really want to know?

He couldn't think of a better way to lose her.

Chapter 12

The wind was a glory in Victoria's hair as she rode next to Danny in the silver-blue Corvette. In one way he felt like he'd abducted her away from the darkness of her shop to the excitement of shopping for what she'd need for the camping trip. In another he worried what was happening to him. The lost moments had to be just the product of a preoccupied mind, like drivers had when they left work and suddenly realized they'd arrived home. There was no way that he wouldn't know if the creature had taken him over—was there?

Damn it, no. He *would* know.

Most of all he would remember if he posed a threat to Victoria. Something like that he sure as heck wouldn't forget.

He glanced over at her as they cruised over the crest of Drought Hill and under the overpass that led onto the Coquihalla Highway, the major connector to Vancouver and the coast.

"We'll be going that way," he said, waving at the highway as they left it behind. "Up top there's a lovely series of lakes off on a side road. There're some great camping areas set back from the road. That's where we'll camp."

"You are sure that I am up to this?" she asked seriously as the sun and wind made wild gossamer threads of her hair that she fought to contain with her hands.

"I guess we'll see, won't we? Everyone says I'm crazy and that it'll be a disaster, but I think they're going to be surprised at how much you enjoy it."

Her expression was dubious. "In Italy we see many campers in their caravans. At their campgrounds they are all pressed together. It does not look like fun."

"You can find that here, too. But not me. I go to the outback and we won't be in a motorhome, we'll be in a tent."

"A tent." She looked at him blankly.

"You know. A tent. One of those nylon, four-person deals. It gives plenty of room for two."

She looked out the windshield, but the way her throat worked, it was clear that she was reassessing her decision.

"Look. It'll be fun. An adventure, and it's only for three days. If you don't like it, we'll pack up and head back to my place, okay?"

"That would be appreciated. I am not sure...where do we go to the bathroom?"

He explained about the outhouses and how they'd bathe in the lake. If it was quiet enough, they might even skinny-dip.

She looked at him out of the tops of her eyes. "Is that what this plan is all about—getting me naked? Because we could just go directly to your house and forget the camping."

"Nope. Not going to happen." They'd passed through West Kelowna and were on the curved approach to the floating bridge to Kelowna.

"Besides, this isn't just about getting to cuddle in a tent, this is about letting go and laughing. There isn't anything better to cut through all the stress than a few days just getting away from it all. You wait. You'll see."

"All right. We will go camping." She looked forward again as he maneuvered them through the traffic and turned into the parking lot at *Clear Air Kelowna*, the best outdoors store in town. Victoria's hands held on tight to the edge of her seat.

"This is the place," he said, exiting the car and coming around to her. He held her door and the door to the shop, where she stopped and looked back at him.

"What is all this?"

"Specialty camping gear and clothing—like what you would wear to go skiing. I'm taking it you ski."

"Very well, actually." She nodded and left him to wander in the store, her face bemused, her fingers trailing over the fabric as if she could read them like fingerprints. When one of the staff greeted her, she looked back at Danny and smiled as if she had made her decision about something.

"I will need a jacket, a warm sweater, t-shirts, shorts, and trousers. Apparently I am going camping," she announced.

She was a surprisingly efficient shopper, getting into the spirit of the event. She bought a pair of dark gray trousers that could unzip the leg to make capris that could be rolled to shorts over her slim legs. Three t-shirts of merino wool in bright blue and pink and black because she preferred natural fabric that would not smell, and a Gore-Tex jacket of dark forest green because, she said, she did not want to frighten any animals. Lastly a pair of sturdy day-hikers and socks because they were surely all she would need. They were out of the store in an hour and headed home through rush hour traffic.

"How about dinner?" he asked as he allowed a motorhome into the lane in front of them.

Sighing, she smiled at him. "I would like nothing better, but I did not finish the transcribing I promised Lila I would do. I heard from my nanny about that old story. I want to get it finished this evening before we leave."

Trying to hide his disappointment and yet knowing the story was important, he nodded. "Then home it is. I'd appreciate you emailing Jas and me the story. Then you can model all your new clothes for the ladies."

She eyed him sideways. "Actually, I will. Tell me, Daniel, are a lot of women attracted to these outdoor clothes?"

He frowned as he changed lanes and then sped up as the road entered the bridge headed south. "I guess, yeah. Skiers. Campers. A lot of women wear leggings, too, of course. And a lot of women here in North America wear them all the time—not just for camping. We're a pretty outdoors focused community in the Okanagan. And people dress for comfort mostly."

"That is what I thought." She nodded, clearly dwelling on something.

"You've got an idea, don't you?"

She grinned and it was like the blue sky got a little brighter.

"Of course. I want to look at these clothing. They are well made. I am thinking that perhaps I can design something more fashionable that offers the same sturdiness, so that it can be both for outdoors and for the city so a woman can be beautiful in both places. Yes?" She arched her brows at him.

"Far be it from me to stop women from being more beautiful. But then, I happen to think they're most beautiful with no clothes on at all. So there's my bias."

That evoked a roll of her eyes, but she caught his hand on the gear shift and held on like she meant it. When he glanced at her as they curved up the hill from the lake into West Kelowna, she was still smiling.

§

At six a.m. the next morning, the *infernale* alarm drilled into Victoria's brain. She groaned and pulled her head under the sheets and waited for the torment to end. Finally she opened one eye and swatted the clock onto the floor. The thing kept beep-beep-beeping until she was ready to scream. She swung her legs out of bed and fumbled the clock into her lap, stabbing at the buttons until the beeping cut off.

The purple-gray room was even more misty at this hour of the day—or perhaps that was her eyes, as unaccustomed as they were to such early rising. Cradling the offending clock in one hand, she ran the other through the tangles of her heavy hair. Light streamed around the blinds above the chair. She stood and shuffled over, only to wince when she peered out at the lake. Yes, this late in the summer the sun was not so high and bright in the sky, but the smooth expanse of the lake caught what light there was and reflected it right into her eyes.

She went to pull back, but it truly *was* beautiful. Peaceful. No people except a lone jogger running down the street. In such peace one could think problems through and also find inspiration. She grabbed her pad and pen off the dresser and pulled the blinds open.

Last night, it had been a wise decision not to go for dinner with Daniel. The transcription of Maria's story had taken more time than she'd expected. After dinner with Lila, Kylee, and Chloe complete with two glasses of wine, she'd kept at it, but Chloe and Kylee were long departed for home and Lila was reading in her room when Victoria finally finished. She'd e-mailed Lila, Danny, and Jas before she went to bed last night.

Unfortunately it had not been a night for sleeping. Instead dreams troubled her—not that she could recall them exactly. Odd images of being trapped in a room, of diaphanous fabric wafting in unseen breezes, of sand blowing, and a sense of doom and breathlessness had interrupted her dreams. Somehow they fit with the story she had translated and made her even more certain that they should be reading the *A Thousand and One Nights*.

And now she should be getting ready for camping because Daniel would be here for her at eight, but she could spare a little time to get some of the sketches in her head down on paper.

She started with a jacket, the same cut as the Gore-Tex one she had purchased, but some time overnight the fabric had morphed into something soft and the hem had lengthened until the piece reached her sketch-model's knees. Instead of zippers there were pearl toggles, and worn with it were shorts or a mini skirt and long flowing top that almost reached the hemline. The jacket had a hood that could be worn up or would accordion down into an ornate collar. Yes. It was good. So were the trousers she drew, complete with many pockets and drawstrings that would allow the wearer to determine the height of the ankles. The shirts were plain, and yet not, with subtle embellishments on the shoulders and tiny sequins on the bodice.

She checked the bedside clock and squeaked her dismay. She'd used most of her first hour and she had promised herself that Daniel would not have to wait for her. She would prove that she was more than some pretty Milanese girl. She could meet whatever challenge he put out to her.

Scrambling for the bathroom, she took a quick shower and went to blow dry her hair, but soon realized that with its thickness and weight she wouldn't have much time left for anything else. She pulled it into a ponytail, threw some mascara at her eyes and lipstick on her lips, forgot the foundation and carefully applied facial contours because, bathing in a lake, there was very little chance she could redo it. Deodorant and her teeth done and she was out of the bathroom, pulling the trousers and a t-shirt on and stuffing toiletries, underwear and the other t-shirts in a small day pack Lila had loaned her. At the last moment she threw in a pair of leggings in case it rained or something and hung the amethyst cabochon necklace around her neck for good measure.

Down the stairs in the sturdy day hikers, her feet felt like she wore lead boxes instead of the strappy Italian heels that she was used to. The trousers felt overlong and baggy and the t-shirts, though they fit, almost formless. But she supposed in the woods she had no one to impress. At the kitchen Lila looked up from stirring scrambled eggs; the air smelled like bacon. Lila's curls pulled up in a ponytail from the crown of her head. She wore leggings and an oversized t-shirt that went down to her thighs, both in a midnight blue that brought out the green in her hazel eyes. Morning light poured through the bank of windows onto the backyard.

"You are up! I did not expect that."

Lila smiled, but it didn't seem to reach her eyes.

"I couldn't sleep last night so I got up early to meditate. When I heard you were up, I made coffee and breakfast. I hope you're hungry." She motioned to the kitchen table already set with three places, complete with the tangerine set of fish that doubled as salt and pepper shakers.

Lila spooned the eggs out onto a platter that she transferred to the nook table and grabbed a platter of bacon and toast from the oven. Two espresso cups she filled from a small metal pot and balanced them over to the table.

"Sit. Eat." Lila slid into the nook and Victoria followed her lead.

"I take it Danny will be here soon." Lila sipped her coffee and spooned a small pile of eggs, two strips of bacon, and a single piece of toast on her plate.

"He said he would be here at eight." Victoria checked the turquoise wall clock. Only a few minutes to go.

"Then I timed the food right. I'm sure there'll be plenty for him."

As if she was going to make him go through inspection like her father had done to all her suitors. Victoria tightened her grip around her knife and fork and helped herself to eggs that she didn't really want.

"Did you receive the transcription I sent you?"

Lila nodded.

"Did you read it?" The bracelet itched on her wrist, but Lila was too intent watching her rub the skin under the silver.

"I did this morning. An interesting read."

"I dreamed of it last night—the fear, the running, the desert. I downloaded *The Thousand and One Nights* to see if there is anything in there that might help us."

"That's good. Thank you." But Lila's gaze was still cool.

From outside came a whistle, and a lean, red-headed figure came around the corner of the house into the backyard.

"Daniel is here," Victoria said, about to stand up and let him in.

Lila beat her up and to the door. "Danny. Come in. I've got breakfast ready."

Her voice was curt, not quite an invitation, not quite an order. He looked from Lila to Victoria and then seemed to sigh.

"All right. I had a piece of toast at home, but eggs and bacon smell mighty good."

He slid in beside Victoria until they rubbed thighs, then he gave her a wink before he filled his plate from the banquet of eggs and bacon.

"Mmm. Good," he said as he shoveled food into his mouth. It was like he couldn't get finished and get them out of there soon enough. Victoria agreed and cocked a brow at Lila. Couldn't she see that nothing was wrong?

"So where are you headed?" Lila asked.

"Up Kane Lake Road off the Coquihalla. Might stop at Kane. Might stop at Harmon. It'll depend on how many people are up there."

Lila smiled. "I haven't been there in years. It used to be a pretty isolated spot from what I remember."

Danny shook his head as he chewed. "A lot's changed. More access for RVs and so on. The place got 'discovered' a few years back by fly fishermen and they've been coming in droves ever since. Place still has its quiet spots, and I thought it might be fun for Victoria to have a chance to see real cowboys."

"Cowboys?" Now that was interesting. As a child she'd always loved the old western movies with Clint Eastwood.

Danny held up his hand. "Whoa. Before you get all excited, this is not like in the movies. At all. But the Valley Ranch is part of Douglas Cattle Company and they still hire real cowboys, not just some kid who couldn't make it in high school. These guys are buckaroos. They know their stuff and they're serious about it. So *if* we see them, you'll have seen a real cowboy."

He turned back to Lila as if steeling himself to face an inquisition, while Victoria considered. This placed another exciting twist on the adventure. Yes, adventure. She no longer felt quite the twinge of dread she'd woken with.

Lila set down her espresso mug and clasped her hands before her like a doctor with bad news. "Danny, I respect you too much not to come to the point. I can't help thinking about how we first met you and the danger you posed to Kylee. How do we know that you won't be taken over again?"

Danny's gaze flickered, but then he appeared to rally. "There's been no problem all summer—not with all the other bracelet wearers. Why should there be now?"

"Come on, Danny. You're too smart to play dumb. You know damn well that this is the first time you've been the love interest where the bracelet is involved. If you'd met Victoria and fallen in love before she put the bracelet on, I wouldn't have this problem. But this...this is too convenient. And taking Victoria out into the wilderness just seems to play directly into what that thing has been trying to do every time—get the woman alone and attack."

Daniel winced as if Lila's words struck a blow on his shoulders. Finally he sighed and nodded. "I understand your concern, Lila. Frankly, sometimes I get scared, too..."

"No! This has gone too far." Victoria grabbed Daniel's hand and laced his fingers with hers. "Daniel has been a godsend. He has been there when I have been frightened. He is not the source of my fears, regardless of this *infernale* bracelet. Lila, I appreciate your concern, but Daniel and I are going, and that is all to be said about it. I have worn Chloe's silly necklace for protection. What more can I do? Now we will finish our coffee and then Daniel and I will be leaving."

Infuriatingly, Lila nodded, but then turned to Daniel. "Please, Daniel. Rethink this and rescind the invitation. If you've had any suggestion that this might be a problem, please don't do this. Wait until we've solved this and the bracelet is off Victoria's arm."

Daniel's jaw worked. Then he slid out of the nook. "Lila, I appreciate your concern, but I think I'd know when I pose a danger to someone I care about." He held out his hand to Victoria and she gladly accepted that warm, strong grip. She stood beside him and looked down on Lila.

"Thank you for breakfast, Lila. I would offer to help clean up, but that would only leave chance for more of these discussions and I am tired of hearing them." She picked up her small bag and leaned up to meet Daniel's lips. "This is all that I am bringing so I hope you brought the rest."

His brow lifted and he grinned, but the smile seemed forced. "I guess we'll just have to see, won't we?" He tossed a less than friendly glanced in Lila's direction. "Maybe all I brought is feathers to get you laughing again."

Chapter 13

An hour later Danny turned his old Jeep Grand Cherokee off the Coquihalla Highway onto the Kane Lake Road. The Jeep was his regular vehicle, used through the winter and on dusty side roads when the Corvette was safely tucked away in his garage. The landscape had changed for the third time, from the deep valley and desert lake of the Okanagan, to the heavily logged tops of mountains, and now to the rolling tree-and-grass-covered hills of the Nicola Valley. The hillside grasses were dry gold from the months of summer heat, but seamed through with the gray-green leaves of poplar following water channels. Here and there the hillsides were dotted with the lazy forms of red cattle, brought down from the higher hills as the autumn rolled around with September. In the towns, schools were getting ready to open.

The sunlight cut through the poplar, pine, and spruce as they turned up and away from the valley floor. The inside of the Jeep held Victoria's faint oleander scent and the smell of old canvas from his camping equipment. It was a nice combination—one that made him smile.

"The Kane Lakes are actually a favorite cross-country ski area. We're going up to the hilltops again, but these hills are a little lower than the mountains we just crossed."

She nodded, her doe-brown gaze wide with excitement as they topped the rise and came face-to-face with an old ranch house, complete with old buckboard wagon set up at the gate and filled with wildflowers.

"This is a wonder. In Europe we grow up seeing photos of such places, but to really be here!" She took a photo with her smart phone and he kept on driving, enjoying her squeals of delight at two appaloosa horses lounging by the fence. She had never seen anything like them. Frankly neither had he, but he remembered an old story from elementary school because a girl he'd had a crush on had been horse crazy.

"I think they were bred by Indians for those patterns of small spots that make them look like equine Dalmatians."

She nodded her appreciation of the information, but hung like a kid at the window to watch the countryside go by. An old snake fence charmed her, so did an old corral and cattle chute. She waxed on about the beauty at a panorama of poplar trees and rolling green-yellow grass that descended to a sky-blue lake and a small herd of horses loafing amidst pale green willows.

The first place he had thought of camping was already taken by a pair of trucks with campers and fly-fishing floaters on a trailer. Another spot he had used had three motorhomes parked and sharing a picnic table. Not what he'd expected. Not what he wanted to see. He wanted a place that wasn't filled with people and all the encumbrances of modern society. Hell, some of the motorhomes had satellite dishes on them.

He kept going. There were camping areas he could get into on the far side of the lake given he wasn't driving a motor home or camper, but he'd still have to look out at the lake and listen to the other voices. He had one more place in mind and kept driving. If the spot was filled, he could always turn around and come back. They left Harmon Lake behind.

Englishman Lake was an often overlooked jewel because there wasn't any campground set up, and that kept the campers and motor homes at bay though the fly fishermen had discovered the lake was a good place to fish. Today there was a camper pulled into the single pullout at the water's side, but he kept going to the end of the lake. As he'd thought, the level ground pullout above the lakeshore was unoccupied and beautiful with pine and poplar to shelter it and a lovely view from the slope down the length of the blue-green lake.

He turned in and turned the ignition off. Then he turned to her, grinning. "Your first surprise awaits you just outside that door. See if you can discover it. Then we'll take a look around and you can decide whether you like it here enough to camp."

She frowned, forming two perfect little lines between her arched brows. Giving him a questioning look, she opened her door and climbed out to stand there. He sat watching her: she inhaled the pine and lupine and black-eyed-Susan-perfumed air. The breeze lifted the golden plume of her ponytail and rippled through the leaves and pine needles of the trees. From the water's edge came the trickle of lake water over the small dam that kept the lake level steady and good for fish. Other than that, there was the call of a cocky, black-headed Steller's jay and the tick-tick-tick of the Cherokee engine cooling. Nothing else.

Victoria turned to him, her brown eyes large. "It is so quiet. I can hear the blood in my ears and the birds and everything!"

He climbed out and came around the vehicle to catch her shoulders, then leaned down for a kiss. In her day hikers she was so much smaller than he'd realized, barely five foot six, he'd bet. Average height, but small compared to his six foot plus. He felt a sudden surge of protectiveness.

Her arms came around him and if the place was silent, suddenly the whole blue-skyed, green-hilled day went away. He pulled warm woman into him, kissed her hard and then released her.

"So what do you think of this as our camping spot?"

He led her to the edge of the flat area that sat even with the road, and the land fell away in a gentle slope down to the water's edge. Water lilies bloomed bright yellow in the deep blue water and a family of Canada geese floated off in a V with squawking protests. Victoria went down to the water's edge and tested it.

She jerked back her hand. "Cold."

Danny shrugged. "What can I say, these lakes are all snow fed."

"But how do we swim? How do we bathe?"

He chuckled. "I guess you could say we suck it up and do it anyway." He'd save the fact that they could heat water for washing up as a nice little surprise.

For a moment she looked horrified and then—he had to hand it to her—she stood and grinned.

"This is truly trial by fire you put me through—or perhaps it is trial by ice water."

He slung an arm around her waist. "You ain't heard the half of it, lady. This isn't a campground, so there's no outhouse toilet."

The horror came back, and this time it didn't go away. "But how will…But what will we…?"

"Before you die of mortification, here are our options. One: we can go back to the camping areas at one of the lakes and have the amenities. Two, we stay here and we do it the old way, which means digging a trench or a hole for our business and having a bag for all tissues. In this part of the world, we don't want to leave anything not biodegradable behind. Not even this cute behind." He lightly swatted her. "So your choice."

Again, she surprised him, for she gave it a lot of thought where other women he would expect to immediately ask to go back to the established campgrounds. But Victoria did a slow turn that ended with her looking out at the lake. Then she turned back to him, her brown eyes sparkling.

"I came on this trip for adventure, did I not? I say we stay here and I will try your old-fashioned toilet." She laughed. "You did not believe I would choose that, did you?"

It was true. He nodded and caught her in his arms to kiss her again—softly this time. "That's the thing about you, Victoria Angelucci. You surprise me and excite me and you make me smile."

She did, too. She was more beautiful today than he'd seen her before. Without all the makeup, her almost poreless olive skin gleamed. Her hair was a wild tangle and her eyes looked as deep as the lake behind them. He looked into her eyes and knew they both felt the longing. They could come together right here, right now, out in the open. A titillating thought, but not exactly what he had in mind.

"How about we get camp set up?"

It wasn't a difficult job and Victoria leapt in readily where she could, assisting with spreading the ground tarp and setting up the tent. Together they chose a kitchen area and set up a tent awning for cover against too much sun or too much rain.

"What about this?" Victoria asked about the cooler still in the Jeep.

"Uh," Danny said, not sure how much to tell her. "It's better off there." He went to turn away.

"Why, Daniel? Why is the cooler better there when it would be more convenient under the awning?"

Danny sighed and turned back to her. "In a word: bears."

All the excited energy seemed to desert her. "Bears? There are bears here?" She looked over her shoulder and he couldn't help himself—he caught her in his arms.

"Yes, there are bears. They live out here. They're just as afraid of you as you are of them and they aren't a problem as long you don't leave food out to tempt them."

He tipped her face up to him. "Okay?"

It must have taken a lot, but she found the strength to nod and swallow. "Then I think the Jeep is absolutely the most convenient place for the cooler."

That settled, they hauled out the fixings for lunch. Then, with the Coleman stove perking coffee, and ham and cheese sandwiches made, he set their chairs up facing the lake and placed a plate and napkin on her lap.

"The coffee comes later when it's done." He slumped in the chair beside hers and grinned. "Pretty cool, huh? All this space and only us and the trees and the wind and the birds."

Victoria followed his arm as he pointed. Then she smiled. "It is better than cool, Daniel. It is like seeing a whole new world. Thank you for bringing me here."

§

Sitting in that chair above Englishman Lake and enjoying the sandwich Daniel had made, Victoria felt the tension of the last few weeks drain out of her. She chewed her sandwich—rosemary ham and Havarti cheese and mayonnaise and Dijon, enjoying the chewy Portuguese buns he'd brought. The sun was warm on her skin and so was the breeze. The lake water rippled around stands of reeds and a black bird with red patches on its wings fluttered among them.

"Do you see that?" Daniel said pointing at the bird. "That's a red-winged blackbird. There used to be a lot of them everywhere, but we keep draining wetlands so they're getting scarcer. They build their nests amongst the reeds. Up here in the hills, a lot of the older species are hanging on. The mountain bluebird, for instance. You might have noticed the bird houses built on the fences—that's to encourage the bluebirds to nest now that so many of the forests have had to be cut down due to the pine beetle."

He sighed and looked sad so she caught his hand. "Things change, Daniel."

He nodded. "It's just that I can't think of a single change for the better—at least not for the wildlife or the country."

She set her plate down on a stump and stood to face him. "I thought this camping was to have fun and make me laugh."

He considered her a moment and then was on his feet. "You're right. And at this moment, I'm thinking a swim is in order. That should make you smile—or climbing out of the water will!"

He grabbed her around the waist and carried her over his shoulder toward the water.

"No! Daniel, no!" she yelled in mock terror. "I don't want to get my clothes wet. I didn't bring enough to do that."

"Well *that's* no good." He set her down in the soft soil at the water's edge. "What are we gonna do about that?"

She tried to escape past him, but he snagged her with one arm and pulled her into him, his other hand coming up to hold her head for him. Then he kissed her again, with leg-melting heat so she sagged into him. His hands found her face and his mouth slipped to her jaw, her neck, as he slipped his hands under her shirt and caressed the underside of her breasts with his thumbs.

Madre di Dio, she wanted him now. She pulled him down beside her in the soft soil, tugged his t-shirt up over his head, and ran her hands over his rock-hard torso. For a redhead, he was surprisingly tanned a light, golden brown that brought out his freckles like golden dust over his skin. She trailed kisses down his chest and fumbled with his belt.

"I'll get it," he said and stumbled up, undid the belt and unzipped, shoving his jeans down over his hips and then fighting to get his boots free of the cuffs.

The water was so blue beyond him. The sky so blue above. Insects hummed in the trees and far above a bird of prey hovered as Daniel danced from foot-to-foot.

"Daniel?"

He stopped, balancing on one foot. "Yeah?"

"I'm sorry," she said keeping a straight face.

He frowned. "For what?"

"This." She rolled onto her knees, put her hands on his thighs, and pushed.

With his legs trapped in his trousers, Daniel didn't stand a chance. One stumbling step back and the lakeshore crumbled under him. He went backward and sat down hard, with a splash that cascaded water.

Spluttering, she sprang to her feet. Daniel was up to his chin seated in muddy lake water, an expression of wide-eyed shock on his face.

She started to laugh. "I got you! I did it!" She danced a little war dance until Daniel got his feet under him and came roaring out of the water. She ran, but he caught her half way up the hill.

"No more excuses for you!" And he dragged her laughing and screaming back down to the water where he unceremoniously threw her in.

She came up spluttering lake weeds out of her eyes and her hair, a thin film of muddy water everywhere.

Daniel roared with laughter on the shore and she had two choices: get angry or laugh with him. She chose the latter and, giggling, came up out of the water.

"Now you have a problem, Sir, because all of my clothes are soaked."

"No problem." He shook his head. "I'll just have you naked in my bed for three days or until your clothes are dry. Or you can lounge naked by the lake and give the fishermen an eyeful. It'll give them something else to do aside from swear at all the gear they lose in such a reedy lake. "

For a moment she wasn't sure if it was a joke or not, but the happy grin on his face told the tale. With his help, she schlepped up out of the lake and together they climbed the hill, where they toweled each other off and stripped out of sodden clothes that they laid on bushes to dry. The contents of their pockets, Daniel placed on a stump in the sun. Thankfully, Daniel *had* brought enough clothing so she wore her second t-shirt over a pair of his athletic shorts that were far too big, so they lounged together on a blanket spread on the ground.

They both had books to read, but instead, they lay side-by side and looked up at the sky.

"Look!" she exclaimed as a bird swept over their campground.

"That's a red-tailed hawk. There're lots of eagles around here, too."

"You know, I never thought I could waste a day like this. Always in Milan it is go-go-go. Yes, we enjoy our meals and our time together, but in the fashion industry it is too dog-eat-dog. We do not relax for a minute. If you do, someone will have stolen your ideas and you will be yesterday's news. Always you run to stay out in front." She inhaled the piney mountain air and relaxed into the sun on her face.

"Don't think of it as a wasted day, think of it as a reset or refueling yourself—like a car. You can't run forever without stopping for gas. Besides, nature is one of the best inspirations there is. Maybe you'll come back from this trip with lots of ideas." His hand found hers and laced fingers as she stared up at the clouds.

"How did you get so wise, Daniel? Tell me more about you." She turned her head sideways to look at him. His profile was strong, his skin covered in tiny freckles, the hair on the forearm under his head, golden.

"Not much to tell, really, like I said before. I'm a cop. Have been for fourteen years. I applied as soon as I was old enough. I went into training at nineteen. They must have had a shortage of candidates that year." He glanced at her and grinned. "I guess I didn't screw up too much 'cause they promoted me to corporal and partnered me with Jas a couple of years ago. Then I met you and that's about the biggest thing that's happened to me in a long time."

He squeezed her hand and she squeezed his right back. Then she rolled on her side to look down at him.

"I think I understand. I feel like something has forced me to stop and take a breath and in that process I've looked around and so I found you. It was not expected, but I'm glad it happened." She nodded down at the lake. "Do you know how long it has been since I did something bratty like that? Since I laughed with my whole body? My sides ache and it was not so long a laugh. It tells me that I am very out of practice."

She stroked his face and leaned in to kiss him lightly. "Tell me about your family. Tell me a funny story. I can imagine young Daniel was a boy always in trouble."

He relinquished her hand and pulled her down to the crook of his shoulder with a sigh. "That's one way to put it.

"Like I said, I'm one of three children. I grew up on ten acres just outside Prince George that was left mostly in trees. There was a creek that ran through the property and I played there a lot with the few other kids in the area. That and rode horses. My older brother, James, was five years older and in a totally different space than I was. My younger sister, Ester, was six years younger than me so I didn't spend much time with her, either. Dad worked for the province as real estate assessor so we weren't poor, and Mom was a stay-at-home mom. We bused it to school every day. Ester was a beauty—Lila reminds me a lot of her—so she had lots of friends. James was good looking, athletic and smart, so he could do no wrong. Me, I was the kid in the middle. To stand out I chose trouble."

She stroked his face, for the lines between his brows said the memories were hard for him. "Not so terrible a trouble, for you are a policeman now."

He nodded. "It was petty stuff, mostly. Pranks that sometimes went wrong. Eventually I realized that what I was really all about was humor. I was always cracking jokes and that made me popular with everyone but the teachers and principals." He shrugged. "So I graduated, took some courses at college, and did volunteer work at the local prison. The next thing I knew, the RCMP came calling and here I am."

He rolled over to look down at her and kissed her again. "And I'm very glad of that." Kissed her again as his hand found the edge of her shirt and skillful fingers trailed too sensually up her side.

She shivered and tried to pull away from the teasing touch. Daniel rolled her over onto her back and slung a leg casually over her hips so he effectively trapped her. He waggled his brows evilly and grinned.

"More laughter. That was what I promised." He set to work tickling her.

It was too easy on the sensitive skin of her sides. She shrieked, and tried to shield herself, but as fast as she blocked one hand, his other hand found a new sensitive spot.

She laughed. She cried. She did both together and could hardly breathe.

"Stop. Please stop!"

The torment of his torture had her writhing and then suddenly he stopped and leaned down to kiss her tears away. Tasted, seemed satisfied, and then kissed her mouth. Lingered there and then trailed kisses down her neck to the top of her shirt. He stopped there and looked up at her.

"I like to see you laugh. I may have to tickle you at least once every day."

As if he intended to be with her always.

She froze a little, but could not meet his gaze. To be with someone always—that was impossible. Her mother had died. Her father was never there. Cesare left her to deal with everything when he ran away. Really, there had been only Maria, and she had been paid to stay.

Finally she managed a smile and palmed his cheek. "It is a very nice thought, Daniel. I would like that."

But the narrowing of his gaze said he read her disbelief and perhaps mistook it as rejection.

A cool wind came off the lake as he rolled away to stare up at the sky again, his arms crossed under his head. "You shouldn't say what you don't mean. Someone might believe you and then there where would you be? Or them? Someone might get hurt."

"Daniel, no. You misunderstand. I do mean it."

But he shook his head and pulled her down against him, then pulled the edge of the blanket over them both.

The brilliant blue of the sky still remained, but the air had cooled as the sun swung behind the nearest hills. The wind rippled the lake and played in the reeds. The trees darkened and draped shadows amidst their creaking limbs. In the distance a cow bawled, the rough cry echoing over the lake like something prehistoric.

They lay there a while with the day ending around them. But something else was ending, too, if she didn't fix it. Perhaps Daniel had felt too much rejection in his life, too. Perhaps that was why she was drawn to him. But how to heal it and what to say? The loose way he held her said he might not believe her.

"I am sorry, Daniel. Truly I am. It is just—so many people who were supposed to always be there in my life have not been. How can I believe you will be?"

He looked at her sadly, then shrugged. "I don't know. Guess I'm being unreasonable, but I expected you to believe me because I spoke from the heart." He shook his head. "First time for me, really—telling someone how I'm really feeling. I thought you'd hear that in my words." He sighed and sat up, setting her aside. "You know what? I'm beginning to think I really am better off with humor, 'cause when I try to be serious, no one believes me."

He shoved up to standing, leaving her on the blanket as he padded barefoot to the car.

"It's getting toward dusk. Up here it comes fast. I think we should start dinner so that we can have the food put away in the car before dark."

And like that, he was busy, his attention elsewhere. Even when she offered to help it was like he looked through her, and she knew that fixing this had to be a priority. She did not want this camping trip to end just when it began. She did not want this man to stop expressing his feelings.

He started a small campfire after carefully scraping away all the forest debris on the ground.

"To stop forest fires," he explained.

Then he placed a grill over the fire pit that would help stop embers and filled a pot with water to place over the fire. When she saw the frying pan, she took the garlic, tomatoes, and onions from him, found a knife, and started chopping. Daniel broke the pasta in two and waited for the water to boil before placing the pasta to cook, then started oil heating in the frying pan. When she was done chopping, she poured the mixture in and Daniel started stirring without a word.

She went to the cooler and dug through for spices finding oregano, marjoram, basil, chili, salt, and pepper. These she brought back to the frying pan and began adding in small amounts as Daniel kept stirring. She found a spoon and tasted. Tested again and the flavor of the freshly grown tomatoes sang through the onions. She put a small amount on her spoon and held it up for Daniel.

"Taste and tell me what it needs."

His gaze met hers, but finally relented. His eyes widened.

"Not a damn thing, I'd say. That's good. Perfect, even." He pulled the pan off of the flame and considered her from across the fire. "How the hell did you do that? I use exactly the same ingredients and mine never tastes that good."

Rarely had anyone ever complimented her cooking—not that she couldn't cook, it was just rare that she had someone to cook for. She smiled and shrugged. "Maybe it is the company that brings out the best in me?"

It was as if the fire stopped burning, the wind quit blowing as his gaze finally met hers again. There was something in his eyes that made her long for his touch, for trust, for the intimacy she had felt with him. She stood up and went around the fire to crouch down beside him.

"I'm glad you like it. On occasion I've been known to add too much salt."

His arm came around her and she leaned her head on his shoulder as the pasta finished cooking. From out on the lake came a wild, lonely cry that she thought might break her heart.

"A loon," he said and eased her back against him. "They're solitary birds and their call is sort of a camping icon."

She could understand why. The soft, painful cry evoked all the loneliness of the world. It seemed closer to the surface out here alone in the wild. Life was like that, too. You were always alone. Her life had been a wild place of concrete buildings and strangers. Even Erminio, who she had thought she knew so well, had turned out to be the kind of person who would steal another's ideas—hers included. Another rejection to deal with.

"I think the pasta's done," Daniel said and released her to drain the water into the soil and then spoon two servings into bowls. The tomato mixture he slathered over the top and liberally sprinkled what North Americans called parmesan cheese over the top. It was mostly tasteless, but it did the trick and with two glasses of wine they settled back in their chairs to consider the lake.

"So what would you like to do tomorrow?" Daniel asked around a mouthful of pasta.

"I am fine with whatever you decide." She caught his hand, still trying to set her faux pas aside.

"We could sit and read and just be."

"That would be fine."

"Or we could go for a hike."

"That might be nice, but nothing too difficult, please."

"Or we could go down to the ranch and I could introduce you to a real cowboy or two."

Chapter 14

Victoria sat up beside Daniel. "Really? For true?"

Whether it was the way her eyes caught the firelight or an internal light that came on in her eyes at his offer to introduce her to a cowboy, Daniel knew he'd done good. If delight was a person, it would be Victoria; and that he had brought her that delight would let him sleep tonight, regardless of what happened or didn't happen between them.

"Yeah. I did some work on a stolen cattle case a few years back and I got to know Matt Stone, who manages this ranch. I stopped in a few times and even rode out with him and his boys on a cattle drive. Took weeks for my poor butt to recover."

"Poor Daniel. So that is what happened to your poor behind."

"What the heck's that supposed to mean?" He feigned injury.

She grinned. "Gotcha! Is that not the word? You actually have a very fine butt, indeed. It looks very good in your trousers—or out of them."

She cocked a brow at him and he pulled her into his lap, the metal lawn chair groaning at the double burden.

"Well, maybe we'll just have to check each other's butts out this evening." He pecked her cheek and pulled a blanket around them against the night breeze and then let his hands roam.

She was all softness and femininity as she turned into him, her scent of oleander with a hint of lake water arousing him as much as the silk of her skin. His overlarge shorts were an affront to the long, curved legs that wore them and he slid his hands over the top of them up under her t-shirt, to caress her loose breasts. Her nipples were taut and waiting.

"Did I ever mention how you turn me on?" he asked.

"Did I ever tell you that I like that I can? That I feel the same?" Her face was so close to him he smelled the tomatoes on her breath, saw the way her pupils had dilated until her brown eyes were black.

She wiggled against him, sitting up and then surprising him with her flexibility as she repositioned herself to straddle and face him, the blanket still around them. Her warmth pressed into his already hard length and she gently rocked against him, sending his heart racing and heat surging through his limbs.

He caught her hands and held them against his chest, feeling the bracelet burning like a furnace between them as if it would sear their flesh into one. The night and the wind disappeared and there was only Victoria gently rocking, rocking, rocking in the most erotic of lap dances. Only his clothes, her single dry t-shirt, and his oversized shorts lay between them and he wanted to lose himself inside her once more.

He swallowed. "You know that this is going to lead to something more, don't you?" His voice was hoarse in his ears.

"I was hoping as much," she said, placing her hands on his hardness and squeezing.

"Damn you, woman. I'll have you right here in this chair if you keep that up."

"And that would be so bad?"

"Well, it would be when the spindly legs gave way. This chair isn't exactly made for athletic sex."

"What about quiet sex?" Her eyes seemed to glow as she unzipped his jeans and fished inside to release him. "Do we have protection?"

"My pocket," he groaned.

She pecked his cheek and grinned. "That is what I like—a man who is always prepared."

"I'm a regular boy scout, all right," he said as she fished the condom from his pocket and erotically rolled it on. Then she pulled the wide leg of the shorts aside to expose herself to him. Adjusted her position and...

"Oh, God." He closed his eyes as he slid into her slick warmth, as she did something with her legs to somehow bring them closer together so he buried himself inside her.

Then she kept rocking, slowly, quietly, kissing his cheeks, his mouth, his chest, his neck. All while rocking and flexing invisible muscles so he thought he might go crazy. He wanted—he wanted to shove her onto the ground beside the fire and make love to her as he had before. But this slow, sweet loving was almost more than he could bear. It brought too much emotion. He fought his hands loose of her grip that had restrained them on the arms of the chair and held her face so he could thoroughly kiss her. Then he slid them down her back, wanted to tear off her t-shirt and feast on her naked breasts, but that wasn't what this was about. Instead he looked into her eyes and saw the longing, the years of hurt, and yet the attempt to trust. She was giving herself to him as a gift.

And such a gift it was. He hugged her to him, then gripped her hips and rose to meet her, slowly increasing the tempo, smiling as small moans of pleasure escaped her. Yes, they were good together. They both gave pleasure to the other one.

But this was not how and where he wanted to finish their lovemaking. Her excitement had increased and she was almost bouncing to thrust their bodies together.

"No. Shhh. Slowly, now. Slowly." His held her hips to slow her and had to restrain himself. Almost impossible.

"The way I see it, we have two choices," he said into the shadowy places under her hair. "We finish here and then have to wait for later when we go into the tent, or we stop now, put out the fire, and then continue this little conversation inside." He motioned at the waiting tent. They would be snug and warm inside and unconstrained by an aluminum lawn chair.

"You think too much." She jerked away from his hands and kept on moving, faster this time so he held her hips and drove up to her. His world collapsed in around them so there was only a blanket-clad woman before him, only her softness and warmth and pressure around him. She threw the blanket back off of them and he barely felt the cold air. He grabbed her t-shirt and ripped it up and over her head, tossed it aside and tongued her bouncing breasts, a pendant cool between them, held her hips as she arched her back and yelled her climax, her muscles rippling around him sending him over the top, a shock of pleasure-pain through his skull.

He shouted release and pulsed inside her. Then, drained, collapsed forward as she wrapped her arms around him. Together they fell, panting, back into his somehow still standing chair. He fished for the blanket and pulled it up over them again, still joined together, as he listened to his pounding pulse, the melded rush of their breathing.

They sat there a long time, the night deepening around them, dew dampening the blanket, and the fire fading, the headache building slowly in his head so he rubbed his temples. Finally, Victoria stirred.

"I think I need to move. My legs have gone to sleep."

With his head beginning to throb he let her leave him, clambering off the chair and taking the blanket with her. He sent her to get ready for bed while he brought a bucket of lake water up to wash dishes, then used it to douse the fire. When the coals were sodden, he tramped them flat to make sure they were out.

He stood on the slope, looking out at the lake. Down at the water's edge, Victoria's naked back made a pale V in the moonlight as she splashed water onto herself. His shorts made a pale jumble on the grass beside her, the blanket pooled around her feet. The sight of her curves and thoughts of what they had just done made him want her again—if his darned head would just quit aching. He'd had headaches before, but this felt like something was trying to crack open his skull. He squeezed the bridge of his nose, but it made no difference. The scene of Victoria washing and the languid, moonlit lake beyond her rippled and swam. A dark fog seeped in around the edge of his vision.

Migraine? He'd heard that the optical centers of the brain could be affected by such things. The way his head felt like it might explode would be consistent, but he'd never been prone to migraines. He sat down on his heels because he wasn't sure he could stand, and watched Victoria's gentle movements and the way they sent rings cascading out and out onto the water.

A lot like the way the damnable bracelet had sent ripples out over the centuries.

What the hell?

He straightened, blinked against the pain, and rubbed at his eyes. The dark fog ate his vision and something wasn't right. No, something was horribly, terribly wrong. He tried to stand, tried to move, but his body didn't respond.

Darkness and a horrifyingly familiar scent of burning.

God, no! Not this!

He wanted to scream. Wanted to shout a warning. Instead, the darkness swept in and held him pinioned. Blind. He was blind until the darkness parted enough to allow a tunnel of vision. Victoria at the water and something inside him pulsing with a sense of satisfaction.

"No!" he tried to shout, but his word echoed silently back at him as his body stood and Victoria looked over her shoulder, smiled, and waved him down to join her.

§

Crouching naked by the lake was the most primal thing Victoria had ever done. A skinny-dip at a private beach on Lake Como, or off her father's yacht, perhaps, but not something like this. The wind caressed her body and cooled it as she sponged herself off. She was damp and sweaty and smelled of sex as she palmed water up over her neck, down her breasts, between her legs, and found herself aroused—again. What was it about Daniel? She had never experienced this constant need for a man.

The water lapped at her toes and the earth was damp and she thought of her ancestors who had doubtless bathed like this in the days before running water, even before buckets were used to bring water to the house for cooking. Had it been a sensual experience then?

More like a vulnerable one. Anyone could creep up on them, and rape was common.

The breeze went cold and from somewhere came a scent of smoke—most likely a vestige of the fire Daniel had just put out—but unlike that pleasant scent of wood resin, this tainted the crisp scent of pine and water. All the hairs on her skin prickled and her skin turned to gooseflesh. The amethyst pendant seemed to warm between her breasts. Ill-ease ran through her and she peered out over the placid silver lake. Nothing but the floating silhouette of a bird. In the sky, nothing but stars and the distant light of a plane traveling overhead.

If she was alone out here...

She shivered. But she was fine. Safe. Daniel was here and she had just made love to a man she truly cared about. Tonight they would make love again and she would learn what loving in a tent was like. She smiled to herself. If this was camping, then she liked it very much.

She glanced over her shoulder up at the camp and found Daniel, like a god, silhouetted against the million stars. Never had she seen so many stars.

He looked so serious as he peered down at her. She smiled, her skin warming at thoughts of him and motioned him down. Perhaps they could swim in the lake together and make love there.

He came down the slope toward her looking slim and virile in his narrow jeans with his bare chest gleaming. Like some hero of a tawdry romance novel, perhaps. But his gaze was steady and filled with intent.

Did he want her now? The thought was exciting, but something about the way he moved wasn't right.

Not the loose-hipped, casual stride she knew Daniel for. This was more a predator. Was he playing another game? She pulled the blanket up around her and stood, suddenly not sure she wanted to go in the water with him. The pendant had turned hot.

"The lake is beautiful, is it not? I see a bird out there." She pointed.

Daniel looked at the lake as if he saw it for the first time. "Sure. Very pretty."

But...his voice was stiff and it was almost unlike him because he always came up with some bit of information about the moon or the lake or the animals or birds.

"What kind of bird is it?"

He shrugged. "Damned if I know."

And that was definitely not like Daniel. Even when he had been injured and distant earlier, he had not been like this. Something was wrong. She caught him staring at the bracelet on her wrist and she *knew*.

Totally knew.

All of Lila's warnings had been true. Regardless of the unbelievable nature of the story, standing next to her was not the Daniel she had just loved in his chair.

Her knees felt weak and watery. She was alone—more alone than she had ever been in her life and, if the stories were true, in more danger. Or else she was imagining things... She probably was.

But her fear told her otherwise and so did the pendant. She might not believe, but her body *knew,* and the pendant burned like a brand.

Her mouth dry and hands shaking, she knelt for the shorts. Used this as a chance to edge away from whoever this was.

He had other ideas and reached for her hand. Resist and run? They might both be barefoot but she seriously doubted that she could outrun Daniel. Don't give her knowledge away and wait until she had a chance.

She looked up at him and found a smile but there was something wrong with Daniel's eyes. Yes, it might be dark, but Daniel's eyes were green—except now they were not green, either. Black pits stared back at her as if she stared into the blackest dye vats ever. On a garment she would want to fasten crystals because the blackness was too stark—the true absence of everything. It seemed to flicker and burn within him.

The bracelet had gone frigid on her wrist until her hand felt numb. She swallowed.

"C-could you do something for me? I have some special soap, but it's up in my pack. Could you get it for me?"

If this was the creature that Lila had spoken of, it could simply strangle her now or do whatever it wanted. But perhaps it was enjoying this. Perhaps it liked to toy with its prey.

"Please?" She pouted coyly, and placed her hand on his chest.

Finally he nodded and turned up the hill.

Every ounce of her being said run—run now. Instead she made a show of returning to the waterside. With the blanket around her hips she tried to hide that she slipped Daniel's too-large shorts back on. She strained to hear the tent zipper, and when she did, she grabbed the blanket and ran.

Silently up the bank, careless of the stone and twig that bit into her feet. She snagged her half-dry t-shirt and her sodden shoes and then dashed out to the road and kept on running. When the road bent away from the campground, she ducked into the brush away from the lake and paused long enough to pull on the shoes and the shirt.

From behind came a roar of fury that froze the night around her.

Braced by fear, she turned uphill and ran.

Chapter 15

The woman was gone and would lead a merry chase.

The thing inside Danny Forester turned from the tent at the pounding of feet, the rustle of brush, and the lovely, tearing, breath of someone deathly afraid. He inhaled the perfume of silver on the stilling night air. The wind was dying and the bracelet so near there was no way that he could lose her scent.

Let her run. Let her hide. It would make the catching, the killing, the final taking all the sweeter. It had been generations since he had made a game of his killing, like a cat with a bird. Easy enough to catch her and dispose of her in this body. It was a good body and he knew it. Easier than most to slide in and out of, though this time the puny creature who was its owner had actually had the audacity to protest. There was other strangeness about this one as well: the fact his mind had not collapsed after the first time he was taken over. How that could be when it had happened with every other body, he wasn't sure, but it did not matter. The man was trapped and helpless and would soon get to watch the woman die at his hands. If that did not destroy his mind—well, then perhaps nothing would.

An interesting possibility. This one—he lifted a hand to study the smooth movement of tendons and muscles under skin as he moved his fingers—perhaps this one would be worthwhile retrieving to Germany. A spare, given the Johan Fehr body was unfortunately becoming too well known to authorities, courtesy of none other than this body. There was a certain charming irony to that.

He set off barefoot down the road, night insects buzzing and biting the skin. The silver was like a thread on the night. These eyes might not see it hanging in the moonlight, but he had other senses to see it and the lure of his power—like to like, still housed inside those cursed silver links.

The gravel road cut the soles of his feet but he shut out the pain and turned uphill where a patch of crushed grass in the moonlit exposed where she had paused. A line of crushed grass led further uphill. Her trail.

"I'm coming for you, Victoria!" he called. "Why run away like this? You know I love you."

The body's voice boomed out and he knew the words were true, though they had not been loosed from the body before now. That should give the bitch pause. They never believed their lover would kill them, and why had he not done this sooner? The power of four links already lost with the opening of the bracelet. It had to be the years that had passed. In all the years in the desert and then in Heinrich and Johan Fehr, he had grown weak and more base. His time in the mind of Johan Fehr had drained him further, for the man was not that bright. Deliciously cruel perhaps, and creative in his cruelty, but not smart. Perhaps he had let that dullness intrude.

But all would be put to rights tonight. The bracelet his. This body his. And the woman's body would not be found for enough days this body and he would be safely beyond the reach of anyone here.

He started through the bushes at a ground-eating lope, branches tearing at his jeans, his bare chest. Ducking the low-hanging pine branches, ignoring the pain in his feet, the blood trickling down his broad chest from the jabbing tree limbs. The forest was rocky here. Rocky soil. Rocky mountains. The trail ran uphill and he felt the pull and release of trained tendons. Yes, a good body. Good strength. More than enough power in these hands and arms to break the neck of a woman.

§

In his cloud of darkness, Danny hunched, protecting himself—or at least the parts of himself that made him the man he was. Around him the thick black fog still roiled, but something kept it from inundating him. He didn't know what, was only glad it allowed what was him to continue to exist—until the tunnel vision through the fog let him hear the roar that his lungs sent into the night. Victoria! Victoria had bested him and escaped—thank God.

Then his body was running down the rough road between moon-shadowed trees. He could hear the deep breaths of his lungs, but could feel nothing. Do nothing.

Then his body stopped and he saw his hands.

They worked with a power he'd never recognized in them before. Threatening. Hands that could do a lot of damage to the soft flesh of the human body. In all his years as a police officer, he'd used those hands many times to subdue a subject. Most had been men, but there had also been a few women who fought with tooth and claw. They had been hard-luck cases, drug addicts mostly. He had had to be careful not to hurt them in the process.

His vision showed dark forest tearing past. He got the sense through the fog of being like a hound after scent.

Bracelet. The image came through the fog. Fury and ancient hunger and a will to succeed.

Damn it, he was after Victoria. Would find her, too, the way the thing that controlled him sniffed the air and seemed to know exactly where to go.

He had to stop it—this thing. But how, when he was cut off from his body? There had to be something he could do.

He shoved against the fog. It was oily and thick and smelled of incense and burning, but there was no heat. Cold, colder than anything he'd ever felt. Cold enough to freeze a heart and yet he had a sense of flames. He yanked back, shuddering, frozen.

"Victoria, run!" he called, but his words echoed back at him, his lips never moved.

Around him something evil laughed.

Trapped. He was trapped and there was nothing he could do to stop the thing from killing Victoria with his hands. If it succeeded, it would also destroy his soul.

§

The night was a blur of dark shadows under trees and pools of moonlight as she ran, stumbled, clawed her way up the hillside—to where, she had no idea. Just go. Just run. Get as far away from the lake and Daniel as she could. In the morning, in daylight, she would figure out how to get to civilization again.

Se ha vissuto—if she lived that long.

The scent of pine and dust filled her nose. The sound of her rough breathing filled her ears. Her thighs ached. Her ankles felt like she had almost broken them so many times. She knew a headlong plunge over such rocky ground was risking everything, but she also knew Daniel or whatever was inside him was right behind. Too close for her to slow. Far too close to stop to catch her breath. He was strong and longer legged. There was no way he would not catch her eventually unless there was some kind of miracle.

That was all she had to hold to—a miracle.

Maria Santissima, salva requesta donna stolta. Blessed Mary, save this foolish woman. She had hurt Daniel and perhaps that was what had let this thing loose inside him, regardless of their lovemaking. She had refused to believe Lila's warnings, and look where it had got her. She had trusted someone and here she was in danger...

The landscape began a slow descent. She let momentum carry her, rushing faster down the hill—until, plunging through a copse of trees, she stepped on a rock that shifted under her.

She spilled sideways and landed on her hip, scrambled up in the shadows, but not before she looked up and saw the silhouette of a man on the hilltop behind her. Did he see her? Did he see her go down? She was in the darkness of the trees. Could she try to hide from him?

Looking up at him standing there in the moonlight, he was Daniel. How could she believe that he was trying to hurt her?

But it was not Daniel. It was hard to believe, but she'd seen it in his eyes, had felt it in how he looked at her and how the bracelet burned. The bracelet. She looked down at it and it seemed to hold a glow of its own.

She shoved her hand deeper amid the folds of the blanket she still held. It was nothing but in the way. She should leave it behind. But if she by luck got away, she would likely need it. No, the blanket that had sheltered her and Daniel's lovemaking would stay with her. She hugged it to her and looked back at Daniel.

"Victoria?" His voice was a weird falsetto as if he was playing a children's game of hide and seek. "I am coming for you Victoria. And I will find you no matter where you hide." She huddled a little lower, but up on the hillside Daniel lifted his head as if he scented the breeze. Then he turned toward her and it was as if he could see right into her hidey-hole.

Scent. He used scent to track her. That meant that there was nowhere safe she could be from him. Or was there? Water. Water blocked scent, or at least so she'd been led to believe by every mystery book that involved tracking dogs.

A glimmer of hope ran through her and brought the hint of a plan. She got up and got moving, silently and as swiftly as she could.

Chapter 16

In the darkness of the night, Victoria scuttled sideways through the trees, hoping her motion remained unseen by the man on the ridge above her. That would be the best of all possible worlds: that she escaped right now and he abandoned the chase. But something that had not given up after trying to recover the bracelet from four other women would doubtless not give up in pursuit of her. That meant she had to outsmart him somehow.

The tall pine, spruce, and poplar partially blocked the star-stained sky. The undergrowth was mostly grass but that masked the fact that the ground was deeply furrowed and rocky. She could break a leg if she was not careful. It meant that she had to go slower than she would like, but surely that would mean Daniel would have to go slower, too.

Half-mad laughter floated after her on the midnight breeze. "I'm coming, Victoria."

Please let her be faster. That eerie voice had no hint of Daniel.

She sped up, ignoring the danger that posed. He was on the move and would be coming fast. She had one chance to lose him and that would only work if she could get to water.

She led downhill and eastward, then turned back up the hill and prayed to blessed Mary that he had not simply paralleled her on the slope. The way was steep here, the trees more sparse, but at least she knew there was a lake beyond. If she could reach the crest of the hill, then it was just run down to the water and in. At least that was what she planned.

She hoped.

Breath tore at her throat as she reached the top of the rise. She paused, panting as the land fell away again and the smooth waters of Englishman Lake glimmered in the moonlight. There was safety. There was hope. All she had to do was get there before Daniel caught her.

But the ridge she'd climbed ended at her feet in a sheer, ten-foot drop down into another pine-grown slope. Getting to the lake was not going to be easy. If there had been no moon, she could have fallen and lain there dead or injured until Daniel finished the job.

No, not Daniel. The thing that wore Daniel like a skin. It was horrible, really, when she thought about what he'd become. Not the man she knew. The real Daniel had been there while they made love. Had the creature been there, too? Watching and waiting? Had it been Daniel who had stood outside her shop and scared her both those times? Only to have Daniel come to rescue on both occasions? *Madre di Dio*, was it all a sham? Was Daniel himself laughing at her as she ran?

Heartsick, she stumbled as she followed the ridge edge praying that she would find a way down. But behind her came the sound of something large crashing through the brush. She had no doubt what—or who—it was.

The drop from the ridge top had lessened to about eight feet. Something a youngster would probably brave. The mutters and chuckles of something vicious came from behind and left her no choice.

Another little prayer and she leapt, hit hard on her feet and rolled, slamming her side into the trunk of a tree. Something cracked in her side and pain curled her in on herself, but she could not afford the luxury.

She staggered up. Pain stabbed into her right side and into her left ankle and she clung to the tree until she could breathe again. Then she started off, right arm clamped across her to hold the pain in. She limped-slipped-slid down through heavy layers of fallen pine needles and dried grass toward the unseen lake. Around her the forest seemed to breathe, boughs creaking, poplar leaves softly cascading like water.

No, that *was* water, somewhere off to her left. She edged in that direction and discovered a small creek following an almost-dry creek bed. Here the rocks were smaller, the larger ones easier to spot because there was no grass. Hobbling, she ignored the burning pain in her ankle and hurried down the watercourse. The slope changed, flattening. The trees began to thin.

She came out at the end of the lake into an area of wild pastureland with long grasses flattened by something—cattle perhaps, given the lowing she'd heard. The scent of water hung heavy on the air and the lake glimmered before her. She left the now-meandering creek bed and set out across the grass. Hopefully the flattened sod would hide her passage.

Finally her feet squelched in mud. She pushed through tall rushes that whipped her face, arms, and breasts through the t-shirt and then suddenly she waded through four inches of water. She splashed her way deeper, ignoring the stink of mud and the slime on the reeds. Suddenly clear water lay before her. She threw herself in and then silently, silently swam away from the clear trail she'd left in the reeds.

Breaststroke so she barely rippled the water. She fought to slow the wild stammer of her heart and the urge to swim—just swim as fast and as far out into the lake as she could get.

But she'd heard the stories of how Jas had helped rescue one of Lila and Chloe's friends from a diving accident deep in the lake. Given Daniel's muscles, she had no doubt that he could far out-swim her. That meant she must be stealthy and quiet as a mouse.

She swam along the wide swath of reeds praying he hadn't seen what she'd done and didn't see what she was doing. Then she eased her way among the reeds again, keeping the bracelet deep under water.

Surely the water would confuse him. Surely he would lose her scent. If she could stay here all night, well then, in the morning, she could flag down traffic on the road for help. She'd get back to Kelowna and Jas and the police could catch Daniel and deal with whatever had possessed his body.

And Daniel?

As she quelled the quick rush of her breath, the silence of the night descended. The breeze rustled the reeds.

What had become of Daniel? Not his body, for she felt him lurking somewhere near. No, it was the man she had been with. The lover. The man who had made her laugh. The man she cared for—*deeply*?

You trust no one—how did you allow that to happen?

"Victoria! Come out, come out, wherever you are!" Another caricature of a hide and seek voice.

Worse, it *was* Daniel's voice.

She huddled lower, praying he would not see her while she could see his shadowed form standing at the edge of the reeds—probably where her terrified plunge had crushed everything in her path.

"I can swim, Victoria. This body can swim faster and farther than you."

She crouched lower, but he still had not waded in. That must mean that he wasn't sure where she was. Maybe—just maybe—her plan was working. He looked like he scanned the lake and, like a hound, he appeared to lift his head to sniff the breeze. All her hackles stood on end. The scent of burned-out houses and ash overwhelmed the natural smell of mud and ooze and the algae that slicked up the sides of the reeds. But his gaze slipped over where she hid.

Pausing, he stepped back from the lake edge and followed it to another vantage. The moonlight on the water might show her silhouette. She sank lower in the water, until only her eyes and nose were above its surface. At the side of the lake, he climbed up on the road and looked back. Then he settled down to a crouch where he could scan the lake.

Which meant she dared not move, for in the moonlight any ripples she caused would show.

The water was cold and the mud was thick and slimy, covering her hands and sinking into her shoes and clothes. Gradually the adrenaline wore off and she shivered, the breeze off the mountains freezing her sweat-soaked head. Her fingers clung to the roots of the reeds. They brushed against something cold and hard.

It was a shaft about one foot long, with a vicious hook at one end. What it was, she wasn't sure. Something from one of the fishermen, probably. Danny had said that they were endlessly losing gear in the reeds. Either way, it was a weapon when until now she'd had nothing. Whether she could wield it was something else again.

She loosed the thing from the mud and slipped it inside her t-shirt and the loose waistband of Daniel's shorts. Could she even use it against him? Against *Daniel*?

The thought left her exhausted and trembling. How could this happen, just when she'd found someone she truly cared about? How could he be the one trying to kill her? It was utter wildness and yet she had seen with her own eyes the change come over him. This man chasing her might look like Daniel, but it wasn't him.

Her legs ached with fatigue from crouching, but she could not sit down, for her nose would not be above the water. She found herself nodding. Her head slumped and she inhaled water. Came up spluttering and managed to smother the choking and coughing. The moon had shifted across the sky, leaving part of the lake in shadow. She'd dozed off—the product of exhaustion, probably.

The pine trees on the slopes had moon-silvered needles, but underneath them was only darkness. She couldn't stay in the frigid lake much longer. If she could follow the reeds into the shadowed part of the lake, maybe she could swim farther away—get to the other end of the lake and she'd reach their camp. When Daniel had changed from the dousing in the lake, he had put his keys and wallet on a stump to dry. In her panic to get out of there, she hadn't tried for the keys. Perhaps Daniel hadn't retrieved them, either. If she could get the Jeep started, she could reach safety.

She looked over at Daniel where he crouched by the road.

He wasn't there.

§

He was—where? The essence of what made him Danny was trapped in the fog—no, make that smoke, given the sense of incense and burning it held. It filled his brain. Not that he had any sense of smell. Or of hearing or touch, either. Instead it was as if his consciousness was trapped between writhing walls. Only the tunnel of vision he'd been left this afternoon, as if the creature relished his horror at what was happening. Now, at night, was only black-and-white snapshot images of moonlight fading off of pine boughs and a great many stars.

If he concentrated, he could get the sense of motion in his body. Not the plunging run of his initial pursuit—no, this was a careful stalking, and more than he had sensed the first time he'd been possessed. Something was different. Hell, it was different that he fully recognized himself as separate from his body.

A slight ripple at the edge of the breeze-swayed reeds caught his attention. Algae stirred at their base and then nothing. A frog?

Perhaps.

A duck or Canada goose?

Maybe? He tried to ignore it—if it was Victoria, he did not want to give her away. She'd been incredibly brave and smart to get away at all, and hiding in the lake was a stroke of genius, for it seemed to have stymied the creature as well.

His body stood and Danny froze in his cell of fog.

Please make it just to stretch kinks from his legs. But his heart told him it was the worst of events. His eyes—not his now—had spotted Victoria and now his body further betrayed him. And he could do nothing about it. Damnation, he was not just going to just hide here and let this happen!

This was Victoria—the woman of his dreams, the goddess he might love, the woman he might live with the rest of his life. He was not going to be her murderer.

There had to be something he could do. Something that could stop this thing in his head. Some way to get his body back under his control, though after this terror Victoria would never trust him again. But that didn't matter. Just to know she still lived would be enough.

The fog writhed around him, the cell narrowing as if it reveled in his horror.

"You're one warped son of a bitch. I'll do everything in my power to stop you."

Fine sentiments from a man who didn't even know where he was at the moment, beyond trapped inside his head.

Or did he? His feet—sank? The fact he could feel it was a change. Yes, he walked on soft ground and the fog rippled and stirred in his head. Was that laughter? The creature, whatever it was, was aware of him. Which meant there was at least one-way communication.

There had to be some way to use that, but first he needed to know more about where he was. The thing had left him vision as if to taunt him. Well, he'd find a way to use that gift against the creature.

He decided to follow the vision tunnel through the fog, and the infernal clouds pressed into his awareness, like fingers digging into his body. That was new, too. The first time out, he'd been barely aware except for a foggy memory of what had happened at Moira Burns' murder scene and then coming to awareness as the thing drew on him to impersonate a police officer.

Well, he wasn't going to let the thing have any more access to him than it had. It might control his body, but it was no longer going to control his mind. It was suddenly as if his essence, what made him Danny, was a source of wind. The fog around him separated and he ignored the stench of burning and the fear that what remained of him could be crisped to ash.

[*You are a persistent little human.*]

The words crashed into him from all around, cloying as the sometimes overpowering incense Chloe burned in her apartment.

He ignored them and swept toward the view through the thick curtains of fog.

[*You wish to watch her die by your hands, then?*] A sense of replete satisfaction.

The way cleared before him and he saw: Lakeshore of night-bound trees. Water rippled in the slightest of breezes that maybe—just maybe—he felt. Tall bulrushes in the shallows.

The gaze of eyes he did not control focused on a patch of reedy water, where something humped low down.

It's nothing but a turtle shell. The painted turtle lives in these lakes. So what are you after? Turtle soup?

A low chuckle echoed through his head.

[*It has been a long time since someone made me laugh. Usually the fear crushes their minds.*] A pause and then: [*Her skull will open as easily as a turtle shell against the rocks along the shore. Shall we retrieve her for that? Or would you prefer the smooth length of her neck in your hands?*]

As if he had such a choice. But perhaps the thing had just given him a clue. If utter fear was what allowed the creature complete control, that was food for thought. If not fear, then what? Was there some emotion that the thing could not tolerate? What was the opposite of fear?

Not love. Certainly not hate? Complacency?

[*You think very hard, human. It must be difficult with such a puny brain.*]

Not so hard when I have something like you doing most of the thinking for me. After all, I'm just along for the ride, aren't I? He kept his mental tone light, his thoughts to himself.

There was silence a moment, then a cautious, [*Yes. It is as it should be.*]

I would have thought that a demon of your ilk would have been happiest when he could turn good as dark as you.

Another dark chuckle that stirred the fog around him. [*You amuse me. I have decided that you shall return with me to Germany.*]

Danny almost froze. No way, no how was that gonna happen if he had anything to say about it.

What? Johan Fehr not working out for you? I thought you had him all locked up and obedient.

He was met by silence and a lurch as his body leapt. Water fountained around him, the scene eerie in the silence with his hearing still blocked. The damn creature had played with him!

Victoria was a sudden vision of white shoulders and legs as she floundered up and threw herself back in the water. She struck out in a clumsy crawl—no match for him. Not with all the training the RCMP gave him.

His body tore through the reeds into the water. If he caught her, he'd drown her. He knew the creature's intent. He had to do something.

One stroke, two. His powerful legs churned through the water. Only a few meters separated them.

Let her go and I'll go willingly to Germany.

Silence.

He grabbed for the fog, but the thing had clear intentions as he churned after Victoria. He grabbed for his body the same way he'd found space through the tunnel vision and momentarily felt his shoulders working. His arms. He fought to slow them.

The thing wrenched control away and left him helpless inside his fog-walled prison. The space reeked of fury—his own frustration, but also the creature's.

But his effort paid off! The tunnel vision showed Victoria somehow at the shore. She stumbled up, the half-light catching on her wrist—the bracelet flaring with blue sparks in the darkness.

He was almost there. Body launched from the shallows, his fist closing on her ankle. She turned, her open mouth a silent scream. From somewhere she produced a fallen bough.

Not a bough. He knew it as he caught a flash of hooked steel as it swung toward his head. Fish gaff. He stiffened. His body ducked. If he got inside her guard, she was certainly caught.

Then pain knifed through his skull and everything went dead.

Chapter 17

Time slowed as Victoria stumbled up out of the water. Behind came the beast-man rising out of the lake, the water glimmered black and white in the fading moonlight. His powerful movement sent rings out and out and out over the surface like wind in a curtain. The tree boughs were black against a black sky, but far above a panoply of stars filled the sky. She'd never seen so many.

Then the world slammed into her again and the man grabbed her leg.

Too strong. There was no way she'd get free. She had to. Her hand found the hard length of wood she'd discovered in the water and tore it loose from her clothes. She rounded on him, swinging with all her might.

Daniel, or what once was Daniel.

He ducked, but not fast enough. Two-handing the club, it landed with a thud across the side of his head.

He went down like a truck had hit him. One minute raging after her, the next minute collapsed on the bank of the lake.

She turned and ran, ducking through the trees, plunging along the lakeshore toward their camp and the truck. Finally she slowed, stopped, and clung to a tree to catch her breath. Her heart beat like a hammer. Her breath tore her throat. The forest was filled with the rough sound of her gasping, no sign of pursuit. The night breeze was cold and cut through her sodden clothes. She looked down at the weapon she still held.

Not wood, metal. Eighteen inches long, with a wicked hook on one end, and she'd used it on Daniel. Daniel's head to be exact. Or the thing inside him.

How badly was he hurt? Had she killed him? If he was capable of getting up, he'd have come after her—of that she was certain.

She knew she should just head for the camp and escape, but this was Daniel. He might die from such a blow. Maybe she could help him. Maybe tie him up first. Or go get help. That was it—she should leave him tied up and go get help.

So what will it be, Victoria?

She looked up the narrowing lake's shore toward their camp, then back the way she'd come, weighing the options. She turned back, knowing she was a fool.

Her father would tell her to get to safety first, then get help for Daniel. Erminio would say the same. Lila might say it too, but this was Daniel, not some stranger.

Cautiously, she retraced her steps. He could have come to, he could be after her again, but the farther she went, the less she thought that was the case. She's put her whole body into that swing and she'd connected hard enough that she still felt it in her shoulders. If anything she might have come close to killing him.

She came out at the lakeshore. Daniel still lay where he'd fallen; his red hair looked darker in the darkness, his fair skin paler. Or maybe that was because he was dead.

Of course, he could be playing dead, too. Pretending to be hurt to lure her in. She couldn't take that chance.

Leaning in, but ready to run, she poked him with the metal shaft.

He didn't move.

She poked him again and there was still nothing. Not even a groan.

Take a chance?

Daniel was someone she cared about. Someone who had been there for her, even if something else had been there, too. She could not believe that Daniel had any intention of hurting her. Not the way he looked at her. Not the way she'd hurt him with her casual disbelief that anyone could be there for her.

But this was a different place from Milan and her father's house. This was not Erminio's house of fashion. These people were different. Look at how Lila and Chloe and even Kylee had been there for Reggie. Jas and Danny, too. Even she had gotten into the act and had done what she could to help Reggie, because it was the right thing to do. These were good people and Daniel was one of them—perhaps the one she cared about the most.

She knelt beside him, club close at hand, and pulled his spread-eagled arms behind his back. She used a strip of cloth torn from the hem of her t-shirt to tie his hands as tightly as she could, using knots she'd learned on her father's yacht. Then she tore another strip—this time from his own shirt—and tied his ankles. If Daniel came-to, he might worm his way back into the lake, but otherwise, she couldn't see him going anywhere.

That done, she pulled his broad shoulders over until he lay face up. His eyes were closed, but she could still see a slice of dark iris. Was he breathing? Was his heart still beating?

She'd thought so when she tied him. Now she checked the pulse at his neck. Still there, deep and steady, but the way she'd hit him, she might have done serious damage to his skull and his brain.

"Daniel, it you're there, I am so sorry. I had to protect myself. I had to stop you from killing me."

Now that he was tied up, she should be going. Get to safety. Get help. But he was helpless like this and this was Daniel that she was abandoning in a forest where Blessed Mary only knew what kind of animals lurked. Like bears. They would eat a person, wouldn't they? She looked out into the trees and was aware of the sounds of the night. Bird wings—large. A hoot, a cry as something died. She shivered in the chill mountain air and looked back to Daniel.

He was looking at her.

§

"Daniel!"

Victoria was a shadow above him, her blonde hair a wild mass around her pale face. Her t-shirt clung to her stomach and breasts, his shorts were still ridiculous on her long, curvy legs. The city fashion designer ripped out of her place. And yet she was the most beautiful sight in the world—because she lived.

Her cry was the most welcome of sounds—not filled with fear, but with relief, but it still made the painful pounding in his head even worse. Then her eyes changed again—this time to caution.

"Or is it the other thing inside Daniel that I am talking to?"

"Victoria. It's me." His voice was a croak. All the aches and pains of his body crashed into him, but he still was not alone. How he'd gained control of his vocal cords he didn't know, given the dark coils of fog still dwelt inside him. He tested the bonds on his wrists and ankles. Victoria might be a fashion designer, but she also apparently knew her way around knots. Good. "Whatever I say, don't untie me. The thing—it is still here, but for the moment it's me who's talking."

And then she was weeping above him, huge, slivery tears running down her cheeks to drop onto his face. "Daniel, I've been so scared. You came after me and I knew it wasn't you, but it *was* you, and you were going to hurt me. How could that happen?"

She hugged him and she was warm and alive and—thank you, God—he could feel it. "It—it happened so fast. I don't know how. He was just suddenly there and I—I think that's why I've been having headaches. He's been here, lurking. My body knew it, but I didn't. Lila was right. I never should have brought you here."

A stupid place to bring a woman from Milan, let alone a fashion designer, and one wearing the bracelet.

"Daniel, no. It was a good idea. It is a good place. A place for lovers to be alone."

"A good place to try to kill you." he could taste his bitterness. "You've got to get out of here. You'll never be able to trust me." Not now. Not ever. The thought mbade him feel like crying.

Instead he looked up at her. "Would you go? Leave. Get help. Go to the police. Then come back for me. I'll take the punishment I deserve for assaulting you."

God, the pain in his head made it hard to see. Hard to focus, and he was so damned sleepy, everything seemed to slur together and the roiling fog in his head was waiting for him. Waiting to take over when his body was free.

Not gonna happen, whatever you are. I'll make sure she gets free, first.

[*And I will come after her again.*]

You do that.

Just not today. He needed to sleep today. He might sleep for days.

"Daniel? Daniel?"

Someone slapped his cheeks and poured water on his face.

"You can't sleep, Daniel. If you have concussion, then sleeping is the worst thing you can do."

His eyes blinked open. If anything, her sobs had increased. She worried about him, after all he'd done to her? It had to be simple shock.

He shook his head and instantly regretted the movement. "Doesn't matter. I'd be better off dead. Then the thing can't use me to get to you or anyone else."

She struggled with his bound body to raise his torso and pull him onto her lap.

That roused him. "What the hell are you doing? You need to get out of here. You need to get help. It's only a matter of time before this thing figures out another way to get you. It'll keep coming back again and again as long as you wear the bracelet."

And yet he had control of his body—could feel the pine-littered ground under his back, could shift his arms and legs in their bonds. Could smell Victoria's sweet oleander scent overlaid with mud, sweat, and iron fear.

Instead of doing what he asked, she hauled his body against her breast and wrapped her arms around him.

"I'm not leaving you. You might sleep if I do."

Her arms were warm. Her heartbeat steady and strong. For someone who had not even wanted to come here, he was surprised at her determination. But then, she had spent years in the fashion industry. From what he'd heard, that took an amazing resiliency. She would get over this, and if he died, that was no worse than going to prison for a very long time. As a cop in prison, he probably wouldn't live that long anyway.

He was so tired—so tired of fighting both within and without. Her warmth was a comfort, a reminder of what might have been. He relaxed into her softness...

...and came to as the stars faded.

Gray dawn. The fog in his head had coalesced in corners, seemingly harmless, but he knew better.

The sky overhead was the palest and coldest of blues. Fitting, given the air was chill and puckered his flesh. Dew had kept his clothing damp and cold against his skin except where Victoria's warmth wrapped around him. Long blonde hair tickled his cheek as he drew in a long breath. Soft breast under his cheek, a long, tanned thigh to either side of him. Sometime in the night she had shifted position and he hadn't noticed. Soft, steady breathing ruffled his hair and he knew she slept.

The lake lay as still as glass, a light mist rising, here and there the faint ripples that showed the fish were rising for a breakfast of insects. Through the mist came the haunting cry of the loon and the sound of a car engine. It passed them by, then slowed and stopped. Vehicle doors opened and closed, but the mist masked the occupants.

Fishermen. Had to be. Who else came up this way so early?

The fog stirred lazily in his head and he could figure the worst. A man across the lake, and the creature would shift heads. Then he could come for Victoria and there was nothing Daniel could do about it because the creature could still take him back whenever it wanted.

Victoria's breathing changed and she stirred under him.

"Daniel? Did you hear that?"

He nodded against her and her arms tightened.

"You are okay?"

Another nod.

"Should we call them?"

"I'm not sure," he answered, keeping his voice low. "This thing could jump heads again, and where would we be if someone else came after you? This is why you should have left me last night. You could have won free easily then.”

The fog unrolled in his head, slowly inundating him again, though he still maintained control.

There was a hitch in her breath and then a sniffle.

“Victoria?” He looked up at her.

Her dark eyes were filled with unwept tears. There was fear there, yes, but also something he hadn’t seen before. Grief. She shook her head and palmed the tears away, unshed.

“I’m sorry. You keep trying to send me away, but I am not leaving your side, Daniel. Together we will figure this thing out.” And then she did the damnedest thing—she leaned down and kissed him.

It was like a surge of silver light ran through his brain, dispelling the dark. The fog roiled up in his head with a roar of fury unlike anything Danny had heard before. It tore open his skull and was gone.

He opened his eyes and Victoria’s lips were still on his, soft, seductive, warm. Then she pulled back, smiling, until her eyes grew round.

“Daniel, look.” She nodded down to where her arms clasped around his chest.

There, on his bare chest, rested the heap of links that was the bracelet.

“What the hell?” He struggled to sit up and the cool links slid down into his lap. His hands still bound behind his back, he turned to look back at her. “But how? Why?”

She shifted to hands and knees beside him. Her brown eyes were wide, solemn. “Didn’t your friends say that the bracelet came off when you met your soul mate?”

She spoke so softly he almost didn’t understand, until her arms came around him and she kissed him again.

“Danny! Victoria!” Worried male and female voices drifted across the lake through the mist from near their campsite.

Victoria pulled back from him. “It is Lila.”

"And Jas and Cesare, by the sound of it." He turned to the lake. "We're here on the far side of the lake. We'll meet you at the campsite," he called.

He turned back to Victoria. "Untie my legs and help me up."

Victoria looked at him doubtfully and fingered the pendant she still wore. "I love you, but you said yourself not to trust you as long as I wore the bracelet. But I don't think I should trust you now, either. Not with the bracelet in my possession. If we want to keep it from that thing, then I think I have to leave you here."

Loved him? His stomach felt funny at the words. But her assessment was astute.

"You're right." He had to agree. "You go and I'll wait here until Jas and Cesare come for me. And just so you know, I'm pretty sure that I love you, too."

She leaned down and gave him a lingering kiss goodbye, but then she stood there looking undecided.

"You need to go."

"I—I know," she said uncertainly. "It is just that all my life it has been others who have walked away from me. Not me that does the leaving."

"You're not leaving. You're just going for help. Now give me one more of those kisses to sustain me while I wait and then get outta here."

The kiss was almost enough to make him forget all the pain he'd felt about what he'd done. Victoria Angelucci loved him—or said she did. It was still early in their relationship, but that was a good sign, right?

As she disappeared along the lakeshore, he found himself smiling.

§

Walking toward the campsite, the morning would have been a wonder if she had not woken stiff and sore and scratched to beyond an inch of her life—if she hadn't almost been killed last night. Not just killed, but murdered by the man she cared for. The sun had risen enough to turn the mist golden over the lake as the blue of the sky gradually deepened. Around her the dark pine and spruce were silent, the barest of breezes muttering in the poplar leaves.

The silver bracelet links felt like a loaded gun in her pocket. Or perhaps not a gun. Perhaps more like a target that could draw dangers out of the forest to her. It brought not quite the terror of last night's run through the forest, but still fear. Healthy fear, for whatever it was that desired the bracelet like she desired Daniel.

The thought of him, of their bodies together, made her smile and want more, but what had he become? Could she believe it was truly over? Would she be smarter to do like her father and everyone else and walk away?

But Daniel had not killed her. She was still surprised that she had made it across the lake before him. And then she had stopped him with the club. She hefted it in her hand. She still carried it for protection against anything else that might come for her.

A noise ahead along the lakeshore interrupted her thoughts of Daniel. She eased away from the water and slid into shadows farther up the hill, then crouched down to see who it was.

Three figures shoved through the brush along the lake's edge. Daniel's partner, the tall dark detective, Jas Stone, moved cautiously in front. He wore jeans and a navy windbreaker that hung open revealing a gun in a shoulder holster. Behind him came Lila in jeans and denim jacket that somehow still looked high fashion on her tall, model's frame. Trailing her came the glossy black head of Victoria's strapping big brother carrying a tire iron.

Victoria watched them almost past her. Then she stood up. "Here I am."

All three of them whirled around, Jas already with his gun in his hand. When he saw it was her, he holstered his weapon as Lila and Cesare leapt up the slope to her.

Lila's warm arms came around her. "My God, Victoria. You look like you've been through a war. Are you all right?"

She nodded and Cesare took her from Lila. Victoria sank into the warm embrace and felt the tears threaten again even though with her brother she felt safe. She told how it had been—wonderful with Daniel and then Daniel suddenly wasn't there anymore and the horrible pursuit. Lila and Jas listened as she spoke. "He is Daniel again, now. Or he was when I left him down by the lake. I tied him up and left him that way against my better judgment."

Jas and Cesare were looking at her in amazement. Lila's expression was more admiration.

Lila patted her shoulder. "You did well. Very well. Better than anyone else I can think of."

"Best if you lead us to Danny," Jas said.

"Daniel. His name is Daniel." She nodded and set off down the lakeshore again.

"There is this, too," she said, pulling the bracelet out of her pocket. The early sun caught in the links and sent shimmering shadows over the underbrush, painting the willow and Saskatoon brush with light.

Lila caught her hand to stop her. She looked into her eyes. "It was Daniel all along, wasn't it? Your soul mate?"

Victoria nodded and Lila sighed.

"I guess that leaves me, doesn't it?"

Victoria closed her hand around the silver doors. "That is not a good idea. You see the danger it causes."

Lila's auburn curls looked like burnished copper as she shook her head. "Who else is there? The bracelet has to be on an arm or else he can steal it too easily. Besides, there're only two doors left. After all the trouble all my friends have had, I think it's my turn."

Gently she uncurled Victoria's fingers and the bracelet fell into Lila's palm. Then, under the watch of Cesare, Jas, and Victoria, she clasped it around her arm.

Out on the lake, the breeze and the sun had vanquished the mist and the lake's surface rippled with small waves. Lila waited a moment and then she sighed.

"Well, that's done," she said brightly. "Now let's go get Daniel." She turned and let Victoria lead them along the pine-scented lake's edge to Daniel and the future.

Epilogue

It could not be—could not have happened.

The thing that had been inside Danny Forester once more scuttled into the brain of what had once been Johan Fehr. The man had been a cruel, conscienceless bastard before he took up residence, so the world had not lost much when he took over. Actually they might not have noticed much difference, except that Fehr's business decisions had become as astute as his father's. They had been together for so many years now that slipping into Fehr's brain was like slipping into an old, comfortable slipper.

But the release of the power of the fifth door's opening left him not only depleted from his efforts, but he actually felt the escape of his stored power. The opening door had literally blasted him out of the police officer's brain!

Fehr's body slumped behind the ebony desk of the hotel suite. The glass walls along one side of the massive office were slicked with the gray rain that was deluging sodden Vancouver, Canada. Silver light caught on the distant mountains across the sullen water of English Bay. The silver light reminded him too much of the links of a blasted bracelet. The body's fingers dug into the arms of the chair, tearing through the leather, straining the metal.

He went to stand, but fell back in the chair. Tried again, but though the body might be willing, his will to animate the body wasn't there.

Shaken, he huddled inside the too human skin. What was happening to him? The soulless hotel room art stared back at him. The pristine, pale blue couch and matching chair and curtains were enough to make his skin crawl.

He was strong. He had always been strong, since his birth with the darkness at the beginning of creation. Yes, the infernal tinsmith had done him a disservice, tricking him so that three-quarters of his power was stolen and locked away in the bracelet doors, his magic bound by a curse so perverse that he had never realized the extent of what the tinsmith had done until the bracelet was recovered again.

He inhaled and this time managed to heave the body to its feet. If this was not such a desperate time, he would leave this envelope of meat and bone to rot alone, but for the moment he needed its safety. He needed its power, and most of all, strangely, he needed the comfort of its familiarity.

The world had turned upside down around him. *He* was the holder of dark power. *He* was the one humans had most feared on their dangerous journeys into the depths of the desert. *He* was the one who had blasted the tinsmith into nothing but an essence that was banished to the bracelet in punishment for his betrayal with the lovely Laelia.

All these years he had hoarded his remaining and still considerable power. He had nursed it and used it to gain human power. But now, just when the bracelet had seemed within his grasp, another facet of the tinsmith's insidious plan had surfaced. The man had been devious. More devious than he had credited him with being.

Johan Fehr walked unsteadily across the thick cream carpet to the bar and poured himself three fingers of twenty-year-old scotch. He knocked it back and felt the burn down the throat. In his time dwelling as a human, he had come to appreciate the act of consumption. It was the most like what he had done to humans in his ancient form—devouring their essence—a skill lost to him since the tinsmith trapped so much of his strength. The loss had left him as a wraith, a thing of nightmares that had to be content feeding on human fear.

The glass shook in his hand as he set it down. He splayed the fingers of the hand and a tremor ran through them.

A thin tendril of fear wormed through him like a crack of light in a blessedly dark room. What was happening to him? He could not be failing. He was the oldest creature in the world and he had survived all this time through his wits and his strength.

So just what had happened with the policeman?

He should have had the woman. He was the faster in the water, so how had she made the shore before him? There was only one answer—the opening of the four doors and his efforts to claim the bracelet had weakened him. An ignorant policeman had somehow bested him—slowed him in the water. That was the only explanation.

So he had been weak, then. Weak enough that the opening of the fifth door had thrown him right out of the body and across the distance—to here.

That left only two more doors. If he was this weak after five were opened, what would become of him after the sixth and seventh? It was as if the escape of his immortal power from the bracelet had ripped power away from him, as well.

There had to be something he could do to stop it. He thought a moment. Thought of the next woman to wear the bracelet and his fists closed around the cool column of the glass. Yes, the time for subtleties was gone.

About the Author

Karen L. Abrahamson has explored cultures and countries around the world, but south central British Columbia, Canada is one of her favorite places to come back to. She writes literary, romantic and fantasy fiction including the highly regarded Cartographer fantasy series. She lives on the west coast of Canada with two Bengal cats that aren't quite as well traveled as she is. When she isn't writing she can be found with a camera and backpack in fabulous locations around the world.

If you would like to get an automatic e-mail when Karen's next book is released, sign up at her website, _www. karenlabrahamson.com_. Your email address will never be shared and you can unsubscribe at any time.

A Special Request from the Author: Word-of-mouth is crucial for any author to succeed. If you enjoyed this book, please consider leaving a review at Amazon, Barnes and Noble, or any other e-tailer, or on Goodreads; even if it's only a line or two, it would make all the difference and would be very much appreciated.

To find more of her writing, visit _www.twistedrootpublishing.com_.

Also by Karen L. Abrahamson

and available through *www.twistedrootpublishing.com*

Romance
Ashes and Light
Shades of Moonlight
Judas Kiss
Second Spring
A Different Nightmusic
Shadow Play
Coming Down Christmas
Surviving Safe Harbour

The Unlocking (Peachland) Series:
Unlocking Her Heart
Unlocking Her History
Unlocking Her Grace
Unlocking Her Dreams
Unlocking Her Chances
Unlcoking Her Doubts

Mystery
Through Dark Water
After Yekaterina
Mareson's Arrow

SNEAK PREVIEW
UNLOCKING HER DOUBTS

KAREN L. ABRAHAMSON
UNLOCKING
HER DOUBTS
Unlocking Saga, Book Six

Prologue

After the short flight from Vancouver the *Schwarzenacht* corporate jet settled onto the tarmac of Kelowna International airport—not that the thing in Johan Fehr's head would in any way consider this backwater single-runway airport international. It was international in the same way that a drug runner's dirt runway was international—a suitable surface for take-off and landing for specific cargo that needed to be shipped. In the drug lord's world it was drugs. For Kelowna he hadn't quite been able to parse what the shipment was—unless it was sun-wizened people trying to escape this hole-in-the-wall town. For, compared to Berlin and the cities of Europe, that was certainly all the 'city' of Kelowna could be called. Even Vancouver, the third largest city in Canada, was just a wet-behind-the-ears upstart in the global city department.

The harsh noonday sun lit the sunburned hills of parched grass and drooping poplar and long-needled pine. Dust hung in the air in the shimmer of heat off the tarmac and shivered the air between him and the distant houses set amid the trees. Dry. Inhospitable and yet everywhere there were vivid green lawns, gardens and orchards—the product of irrigation. In some ways it reminded him of ancient times. The Tigris and Euphrates had caused just such a microclimate of fresh green along those storied riverbanks. In the springtime of his youth he had dwelt there, taking his toll of the humans foolhardy enough to venture out between the daytime and the night. That was when he had stirred. That was when he had hunted. That had been when he had fed—until civilization came upon him and he found other, less strenuous ways to hunt, first in ancient walled villages and then in the dark alleys of modern metropolises.

The Lear jet swayed to a stop and the engine cut off. The steward unstrapped from his seat near the front—the cabin staff knew to leave their betters alone unless called. The mahogany paneling glowed in the light through the window. The scent of recycled air still held the memory of the steak the body, Johan Fehr, had eaten as his in-flight meal and the red wine he'd drank with it. Unfortunately, regardless of the reasonable food and the light doze he had managed on the flight, the body was still tired. A full sleep had eluded him for the past few days because the heart of this body had pounded, the blood rushed through the veins, all out of the excitement that came with the decision that Johan Fehr himself would take action. He had wasted too much time waiting for others to complete the job that must be done. This time it would be completed.

He would recover the bracelet and his power would return, for surely if he salvaged the power remaining in the two unopened doors it would give him the strength to reclaim that which had been lost at the opening of the five other doors. He would feed in the old ways once more. The power of two doors was not inconsiderable. This close to the woman who wore it, he could feel her heart beating in sympathetic rhythm to his own.

He closed his eyes, taking the moment to revel in the intimacy. It was the sensation he had always relished before he killed.

The steward checked on the pilots and then cracked the door to the tarmac. Dry air rushed in carrying with it the scent of sage and airplane fuel. The Johan body inhaled.

"Ready to deplane when you are, sir. The pilot reports that the limousine is waiting."

The steward's footsteps retreated to his cubby at the front, leaving his master to do what he wanted.

With a sigh he opened his eyes and scanned the file he'd been reading, his finger trailing down the photographs of the six women. After a thousand years of no news of the bracelet, so much had happened in the barely three months since the bracelet had been found. All his attempts to retrieve his treasure had been blocked at every turn. His bodies stopped, some actually killed— him forced to abandon them and return, depleted, to Johan Fehr, until the only way he could return was to fly like some common human, trapped in this body.

All caused by these women. His jaw clenched.

Each was lovely in her own way. Lovely enough he would enjoy their death, but truly it seemed he had saved the best for last. He ran his fingertips over the photo again imagining the silver singing on her wrist, imagining the sweetness of the fear he could evoke in her through his little jokes. Her fear would feed him and make him strong again. Auburn haired and with hazel-flecked eyes, she was the only one left amidst the bevy of beauties who had not already worn the bracelet. There was one way to be sure, for just the sound of her voice would tell him.

He picked up his cell phone from the table beside him and dialed the number his investigator had listed in the file. Not that he needed the file. He'd stolen the number already from the mind of a policeman.

The telephone purred at the other end. The best for last and he closed his eyes at the pleasure the thoughts of her death evoked. The body's fingers worked, the large knuckles cracking. It had been a long time since the Johan body had taken direct action.

It had been even longer since he was directly involved in killing.

Chapter 1

Six-thirty in the morning and Lila Weber sipped a cup of maple-flavored milk tea as she stood on the wide front porch of the large red and white heritage house that had belonged to her grandparents. This late in September, along the porch edge bright copper pots held fading displays of red and white petunia and purple heliotrope that scented the air like baby powder. Across the street, beyond the white gate and hedge of the house's yard, lay the uneasy waters of Okanagan Lake, still dark from the night. It was the last of the dog days of summer and the days were shorter, the dawn later, the nights—thankfully—cooler. But it also meant fall was here and the long gray days of winter would follow all too soon.

The rush and hum of the highway traffic at the base of the mountain behind the strip of flat land that held the sleepy town of Peachland had increased with the onset of September's work days so it was no longer just white noise. A breeze from the south picked up moisture, the scent of sage and pine, and an unusual coolness as it ran up the long narrow lake. She shivered.

She still wore her clothes from her morning yoga—navy leggings and a lavender sports bra—both still damp from her workout. Her thick auburn curls were a damp, tangled ponytail on the top of her head, so the breeze cooled her neck.

Cold, actually. Soon the wind would come from the north all the time and it would be too cold to do this. The thought saddened her. Something about this time of year always brought thoughts of endings. Maybe it was the fact that the summer people who usually staked out their piece of beach even this early in the day, had mostly departed with Labor Day. The number of morning joggers had decreased to a trickle on the promenade along the water. Maybe it was because all the important things of her life had mostly happened at this time of year—the death of her parents and grandparents, other things that had been less painful but no less important.

Her fingers strayed to the silver links of the bracelet around her wrist.

Or maybe it was the bracelet. God knew the troublesome thing caused strange reactions within its wearer. The darn thing had been nothing *but* trouble ever since she brought it into the house. She'd like nothing more than to get it off. After causing innumerable problems for her friends, who had, one-by-one, put the bracelet on, the time had come for her to face the music and wear the infernal thing. She had no time for this kind of thing—not with a business to run.

She sipped her tea, savoring the smooth tannins and the slight sweetness of sugar. Soothing. That was what she'd been going for. Something to soothe the bad dreams that had been disturbing her the past three weeks. So far it wasn't working.

And this month was supposed to be one of beginnings—the opening of the new clothing store that she and Victoria Angelucci had partnered on. It would bring Milanese custom fashion to the Okanagan, the first of its kind, and would build on the jewelry store, *This and That,* that had already made Peachland a destination.

The first rays of sun over the bald gray mountains across the lake shattered golden in the lake's small waves and caught on the silver of the bracelet.

No, she was not going to dwell on endings, though wearing the bracelet meant she wore a target on her back. It was her turn, that was the only reason she'd put the darn thing on. That and someone had to keep it from the reach of the creature that was seeking it. The trouble was, she'd put the bracelet on three weeks ago after it fell off of Victoria Angelucci's wrist, and too many nights of dark dreams had followed.

A sound from the house brought her around and a sleepy blonde figure in violet satin pajamas and robe padded into the *This and That* jewelry shop that occupied the front of the house. The front door opened with a little ding-a-ling from the silver bell above the door, releasing the scent of incense as Victoria Angelucci stepped out onto the porch.

She was a beautiful woman of lush hair and lusher curves à la movie stars of the Bridget Bardot era, but sleep still muddied her features. This was her last morning as a guest of Lila's. After a month and a half staying in Lila's guest bedroom, she had leased a condo just down the street and above the clothing shop that she and Lila were opening. It meant that Lila would get her house, her sanctuary, back to herself. After the events of the summer she couldn't say she wasn't looking forward to it.

Victoria slumped onto the turquoise and mandarin cushioned wicker loveseat that was part of a grouping of wicker furniture on the covered porch. She put her slippered feet on the cushioned ottoman, closed her eyes and held out a phone.

"This—this thing would not stop ringing. It is for you," she said in her Milanese accent.

Frowning, Lila accepted the phone. A call this early in the morning did not bode well. In fact the phone call on top of the queasy feeling she'd had in the pit of her stomach since she finally got up this morning had her hesitating to answer.

"Man or woman?" she asked, but Victoria had laid her head back to catch the first warm rays of sun and simply waved the question away.

Bracing herself, Lila brought the phone to her ear. "Hello?"

There was silence a moment, but the sound of breathing came over the phone.

"Hello? This is Lila Weber."

The line went dead.

She looked at the phone before clicking it off, a tingle of dread pooling in her stomach as she sank onto the fan-backed, peacock chair that others called her throne. The phone felt unfamiliar and unwelcome in her hand. She set it on the ottoman and scrubbed her hand on her thigh.

"Who was it?" Victoria turned one bleary eye toward her. They had both been up late the night before with discussions about the store's grand opening and dealing with issues about Victoria's visa.

Lila shook her head, the chill she'd been feeling coalescing into cold even though the sun was finally warming the air. "I don't know. Whoever it was, they hung up as soon as I said who I was. It's odd. I had a similar call yesterday."

"He. It was a man that asked for you."

If anything the day went colder. Lila rubbed her arms and wished for a sweater.

"I don't suppose that bodes well either, does it?"

Victoria sat up and pulled her dainty muled feet onto the floor again. "Do you think this has something to do with that thing again?"

She nodded at the bracelet, shuddering delicately.

"Do you? But why would the creature call me? It's done things much more insidiously up until now—it doesn't phone to announce itself."

"Would it not call if it knew it could upset you?"

Lila didn't know how to answer. The creature that was somehow connected to a German named Johan Fehr, had dogged them all summer since the bracelet came into their possession. The bracelet, however, seemed to have a mind of its own, refusing to come off the wearer's wrist until the woman had found her soul mate—a man associated with one of the ornate doors that formed the links of the bracelet. So far five of her friends had found love and happiness and she was happy for them, but love—well love wasn't what she was looking for anymore. She'd long ago given up on love for herself. If anything, she was married to her store.

She held out the bracelet to catch the sun's rays and the link shaped like an arched door with ornately-filigreed, scrolled-iron hinges, momentarily blinding her.

With this store and the grand opening of the new one and trying to research the story behind the bracelet she was busy enough.

Love was definitely the last thing she had time for.

§

For the umpteenth time Nathan Moon hung up the phone and wondered what in god's green earth he was doing. He sat in his room in the Kelowna Marquis hotel, supposedly enjoying the blue and white view of the lake and the marina that sat at the base of Kelowna's most prestigious hotel. Instead, here he was in the glass-walled room, agonizing over whether to actually talk on a phone call.

With a groan he tossed his phone on the white leather couch and stood to pace the length of the white plush carpet to the base of the baby grand piano one more time. Money might get him the best room in the house, but apparently it didn't get him the balls to talk to a woman he hadn't seen in about fifteen years. Stupid. Idiot. Disgusting. Sissy.

"What are you, Moon? A momma's boy? A weak-willed, lily-livered coward?" he said choosing dialogue straight out of one of the nineteen forties movies that he'd cut his teeth watching in Hollywood.

He strode across the room to the bar and poured himself a glass of orange juice from the carafe that room service had delivered this morning. He considered adding a shot of vodka but wasn't this just the kind of thing his father had done that had led to his parents' divorce? Damn it. A drink would help to work up the courage, but the sun was barely up over the mountains let alone over the yardarm. Surely to goodness Lila Weber wasn't that daunting and the two of them *had* been rather good friends, but this time—this time he'd like things to end differently.

And if you want that to happen, then maybe you have to start somewhere? Like a screenwriter starting a script, the hardest thing was the empty page. In this case it was all the empty years between them.

Orange juice in hand, he crossed back to his phone and slumped on the couch. The view truly was stunning—blue lake and green mountains, a single stately sailboat running up the lake before the morning wind. In front of the hotel the huge, shaggy cottonwood shaded a waterside walkway. The kind of view people would play top dollar for, even more so for top billing in a penthouse suite like this. He was a man with enough confidence in himself he'd told the big studios to piss off and had gone independent. Surely any woman would be impressed by this address.

Except maybe Lila Weber. That was one of the things that had always impressed him about her—the trappings of Hollywood power really hadn't seemed to mean anything.

He stabbed redial on his phone.

The line hummed in his ear and then began to ring at the other end. What the hell he was going to say after all this time he wasn't sure, but he'd think of something. He and Lila had always been good at conversation while they stood around on the set between takes. He remembered the girl-woman dressed as a goddess, with Grecian toga flowing around her slim figure, the cording of the toga tied up high under her breasts, her auburn curls tumbling about her neck with a fine netting of jewels across her forehead and makeup that glittered on her high cheekbones. Her eyes had been huge and liquid. Her lips the color of wine so that every time he'd been with her he'd wanted to kiss her.

He hadn't of course. He'd been living with Celia back then and he was loyal to her even if he'd already had the feeling that she wasn't the one. Besides, Lila Weber had only been seventeen, seven years his junior and too close to jailbait at the time.

The phone clicked as someone picked up and he held his breath.

"This and That, Kylee speaking." A bright, but harried female voice at the end of the phone.

Not what he was expecting. He almost hung up again.

"I'm sorry. I was looking for someone. A woman named Lila Weber. I'm an old friend from her Hollywood days and a mutual friend gave me this number." Mutual in a pig's eye. He'd spent weeks digging around for her number, had been close as damn to hiring a private investigator to find her.

"Who's calling please?"

So the voice on the phone did know something.

"My name's Nathan Moon. I worked with Lila on a movie a long time back. Maybe you saw it—*The Battle for Olympus*?" That usually impressed the locals.

He settled back on the couch. This was going to work. Lila'd come on the phone and he'd arrange a date to take her to dinner. Sort of sweep her off her feet.

The pause on the phone lengthened, but then the chipper voice returned. "I'm sorry, Mr. Moon, I know Lila Weber and I'm also aware that she really would like to forget her short period of fame and be left in peace. Thank you for your call. Goodbye."

The connection went dead leaving him eyeing the phone.

"What the hell was that?" he said, dropping the offending handset in disgust.

Heck, where the hell was that? He knew Peachland was a backwater town in a backwater eddy of British Columbia, Canada, but the way the woman had answered the phone it sounded like she was in a store of some kind. Was Lila reduced to a store clerk now?

The thought was almost impossible to believe, but maybe he could make like the hero in *Pretty Woman* and ride in and sweep her off her feet—rescue her as the case may be. Poor kid. Things obviously hadn't gone well for her. Fifteen years—a lot could change. She could be married with six kids by now. Hell, the voice on the phone could be her daughter! But he just couldn't picture Lila Weber like that. No, Lila Weber had been too much like the goddess she played in the movie—too far above most mortal men. He was probably a fool thinking he could woo her even now, but hey, didn't most of his movies feature determined men who overcame the odds?

He pulled up the search engine on his phone and stabbed in *This and That* and *Peachland*. The system sought and then brought up the option for *This and That: Jewelry and Unsung Treasures*. That had a Lila Weber ring. He brought up the website.

A background images of a lake—probably this one—overlaid with a misty image of the inside of a store with dark wainscoting and gleaming glass cases. Then writing faded into existence as the misty image faded further.

This and That provides custom-made jewelry of precious and semiprecious stones from around the world. The proud home of Regulus Designs, come and see the latest stunning pieces destined to grace the runways of Europe.

This and That Jewelry and Unsung Treasures: Open Monday to Friday 9:30 am to 5 pm. Open Saturday 10 am to 6 pm. Phone to arrange a private viewing outside these hours or contact the store to arrange a jewelry party at your home.

Links at the top connected to a gallery, a page on arranging a private party, and a page on Regulus Designs, as well as an About page. He clicked on About and a clearer image of the store appeared and began rotating to give a full view of the interior—much like real estate used for a three-sixty degree tour. On top of the image more writing appeared.

Opened in 2010 at its current location at 1735 Beach Avenue, Peachland, This and That is the lovechild of three friends who love beautiful things and who are determined to share that beauty with the world.

Hardly a Hollywood headshot and credit sheet. He tossed the phone on the couch again, then scooped it up and headed for the door. He was not going to sit here like some jilted ex-lover. Even if things didn't work out with Lila the way his far-too-vivid imagination had envisioned, he still would like to see her again—even just as a friend.

Down the elevator and through the lobby to the heat that was a lot like Los Angeles on the very best days—no pollution and very little humidity, but with a breeze off the lake that kept things downright pleasant. In the parking lot he climbed in the dark gray rental Mercedes. Hot. He keyed on the car and opened the sunroof to let out the heat and catch the breeze. Then he tapped the voice recognition GPS and turned on the air con.

"This and That Jewelry and Unsung Treasures. 4246 Beach Avenue, Peachland."

The GPS computed and provided a map of the turns he needed. If only it would be as easy to secure a route to Lila.

Chapter 2

Returning to the store from a run to the printer's in West Kelowna, Lila parked her Ford Escape in the carport at the rear of the house and hauled the box of cards and pamphlets from the back. The final announcement cards for the grand opening of the clothing store had finally arrived—late of course. In addition, Chloe and Kylee had been planning informational brochures about the proper care of individual jewels or crystals that they could provide to each customer. Chloe was a crystal healer and believed that a jewel's owner should understand how to maintain the positive vibrations of their stones. So far their test run of brochures had been eaten up by store patrons, so they'd finally committed to the not inexpensive full printing.

She lugged the box around the car and across the flagstone back patio that was unusually silent since Reggie—Reggie Lewis of Regulus Designs—had taken a day off from her design studio to be with her daughter at a horse show. Her sweetie, Cesare, was off in Milan supposedly dealing the final death blow to the lawsuit that had haunted Reggie. The turquoise and yellow wicker patio furniture beckoned for her to just sit and take in the sun, but she had no time. In fact it felt like years since she had. She might live in one of British Columbia's summer playgrounds, but she rarely played herself. As a business woman who had time?

Balancing the box on her hip she opened the back door to the kitchen and stepped inside into coolness. The kitchen was her favorite room of her house. It was her grandmother's old summer kitchen with a bank of windows that spanned the entire back of the room, including the door. Broad marble counters spread under most of the windows except at one end of the room where there was a comfortable old fashioned nook with more turquoise and yellow and tangerine cushions. The room's walls were , but the cupboards were . Stainless steel appliances were an update along with the copper fan hood above the gas range that sat in its own alcove.

Lila set the box on the table and eased her back, then went to the fridge. She was just pouring herself a lemonade when Kylee appeared from the darkened hallway, Chloe on her heels. Both women looked concerned. Kylee was the latest addition to *This and That*. The petite blonde had been Lila's high school best friend and had turned to Lila when her latest love had gone wrong. She'd since partnered up with Chloe's vintner brother, Brett. As usual, today she wore a brightly colored floral dress, her bright hair in a cute cut that just skimmed her chin.

Chloe was everything that Kylee was not, average height with hip-length brown hair that she tamed in a braid, her uniform was a caftan tunic with matching leggings. Today they were in a pale lavender that brought out the hints of violet in her eyes. Chloe was a long-time friend with a passionate belief in psychic talents.

Lila looked from one to the other and sipped her drink. "What?"

She looked down at herself. Was something wrong with her outfit? She wore a sleeveless navy shift that skimmed her body and navy and white spectator flats. "I haven't peed myself. And I'm not wearing my breakfast. What gives?" Another sip of the thirst quenching lemonade as Kylee and Chloe looked at each other.

Kylee crossed the room to catch her hand.

That someone had died was the first thing that crossed Lila's mind.

She set down her glass and felt suddenly afraid. "What's happened? Who's hurt?"

Kylee shook her head. "It's nothing like that. But Victoria mentioned those two weird calls you've had." She swallowed. "Another call came while you were out. I don't know if it means anything but—well I gave him the kiss off."

"Tell her what he said," Chloe urged.

"He said he was looking for Lila Weber, and all I could think of was the bracelet you're wearing." She nodded at the silver links gracing Lila's wrist. "He said he worked with you on a movie a long time back and he mentioned *Battle for Olympus*. Knowing the problems you've had with fans in the past, I told him that was part of a life that you'd put behind you and that you'd prefer to be left in peace."

Lila nodded. That was the instructions that all her friends had. All of Peachland, too, at least all of the old timers, and they guarded her privacy from the fan boys and fan girls who still showed up occasionally. Unfortunately that single film had gone on to be a cult classic that had made the careers of most anyone associated with the project, but all it had done for her was make her very certain that the Hollywood lifestyle was not for her.

"It sounds like you did exactly right." She took another swallow of the lemonade and felt the heat from outside dissipate.

Kylee shrugged. "Maybe. Maybe not, too. You see this one wasn't exactly like all the usual fan-boy calls. This one introduced himself and he said he worked on the movie with you. He said his name was Nathan Moon."

Lila almost dropped the glass. No way. No how. It couldn't be. That blast from the past just couldn't be here—unless...

She turned to lean on the counter and peer out the window into the backyard. Nathan Moon. Nathan—handsome-beyond-belief—Moon. The man she had thought she might love but never done anything about it because she'd been seventeen and stupid enough to already have been swept off her feet by a Hollywood producer who'd turned out to actually mean it when he said he was going to make her a star. She and Nathan had spent three months sitting in lawn furniture getting to know each other while the piece was shot in the desert outside of L.A.—standing in for

Greek highlands. Nathan Moon who she'd dearly wanted to run away with, but who treated her like a big brother. Nathan Moon who she had finally, after fifteen years, put out of her mind.

"Why would he want to find me?" she asked no one in particular.

"Maybe he realized he missed you," Kylee offered.

Lila shook her head. "Why would he want to find me now? After all these years? That makes no sense."

She turned back to then, her hand covering the bracelet. "Don't you think it's a bit strange he calls me now? After all the trouble my friends have had when they wore the bracelet? A blast from the past just means danger, doesn't it?"

"Could be," Kylee said.

"What I want to know is just who is Nathan Moon?" Chloe said. She drummed her fingers on the counter and arched one eyebrow. "Long as I've known you, I've never heard of Nathan Moon and I've certainly never seen you go wonky like this—especially not at the mention of a man. So just who was this guy to you?"

That was the thing with Chloe, far too astute and once she got an idea in her head she was like the proverbial terrier that wouldn't let go.

Sighing, Lila leaned back on the counter and took another sip of lemonade seeking her steady, clinical self."Nothing more than a friend, really. He was an assistant director on the movie I did. We spent a lot of time talking, that was all. Okay?" She went to push past to the door but Chloe had her by the arm.

"Nuh-uh. Not going to happen, sister. The look on your face says there was something more—a lot more about this guy."

With a roll of her eyes Lila turned back to her. "Damn it, Chloe, why don't you learn to leave things alone? There was nothing else. He was nice to me, the one nice thing in a situation I would rather forget ever happened. Making *Battle for Olympus* was not my shining hour, okay? And now I think I need more than this lemonade. I'm going for a walk to stretch my legs and get myself an iced coffee. Anyone want anything from the café?"

When both women just shook their heads she abandoned her lemonade and headed for the front of the heritage house with a growl. "Damn women and their stupid suspicions."

As if there was something between her and Nathan Moon. It had been so long she could barely remember what he looked like—except his almost turquoise-blue eyes.

And then there had been that grin of his.

Would you just stop! You are a business woman. You have better things to do with your time.

She shoved out the front door of *This and That* after switching the little open sign back on because Kylee and Chloe must have switched it off before they came to talk to her. Then she half ran down the porch steps. Darn friends, anyway, thinking they could grill her like that. Not that she hadn't done some grilling herself over this very romantic and very dangerous summer.

Away from the shade of the porch the heat fell on her head and shoulders like a hammer. Her dress might be lightweight cotton, but navy blue wasn't exactly the most cool color she could be wearing. She crossed the street for the promenade, thinking to distract herself with the last antics of the toddlers and pets that played in the water. That was half the fun with living so close to the lake. Water was like a magnet for all the best things in her life. Chloe, Brett and Kylee were all part of her summer memories from long ago.

She headed north along the water, letting the sound of the waves and the remaining summer people and the faint scent of suntan lotion ease away her frustration. It was only a block and a half until she came even with the bakery café that leaked delicious aromas of fresh bread and cookies and the pungent promise of fresh coffee. She could have made equally good coffee at home, but that would have required her to continue to face down her inquisitors.

The café sat in the corner of a newer development with expensive condos up above, one of which Victoria was subletting fully furnished until all her residency documents came through. The building also housed the clothing shop that Victoria and

Lila were opening and there was already a buzz about the event. As she stood there, a couple of summer people paused to read the announcement in the fledgling store's front window. It was designed by Kylee and showed a few of the pieces that would be available along with the grand opening date. They'd also named the shop *The Next Thing: Victoria's,* playing off against the association with *This and That.*

Everything was in place for the opening. Victoria's seamstresses were busy finishing off the last few pieces, the music was arranged, as was the food. The Peachland Mayor, Haifa Samuels, had been invited as had City Council and so had the local media including *This and That's* longtime client Marcia Oldstrum, publisher of the Kelowna Herald.

Lila stepped off the curb mulling over all the things that remained to be done before the opening—pick up garment covers for purchases, ensure the credit card hookups were working, ensure that there were tables and chairs set up on the sidewalk outside, and that there was a ribbon for cutting.

The nearby roar of a car engine caught her attention. This wasn't a drag strip—the speed limit was a sedate thirty kilometers an hour along Beach Avenue.

A dark SUV squealed away from the curb three cars down. It shot across Beach Avenue's centerline directly toward her.

Leap forward? Leap back? Someone on the sidewalk screamed. She tried forward and the SUV seemed to swerve to keep her in its sights until suddenly she was picked up and thrown to the curb. She landed on her hands and knees as the car roared past and was gone like a bat out of hell to disappear around the curve of the shore line.

Lila rolled to sitting. Her knees bled. So did her palms. One of her shoes sat in the middle of the street and her heart was pounding. There were people crowding around her asking her questions, asking if she was all right? Okay? Injured? Hurt?

It was all too much. She blinked, trying to make sense of it all and considered the blood seeping from her grated palms, the bracelet gleaming around her wrist. Darn thing still hadn't come off. Someone cut through the crowd and cast a shadow over the sun. The figure knelt in front of her and caught her hands, gently using a tissue to wipe the blood off, and then cleaning her knees of gravel.

When she looked up it was to peer into perfect turquoise-blue eyes, the kind you could swim in. Nathan Moon knelt before her like some kind of knight.

That was when the shaking cut in.

§

Holy hell that had been close. The dark blue SUV hadn't even slowed. If he hadn't been hurrying to catch up to the woman he thought was Lila, he never could have caught up to her in time to help her. The roar of the engine had seemed to freeze her just long enough that there was no way she was going to get out of the way in time. He'd barely had time to grab her and throw her and himself out of the way. Where he'd got the reaction time for that, he couldn't say. He was no hero.

"Lila, your hands and knees are scraped but otherwise you look okay." At least physically. By her thousand yard stare she might have hit her head, or she was in shock, at least. "Is there somewhere else you're hurting?"

She licked her lips and then her gaze shifted, slowly coming into focus on his face. "My pride?"

A glimmer of a smile appeared on her lips and suddenly she was Lila again—just as he remembered.

"Could you give me a hand up?" Her voice was stronger, as she got her legs under her.

"I've called the police," said a spandex-clad, male jogger. "I got most of the license plate—I think."

The barista from the coffee shop appeared with a white metal first aid case and Nathan wanted to sweep Lila off her feet to the nearest chair, but had to content himself with his arm around her waist. She felt slim and fine as a reed in his grasp, though she was limping. Her scent of baby's breath and roses caught in his nose.

On the sidewalk patio in front of the café he settled her in one of the wrought iron chairs in the shade of the awning and sat down across the table from her, the breeze ruffling his hair. Someone brought them both water and she sipped, holding the glass with shaky hands. She watched him over the rim as he set to cleaning her knees for her.

"So is this one of those meet-cute situations?" Her brows rose in speculation.

"Could be, if you want it to be. I guess it depends on what happens doesn't it?" And just like that it was like they were fifteen years younger and the world was their oyster—a young star in the making and a top director-to-be. Except it didn't happen like that, because Lila walked away and now she didn't respond—just seemed to be contemplating what he had said.

"So how have you been? It's been a long time," he said to break the awkward silence and distract her from the sting as he used antiseptic wipes on her injured knees.

She shrugged and held out her palms for his ministrations. "And how has Hollywood been treating you? Wait—don't tell me—I've managed to see all your pictures, I think. I really enjoyed *The Sultan Shuffle*. It was my favorite."

"You saw *Sultan?* Heck you and about fifteen other people. It was my first indie film and never got picked up by the theatres."

"I saw it at an indie film festival here in Kelowna, so someone must have liked it enough to bring it in."

He grinned and spread salve on her scrapes. "One of the other fifteen people. But thanks. Your opinion means something. It wasn't quite what I had set out to make, but it was close." Before expediency demanded that he compromise a little to succeed commercially. Like that had worked.

"So what brings you to the Okanagan? A shoot?"

'You' was the answer he wanted to give, but he was saved or prevented from revealing himself by the arrival of the ambulance. Under the force of blue and white clad paramedics he was shoved aside while they checked Lila over. Over her protests they concluded that she should come with them to the hospital to make sure everything was okay.

"But I don't have time for this! I was just going to get a coffee and head back to my office."

The paramedic, a burly, middle-aged blonde eased her onto a stretcher and strapped her down. Panic filled her eyes and she reached for Nathan.

He was more than glad to take her hand.

"I hate to ask. Would you go down the street to my store, *This and That?* Tell them what happened and they can come and pick me up at the hospital. Okay?"

The paramedic was levering her up into the ambulance.

"You really don't need to do this. It's just scrapes and bruises, I'm sure," she said to the paramedic.

He slid the stretcher the rest of the way into the vehicle and , then grinned at Nathan. "Some people just don't know how to take care of themselves."

He could believe that about Lila. She always pushed herself to give everything she had.

"Which hospital?" he asked. In L.A. they were too many to count.

"Kelowna General, where else? Check Emergency. They probably won't keep her, but better safe than sorry."

The blonde paramedic joined Lila in the back and slammed the doors behind him. The driver set out for the hospital. Nathan watched them turn onto the highway and then turned back to Beach Avenue.

The red and white house waited. He'd talk to her boss. Sighing, because this wasn't exactly how he saw himself reentering Lila Weber's life, he headed down the sidewalk.

The red and white house was the kind of place that a location scout would take note of. Its broad covered front porch that spanned the entire breadth of the place, and the copper hanging baskets overflowing with fading red, white and purple flowers gave it a heritage feel and a gentility equated with the old south. And yet the two-storey structure had a sense of *gravitas*—of being a serious part of the town's history, even if it was just a house. This house belonged, not just to whoever owned it, but to the town. And while Peachland looked like it was gradually being rebuilt to fit the current preference for concrete condos and townhomes, this house held onto the grace of the past and had a presence that wasn't going anywhere anytime soon.

Odd, that he got all that from the place, but there were some places that just spoke of—home. A beloved home.

He let himself in through the little white picket gate and climbed the porch stairs two at a time. The place looked just as well groomed up close. Comfortable wicker loveseat and chairs decked out in bright summer colors. Squeegee clean windows and discreet little "open" sign by the door.

He shoved inside and caught a face full of incense as a bell tinkled above him. Then he was inside and found himself facing two women, one of whom was serving a customer. The other—brunette with a long rope of braid—eased herself from around the dark wood and glass cash counter where an incense burner before a small brass Buddha released a thin coil of smoke toward the ceiling's crown moldings.

"Welcome to *This and That*." she said. "May I help you?"

He felt totally out of his element because the place felt so—well—other. Feminine. New-Agey. Misty, as if it existed in both in this and another dimension—an effect it achieved through gray-lavender paint and dark wainscoting that he'd have to remember for future movie sets.

"Um. Yeah. My name's Nathan Moon. I'm looking for the owner. I was just down the way at the coffee shop and there was an accident."

The women in the shop seemed to take a collective breath, both the customer and the small blonde clerk turning to him.

"Lila," said the brunette with eyes that had turned the most amazing violet.

Nathan nodded. "Yeah. She was almost hit by a car and she seems only scraped up but the paramedics thought she should go into the hospital for a check-up anyway. She asked me to come let her boss know what happened. I gather she was on her coffee break."

The brunette and the blonde looked at each other as if he was missing something.

The brunette held out her hand and he shook it. A small tingle ran up his arm.

The woman's concerned face eased into a smile. "Pleased to meet you, Nathan Moon. I'm Chloe Main. This is Kylee Jensen and this is Franny Graystone, one of our favorite customers."

Chloe almost looked like she was gloating.

"So you own the store?"

Chloe Main shrugged. "Sort of. In partnership with Lila." She arched a brow at him. "So Lila's okay?"

Nathan inhaled and sighed. Of course Lila'd own the store. She wasn't the kind to be satisfied being a clerk. "From what I could tell. I checked her out right after it happened."

"I'll just bet you did." The sotto voice comment came from the small blonde.

When he glanced at her, she met his gaze innocently.

He turned back to Chloe. "Lila said she was going to need a ride back from the hospital."

"Uh-huh. Did she now." Chloe checked her watch. "Gee, that could be a problem. I've got some healing sessions booked and Kylee has to watch the store. I guess we could call Reggie..." She glanced at the little blonde who nodded.

"If it would help, I'd be happy to pick Lila up," he offered.

"Really? That's a very kind offer, Nathan. If you wouldn't mind. But just so you know, Lila can be kind of bitchy when she's surprised by something and you picking her up will definitely be a surprise to her."

Forewarned was forearmed. He nodded. "Okay. That's good to know. I'll head into town then. See you in a while."

Chloe preceded him out to the porch. "Thanks so much for helping us out. You know, I think Lila's mentioned you. You're a friend from way back, aren't you? Someone she knew well, but not well enough?"

What could he say? A small flush of heat ran up his neck as he shrugged.

The darn woman smiled as if she knew better, so he hurriedly left her on the porch and headed out to the Mercedes. Funny thing was, he was almost sure he heard her chuckle.

§

Chloe reentered the shop feeling a sense of satisfaction.

"You are a very bad woman," Kylee said from the cash counter as she rang in Franny Graystone's latest purchase.

"Funny, I always thought of Chloe as an agent for good," Franny said as she punched in her credit card code.

Chloe drew herself up to her full five-foot-seven. "I *am* an agent for good, but it's about time Lila Weber got as good as she gives. She's always nudging someone along into romance. Now it's her turn. Didn't you hear who that was?"

"I heard. Nathan Moon," Kylee said.

"And who's Nathan Moon aside from a man good enough looking to leave me fanning myself," Franny asked, demonstrating her bright blue eyes flashing under her stylishly cropped gray hair.

"Someone from Lila's hidden past," Chloe said with a dramatic flourish of her arms. "Someone who got away before Lila ever got to express what she felt for him—or that's what I'm thinking. 'Course it was a long time ago and chemistry can change, but him showing up right now? Well, what do you think?" she asked Kylee.

"Could be a coincidence."

"Or good timing. Just when Lila Weber needs to find her soul mate Nathan Moon comes calling. I'd say that's a pretty good omen, wouldn't you, Franny?"

Franny nodded and took her leave. Chloe watched her down the porch and turned back to Kylee. "Perfect timing, given Lila's wearing the bracelet. And there's something else. I was worried when he walked in that he might be Fehr's latest victim, but he's clean. More than that, when I touched his hand, I got 'True'." Chloe often got a single word description of a person the first time she met them. "How's that for an auspicious beginning."

"Lila's still going to be *pissed* at you." Kylee shook her head with admiration.

"Let her be. She didn't make things easy for me when Jas came a-courting. Now's payback time."

She was still chuckling an hour later when she went for lunch.

Look for *Unlocking her Doubts* coming February 2016.

**Romance, Mystery and Fantasy
from Twisted Root Publishing**

If you enjoyed this book, you might enjoy other titles available from Karen L. Abrahamson in your local bookstore or wherever e-books are sold.

www.karenlabrahamson.com

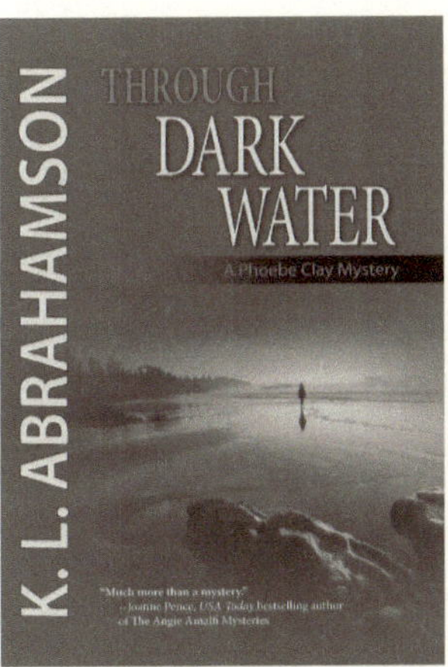